break a leg

Polyam Fam
Book Two

phoebe alexander

Mountains Wanted Publishing

P.O. Box 50

Harbeson, DE 19951

www.mountainswanted.com

Paperback ISBN: 978-1-949394-76-4

Cover design by the author

Editing and proofreading by Mountains Wanted Indie Author Services

�֍ Created with Vellum

To Chris, who first taught me the word "polyamory."

And a very special thank you to Kelli and Tina for the rush proofreading jobs! Love you both <3

one

. . .

aris

IF YOU WOULD HAVE TOLD me I'd start my thirties by moving in with my boyfriend and a few friends to form one big happy polycule, I'd have said you were crazy.

But here I was, looking around the dinner table at my new family: Noah, Cynda, Jason, Darth, and our new rescue kitty, Sushi. Noah was the man I loved, but right now Cynda was my favorite human. She was the best cook in the universe, and this meatloaf was out of this world.

"How was work today?" Jason asked as he passed the mashed potatoes to Noah.

"Oh, nothing exciting. Just seeing patients. Tomorrow morning I'm in surgery though—deviated septum," my handsome boyfriend explained. Noah was an ear-nose-throat specialist who tolerated seeing patients but was most passionate about surgery.

"What about you, Aris?" Jason liked to take on a fatherly role in our found family, and his girlfriend Cynda, who was older than him by about ten years, was definitely our matriarch. Darth made up the other third of their triad and—well, he didn't talk much, but he had a dry sense of humor and a sharp wit. A bit of an acquired taste, but I was getting used to him.

"Oh, you know, pretty much the same as Noah's, only I love seeing patients, and I'm glad I don't work in surgery." I turned to my love and gave him a smirk.

Noah smiled, but it seemed forced. He was being awfully quiet this evening, even for him. I wondered if something happened at work to upset him. He only took a few more bites before he scooted his chair back from the table.

"What's wrong?" I turned concerned eyes on him.

"Nothing, just not very hungry this evening, and I need to get to bed early. Tomorrow's surgery is at the crack of dawn," he explained as he stood up. "Dinner was magnificent, Cynda. Thank you so much."

He gave a little bow of gratitude, patted me on the shoulder, then padded down the hallway to the room we shared across the hall from Cynda and Jason's. Darth stayed in the room down the hall because he enjoyed having his own space. There were four bedrooms total, and we used the spare one as an office of sorts.

The other occupant of our quaint homestead was the cat Jason just brought home from a local rescue organization earlier this week. Sushi was very shy and had spent most of her time so far hiding behind and underneath various pieces of furniture. Maybe I'd try to coax her out later with a toy and a treat. Jason and Darth had practically bought out the pet store making sure she had everything she needed.

"Is Noah okay?" Cynda dabbed at her mouth with a napkin. "He seems a little…off tonight."

"I thought the same thing. Glad you said something." I smiled back at our resident "mom." As an empath, she was adept at picking up on people's emotions. I didn't know if I qualified as an empath, but I was very in tune with Noah, even though we hadn't been dating that long.

"Maybe you should go check on him?" Jason suggested as he began to clear the plates. It was his and Darth's turn to do the dishes tonight. Cynda cooked, and we all took turns cleaning up afterward. It was only fair.

"Yeah, I will, as soon as I demolish these potatoes." I winked at Cynda and stuffed my mouth full of several consecutive bites, followed by the rest of my green beans and a few meatloaf crumbs. "Mmmm, good stuff." I glanced around the table. "Wish me luck."

"You act like Noah is an unreasonable person," Darth commented, his first foray into the conversation.

"That's the problem." I shook my head. "He's too reasonable!"

"You're Captain Kirk to his Spock." Darth leaned back, satisfied with his geeky assessment.

"Wouldn't he be Bones?" I questioned. "He's a doctor, after all."

Everyone chuckled as I pushed my chair back in and headed down the hallway toward our room. We shared it, but I knocked anyway, so I didn't burst in and interrupt anything.

Not sure what I thought I might interrupt, but—

"You don't have to knock, you know." Noah's eyes trailed up and down my figure.

He was sprawled on the king-sized bed, his dark skin contrasting with the white comforter. Propped up by several pillows, he hunched over a tablet, his broad shoulders looking tense.

"Are you okay?" I'd asked him in front of the polycule, but I might get a different answer now that we were alone. I hoped he didn't regret moving in with Jason and Cynda. Not only was it saving us a ton of money, but we'd both had somewhat homophobic roommates we wanted to escape, which was a whole other story.

"Yeah, I will be." He laid the tablet face down on the bed and patted the space next to him. Then he spread his arms out, inviting me to cuddle up with him.

Cuddling with Noah was one of my favorite pastimes. Being in his arms felt safe. He had a quiet, sane security about him that set me at ease. Always steady. A rock.

How could I not fall in love with someone like that?

I climbed onto the bed and rested my head on his massive biceps, then wrapped an arm across his chest as I snuggled close to him, breathing in his fresh, clean, citrusy scent. He lowered his chin and pressed a kiss to the top of my head.

"You know I love you, right?" I looked up to meet his dark eyes, and the corners of his lips turned up at my declaration.

"I love you too, Aris. Don't mind me…just been a long day. Okay?"

I nodded. "I understand. I just want to make sure there's nothing we need to talk about. Communication is the foundation of a healthy relationship, you know."

"Is Cynda sending you poly articles again?" Noah teased me.

"Nah, I'm following a lot of poly folks on Instagram and TikTok," I admitted. "This is all new to me, you know."

"It's new to both of us, and you're right. Communication is paramount. If there was something I thought we needed to discuss, I wouldn't hesitate to bring it up. I'm just tired tonight, and it has nothing to do with you."

"Okay, then, how about a nice massage, and then you can get some rest?" I stroked my fingers down his chest. His gray V-neck shirt was soft and cozy, but I really needed it off him.

"Well, how can I pass that up?" A smirk flashed across Noah's face as he grabbed the bottom hem of his shirt and lifted it over his head, almost like he read my mind.

He turned over onto his stomach, his bare back and the very top of his ass crack on display. I needed to see more, so I pulled his soft jersey lounge pants down until they were right under his cheeks. The firm globes of his ass were just too tempting, and I sank my fingers into his flesh, rubbing.

He moaned softly, and then, "Wait, I thought you were going to rub my back? That's not my back."

I chuckled. "I said 'massage.' I did not specify which body part I'd be massaging…"

"Fair enough," he murmured, the sound muffled by his pillow.

I worked my way up his taut muscles, kneading and digging deep, trying to release the tension I felt knotted up under my fingers. Noah was a Type A person—there was no doubt about it. And he often let stress build up in his body. Sometimes he took that out on me—he loved rough sex. Maybe he needed that tonight and just didn't know it. I would be happy to coax that release out of him if that was what he needed. In fact, that sounded like a win-win to me.

I straddled his ass, firmly massaging his trapezius muscles where his neck and shoulders met. The tension was dissipating as his muscles began to melt and loosen under my touch. The sexy groan that left his lips went straight to my cock, and I leaned slightly forward to press my groin to his ass.

"Mmm…you getting a little distracted there?" He lifted his head to look over his shoulder at me.

"Maybe a little…"

"Your hands are like magic, mmm…" He rolled over onto his back, his dark eyes shining with desire as they met mine.

Sure enough, the front of his lounge pants was tented. My guy was magnificently endowed, a beautiful uncut cock, a shade darker than his mahogany skin. I worked the pants over his manhood, dragging them down his thighs.

He cocked his head, a smirk lifting one corner of his mouth. "Well, you succeeded in getting me naked…"

"You act like that was my plan all along!" I bit my bottom lip.

He scoffed. "Wasn't it?"

"Well, I just know you work so hard taking care of me and all your patients, sometimes you forget to take care of yourself. That's all."

"So, this is a purely selfless act…?" His brows quirked as he studied my face.

"I mean, maybe not 'purely,' because I feel pretty damn good when you feel good, but your tight muscles are telling me you need to get off."

"Is that so?" A sharp, staccato chuckle shot out of his mouth. "I thought I was the doctor here."

"Well, I may not be a doctor, but I am a nurse. I have a pretty good handle on anatomy and physiology." With that, I gripped his cock firmly in my fist, making him gasp. I squeezed as I stroked from base to tip, bringing a dewy drop of pre-cum to the slit on his crown. "Hmm, just as I suspected…"

"What?"

"You need a release." I used my other hand to cup his balls, gently massaging them. "Mmm, yes, these balls need to be drained."

"You think so?"

"That's my official diagnosis and cure right there, all rolled into one." I winked as I settled between his legs, my light hazel eyes landing on his dark brown. As if I needed to further corroborate my claim, my tongue darted out, sliding up his shaft and circling under the glans until his back arched. "I rest my case."

"That sounds like law instead of medicine…" His words came out needy and raspy.

I shut him up when I wrapped my lips around his cock and took him deep into my mouth. Sure enough, no more words slipped out. Instead, his head fell back against the pillow, his eyes closed, and his breaths turned into shallow puffs as I began to work my mouth and hands up and down his shaft with a slight twisting flair I knew drove him absolutely wild.

No longer able to speak actual words, Noah's throat produced an array of lusty, gravelly, animalistic groans and moans, all of which made my cock ache. But I kept at it, desperate to taste his cum, swallow down his load and feel him relax in my arms. When his hips began to rock, thrusting up into my mouth in a faster rhythm, I knew he was close.

He grabbed on to a pillow, bellowing his release into the fluff as thick ropes of his seed rocketed into my mouth. I held his hips in place, taking him deep as he emptied his balls down my throat. Fuck! I was so turned on by swallowing his load, I had to reach down and stroke my cock through my jeans. It wasn't nearly enough, but it relieved a bit of the pressure.

While Noah recovered, his body stilling as the last few spasms jerked his cock in my mouth, I unzipped my jeans and pulled my own cock out. Where Noah had a long, elegant magic wand of a cock, mine was shorter and girthier. I fisted it, squeezing a pearly bead to the tip just as Noah's eyes fluttered open. They immediately snapped to my torso, watching me fuck myself.

"What are you planning to do with that?" he asked, his voice still sounding a little raspy after his orgasm.

"You made me so fucking hard," I stroked from base to tip again, nice and slow for his viewing pleasure, "and I'm gonna have to get off too if I have any hope of falling asleep tonight."

"Come here," he gestured to his body, "and I'll take care of you."

I straddled his face, feeding him my cock as his pink tongue came out to sample a bead of my essence. His tongue twirled around my head, and a breathy sigh floated out of my mouth. "Fuck, it's not going to take me long."

"Let's see how fast I can suck you off." He took me deep into his throat, making all the muscles in my thighs clench tight.

When Noah set his mind to something…well, there was no doubt he would not only finish, but he'd do it in the most excellent way possible. It was the way he approached every-thing in life: with diligence and determination.

Those powerful qualities went to work as he used his mouth and hand in tandem to bring me to the brink. As I rose up on my knees to thrust down his throat, he gripped my balls, milking the cum right out of me. I shot my load, and he enthusiastically swallowed it down, his Adam's apple bobbing as he consumed every drop.

Satiated, I rolled off him and cuddled up in his embrace, my head on his shoulders.

"I like us," he declared, pressing a kiss to the top of my head. "I like this. We are perfection together."

"We sure are." I kissed his cheek, and next thing I knew…

It was morning.

two

. . .

danielle

"I'LL BE FINE," I insisted, but I could tell my best friend and roommate wasn't buying it.

"Your audition is next week," she fired back, her jaw set firmly. "Don't risk it. You've been hacking and clearing your throat for weeks, and you might get worse before you get better."

"But I don't want to go to the health center on campus. They'll just tell me to take some Tylenol. Or they'll want to pump me full of antibiotics. I'm allergic to everything. Besides, I don't think I'm sick. I just have all this annoying drainage…"

"Dani, you've been complaining about your voice all semester," Raine reminded me. "You got that sinus infection after winter break, and it's never fully gone away. Why won't you just listen to me for once and take care of yourself?"

I wrapped my arms around myself. I didn't want to tell her the real reason. I hated doctors. Like *loathed* them.

I couldn't think of anything I'd rather do less than see a doctor. I'd prefer hearing hours of nails on a chalkboard or repeatedly getting poked in the eye by a sharp stick. Seriously, doctors were the absolute worst.

"You're such a diva!" Raine's fists flew to her hips, and she rolled her eyes. "Look, my friend Aris's boyfriend is an ENT. Let me text him and see if there's any way to get you in for an appointment."

"Wait…Aris that we met at Bonnie's party a few weeks ago? The hot Greek guy with the man bun?" I blinked a few times as the memory of him filled my mind. I'd seen him across the room and asked Bonnie who he was.

"That's the one. He's gay, but, damn, isn't he a hottie?" She fanned herself. "Anyway, his boyfriend is an equally sexy ear-nose-throat specialist."

"Of course he is." I rolled my eyes. Hot gay guys did often turn out to have hot gay boyfriends. *Sigh.* "Well, do you think he'd really be able to see me before my audition?"

"There's only one way to find out. I'll text Aris." She shifted her weight from one foot to the other. "Now, you better go get some sleep. It's already midnight!"

I rolled my eyes for approximately the hundredth time this conversation. "Sheesh, when did you become my mother?"

"Since I got tired of hearing you clear your throat and complain about not being able to sing every three minutes." She reached out and put a hand on my arm. "Seriously, Dani, I care about you. And I want you to get a good part in the spring show. Your whole thesis depends on it, right?"

Raine and I were both grad students at Indiana University. Her specialty was costuming, and mine was musical theater. We met as undergrads and both worked for a couple of years before deciding to come back for our master's degrees. We always got along back then, so we decided to get an apartment together. We'd grown close since we both started our MFA's. I was sure she was worried if I didn't figure out what was going on with my voice, it might keep me from getting my degree—or even sidetrack my whole career.

She wasn't wrong.

She just didn't know how much I hated doctors. However, the idea of seeing someone we sort of had a connection to made it a little better.

"Was this guy at the party too?" I asked. "The doctor boyfriend?"

Raine shrugged. "I don't think so. I think Bonnie said he's super serious and really focused on his work. But that's good for you if you want to see him in a professional capacity."

I laughed. "Well, what other capacity would I see him in? You already said he's gay."

She elbowed me, joining in with her own airy cackle. "You're right. I'll go text Aris right now."

"Can you go see Dr. Evans at eleven forty-five?" Raine asked, poking her head into the bathroom, where I was taking a steamy shower and trying to do some vocal warm-up exercises.

My throat was still full of phlegm and ickiness.

"I have class then, but, yeah. My audition is going to suck if I can't get this under control." I flashed her a grateful smile. "Thank you for arranging this for me. You're the best!"

"I know," she agreed with a smirk. She loosened the scrunchie that held her wild mane of jet-black curls in a messy bun on top of her head. "And for my reward, I'm gonna sneak in here and brush my teeth real quick while you're in the shower."

I rolled my eyes. Sharing a bathroom was the only thing I didn't like about living with Raine. Considering she'd just done me a favor, I decided to spare her eardrums and stop my warm-up exercises. I finished rinsing the conditioner out of my hair, which was so flat and non-descript next to Raine's, just a mousy brown with nary a wave or curl.

"Let me know what Dr. Evans says, okay?" She rinsed her toothbrush and set it in the holder. "I'm going to be home early tonight. They canceled the dress rehearsal for *Summer and Smoke*. I guess the director and tech director got into a huge fight."

I couldn't help but giggle. "Wow, nothing like a little theater department drama!"

"Right? It's so cliché...I guess their visions didn't 'match.'" She laughed. "Well, good luck today at the doctor. See you tonight."

As she left, I called down the hall, "Thanks again for the hookup."

I realized what a relief I felt at not having to go through the trouble of finding a practitioner and calling to set up the appointment. Just thinking about those steps provoked a wave of anxiety to pass over me. Now I got to skip ahead to the *real* stressful part: actually seeing the doctor.

To be honest, there was another step that was even worse: being greeted by the nurse and immediately ushered to the scales.

Could I stand up for myself and tell the nurse that my

weight had nothing to do with my voice, and it wasn't necessary to weigh me for this appointment?

I tried to convince myself I could.

Panic truly set in while I was waiting for the nurse to call my name. The waiting room felt like purgatory with its muted pastel decorations. I couldn't tell if it hadn't been updated since 1990, or if it was new décor, and they were going for retro vibes. Either way, it was not vibing with me.

I cleared my throat for the four hundredth time this morning. It had gotten to be a reflex. There was always some sort of ickiness stuck at the back of it. Raine was right; it was time to get this taken care of, and going to the health center would have been a bad idea. Seeing a doctor who specialized in this part of the anatomy was the right choice.

I just wish I didn't hate doctors so much.

It didn't help that, no matter what I saw a doctor for, they always had to bring up my weight. That judgmental way their eyes darted between the chart and my body, as if I were nothing more than a giant slab of adipose tissue and not a human being with a heart and a soul, it sent me into a dark place.

I'd even had *overweight* doctors fat-shame me before.

And recommend losing weight for maladies ranging from chronic headaches to a twisted ankle.

"Danielle?" a soft voice came from the doorway at the front of the room.

Fear rippled through me as I stood on shaky legs and made my way toward the door, which seemed very much like a portal to hell.

The nurse, who was petite with matching features and mousy brown hair, smiled. "This way please." She led me down a hall, around a corner, and there it was: an electronic scale. My nemesis. "Do you mind getting a quick weight please?"

At first, my protest was trapped in my throat. But I cleared it again and slowly turned to her. "Is it truly needed? I'm here for my throat."

"It's in case we prescribe medication," she explained.

"I can give you a recent weight," I argued, starting to feel flustered. "I just—I don't—"

She smiled. "Okay." She wrote something in the chart before her green eyes settled on me. "Right down the hall here. Room 4."

Did I just win that battle?

Feeling slightly puffy with pride, I traipsed down the hallway to the room marked with number four. She gestured toward the paper-covered table. "Do you object to getting a temp, heart rate, and blood pressure?"

She didn't sound sarcastic, but it would have been easy to read that into her question. "I do not object."

She smiled again and whipped out the thermometer and the blood pressure cuff. She frowned as the cuff tightened around my upper arm. "It's 135/85. A little high."

"Sorry. I don't like doctors, so my blood pressure tends to go up when I'm seeing one," I admitted. "No offense."

She ignored my statement. "How tall are you?"

"Five-five."

"And that weight you promised?" Her eyes were fixed on the chart, not at me.

I gulped. "Two-seventy-five."

Her face remained neutral, which impressed me.

She made eye contact with me finally and said, "Dr. Evans will be in to see you shortly."

She headed out with the chart tucked under her arm and a pleasant smile. I guessed I didn't need to take off my clothes for this appointment. He was, after all, going to be concentrating on my head. That was welcome. So far, this hadn't been as bad as I feared.

But, as I waited, my unease started to rise again, making my heart flutter and my palms sweat. I hoped the doctor didn't want to shake my hand or something. Swiping them both down my pants, I swallowed hard as the door handle turned.

The kindest pair of brown eyes I'd ever seen met mine. A tiny smile curved his full lips, and his jaw was outlined in a neat beard. He was a tall, broad-shouldered Black man wearing a white lab coat over a shirt and tie and charcoal-gray trousers. "I'm Dr. Evans," he offered, extending his hand. "Nice to meet you, Danielle."

He'd looked at my name before coming in. He didn't have to look down at his chart to remind him who I was.

"Uh, hi." Well, the fact that he was so handsome didn't make this any easier. But he was gay, right? Aris's boyfriend? Working in the theater, I was used to that kind of disappointment, but this one stung a little because, damn, he was scorching hot.

"Tell me what's going on." He pulled out the rolling stool and spun it to the center of the room before sitting down on it. He looked at me, not at my chart, while I spoke.

I described my symptoms, and he asked me how long I'd had them. All the standard medical interview stuff.

Then I watched the way his hands held the chart as his eyes scanned the documents inside. They were strong and manly with long fingers and nicely manicured nails, but there was also something…precise and exacting about them.

He finally looked up from the chart, meeting my eyes again. There was such kindness, such care etched on his face, my breath nearly hitched with surprise.

"I'm going to examine you now," he announced, rising from the stool and placing the chart on the counter.

Those strong hands I'd just admired were warm against my skin as he palpated the glands in my neck. He pressed his thumbs to my forehead and sinuses. "Any pressure here?"

"Yes, some." I expected to feel uncomfortable with his hands on my face, but his touch felt unexpectedly nice.

"I'm going to take a look in your nose, ears, and throat now." He whipped out a tiny light from the pocket in his coat and explored each of the features he'd mentioned. His face gave away absolutely nothing as he concluded his exam with my throat.

He sat back down and pulled the chart into his lap again, jotting down a few notes.

Damn. Way to hold me in suspense, Doc. Everything he did was deliberate and methodical.

"I think we need to do some more testing," he finally broke the silence. "But I also think you have a low-grade sinus infection that's causing some of the drainage. Have you ever had allergy testing?"

I answered his questions, but I wasn't sure I was hearing his words. There was something so capable, so skillful in the way he did everything. The tiniest movement of his hands, eyes, mouth seemed perfectly orchestrated to deliver the results he was aiming for, which was taking care of me.

I'd never had anyone want to take care of me.

So I'd learned to take care of myself.

"You can schedule the CT scan and endoscopy with the front desk, and I'll see you back soon for the endoscopy, which we do here in the office. Make sure you take the entire round of antibiotics, okay?"

The careful way he enunciated his words contributed to the overall effect. I took the prescription from him as he stood up and took two steps to the door. "Have a good day, Danielle, and call the office if you need anything else."

Then he was gone.

I was still contemplating the smooth, debonair demeanor of Dr. Evans when I left his office and headed toward the exit. I pressed the button for the elevator, which was stopped on the floor above me. Next thing I knew, the doors were sliding open to reveal a familiar face.

"Aris?" I choked out when he came into view. He was wearing pale blue scrubs that made his olive-colored skin look tan against the light fabric. His long brown hair with caramel highlights was piled on top of his head in a messy bun. I'd never seen a sexier man, and that was saying a lot since Dr. Evans was pretty fucking sexy.

Sigh. They're perfect for each other.

"Hi!" His face immediately scrunched up with confusion. "I'm sorry… Have we met?"

I smiled. "Yes, at Bonnie's party a few weeks ago." I was already envisioning him and Noah side by side. What a striking couple! "I'm Danielle Delacroix. I actually just had an appointment with Dr. Evans. Isn't he your partner?"

"Oh, yeah! I remember you now. I saw you across the room, but I didn't get a chance to say hi. My loss, obviously.

You're Raine's roommate, right?" When I nodded, his smile could have lit a thousand stars. "And, yes, Noah is my boyfriend. But we're poly."

"Poly…really…" It was a statement, not a question, but Aris's eyebrow quirked.

He leaned forward, his lively hazel eyes roaming my face. "Surprised by that?"

"No…" I giggled but then realized I sounded like a silly teen. "I think it's great. Not sure I could do poly, to be honest."

The elevator opened to the lobby, and we both stepped out. I already regretted saying that about polyamory. Not only was it dismissive and judgmental, but—

"Yeah, I get that a lot, to be honest," he said. "Poly doesn't work for everyone, but it works for us."

"That's great. Love is love, and all that." I nodded, still feeling flustered but glad he didn't seem upset that I'd stuck my foot in my mouth. "So do you have other boyfriends too?"

As soon as the words were out of my mouth, I realized I was not only still being rude but nosy too. "Oh my god, I'm so sorry! You don't have to answer that. I'm being a complete idiot today. Going to the doctor does that to me." I waved the prescription Dr. Evans had written for me. "Hopefully this will cure me."

He chuckled as we reached the automatic door, which slid open to let us out into the brisk late winter sunshine. "No other boyfriends…or girlfriends, for that matter…"

He winked before unlocking a bike from the nearby rack. He swung his leg over the frame and shot me a devastating smile. "Gotta run. See ya around, Danielle!"

three

. . .

noah

I MET Aris for lunch at our favorite café about a block from the medical office complex where we both worked. He was sitting in what was widely considered to be "our booth" in the back, and he'd already ordered my veggie panini.

"You're on top of things today," I praised him, which made him grin like a fool. "Thanks for ordering for me. I got out of the office a little later than I hoped because I had an unexpected patient right after I got back from surgery. I thought Karla had cleared my schedule until one o'clock, but I forgot I'd agreed to a last-minute consultation."

"Oh, you must be talking about Danielle." He took a bite of his meatball sub.

"That's right… I almost forgot Raine texted you first to ask if I could squeeze in someone as a favor." My boyfriend was always connecting people. Aris was gregarious and knew how to work a room. And with his gorgeous Greek heritage, signature man bun and dimples, he always left quite an impression on folks.

I know he did on me.

"How did you meet her again?" I took my first bite of panini. So good.

He grinned and was adorable, even with a tiny bit of tomato sauce in the corner of his mouth. "Yeah, I met her at Bonnie's party a few weeks ago. She's Raine's roommate."

"I almost forgot you know Raine too, but of course you do." He rolled his eyes in a playful way as I reached across the table to wipe away the sauce with my napkin. "Well, I can't share the details—HIPAA and all—"

"But will you have another appointment with her?" Aris set his sandwich down and leaned forward, seeming invested in my answer.

"Again, HIPAA." I wagged a finger at him. "Why do you care, anyway? Did you see her today?"

"We shared an elevator after her appointment. She told me she'd seen you, but she didn't say what for. She seemed very intrigued when I told her we're poly."

My brows wrinkled. "You told her what?"

He blinked a few times. "I told her we're poly."

When I continued staring at him, he added, "Because it's the truth?"

I sighed. It was the truth, but it wasn't something I liked to advertise, especially to patients. I was already in trouble for—

"Do you have a problem with that?" His gaze sharpened. "She's gorgeous, don't you think?"

I shrugged. "She's fine."

"That long brown hair? Those curves? She's a goddess," Aris insisted. "I wouldn't mind worshipping those curves."

"Are you saying you want to go out with her?" I asked him point-blank. I didn't see any reason for beating around the bush.

His lips pursed as he appeared to consider my question. "Well, I wouldn't be opposed to it. But I won't ask her out if you have an issue with it."

Aris wore his heart on his sleeve, and it was easy to see he was disappointed by my reaction. I scrambled to come up with some talking points about why it might not be the best idea. "Well, first off, she's my patient, so I can't really get involved with her. Not that I have to if you're dating her, but —well, you and I are so new, and…"

"And what? You don't know if you want to share me yet?" Those long-lashed hazel eyes blinked rapidly, but he wasn't going to drop this conversation without an answer.

Was that what it was? Or was it the issue I was facing that I hadn't told Aris about yet and, frankly, I wasn't quite sure how to broach the subject. I hadn't been able to think of much else, yet I didn't want to talk about it either.

Maybe encouraging Aris to date someone else was actually in my best interest. We were still establishing our relationship, our routine, and we'd only been living together at Cynda and Jason's for a month. But, at this point, I was unsure what the next few months would bring.

"I love you," I took his hands into mine, "and I'm not going to stop you from seeing other people. Love doesn't have to mean ownership. In the truest, freest sense of the word, it *shouldn't* mean ownership."

"Why do people equate love with possession?" he wondered, but there was a playfulness dancing in his hazel orbs.

I shrugged. "I think it's insecurity. The fear that letting your love explore other relationships puts your own in jeopardy. But the truth is: love is a risk. Any time you give your heart to another person, you risk them breaking it. Holding on too tightly doesn't change that."

"You're so right." He squeezed my hand, and I saw the wheels spinning in his mind. "I do think I might ask Raine for Danielle's phone number. If you're sure you're okay with it."

I smiled. I might not have been one hundred percent okay with it, but I reminded myself of the words I'd just spoken. Their veracity. And how my present circumstances might distract me from being the best partner I could be.

"She is really pretty," I agreed. "I don't blame you for wanting her."

He grinned as a deep breath puffed his chest out. "Maybe she's into sharing too?"

I had a huge headache after seeing my afternoon patients, so I went home after my last consultation. Aris was headed to the gym after work, so the only person in the house was Cynda, who was making her famous lasagna.

"God, it smells like heaven on earth in here!" I exclaimed as the smell of garlic and cheese filled my senses. "You sure do spoil us, Cynda."

She came out from the kitchen, wiping her hands on her apron, which read, *Kiss me, I'm bi and poly!*

"Love that apron. If I cooked, I might need one like that too."

She wrapped her arms around my waist and gave me a hug. "How was work today? You didn't go to the gym with Aris?"

I shook my head. "Nah, I'm going to take a couple ibuprofen actually. I had one or two challenging patients this afternoon, and my head is pounding."

Cynda's lovely face scrunched up with concern. "I'm sorry to hear that, Noah. Go sit in the living room. I'm about to have some coffee while this lasagna bakes. I'll bring you some painkillers and a coffee—the caffeine will help your headache."

"You're the absolute best, Cynda. You would make an incredible doctor. Has anyone ever told you that?" I patted her shoulder affectionately. "I have to admit, your bedside manner is a lot better than mine."

Her contagious laugh spilled out, warming my soul, before she returned to the kitchen to complete her tasks. In no time, she was serving me coffee, ibuprofen in a small paper cup, and a glass of water. I owed this woman so much —Aris and I would have probably never gotten together if not for her. She helped us both admit to each other we were bisexual, and that we were wildly attracted to each other.

"So, tell me what's new with you, Noah. You seemed a little upset at dinner last night." She settled down in the armchair and took a sip of her coffee from a mug that said *Sharing is Caring!*

"Oh, it's nothing. Don't worry about it." I brushed off her concern, though she was right that something was bothering me last night—and today. If I were being honest with myself, my headache probably had more to do with this cloud hanging over my head than it did my afternoon patients.

"Are you sure you don't want to talk about it?" She tilted her head, and her honey-brown eyes honed in on me. It was like she had lie detectors in them, and they could see straight through me.

Well, telling Cynda would be safer than telling Aris. Aris had a tender heart. He was a notoriously positive person, but he didn't handle stress well.

"I probably shouldn't say anything until after I meet with

my lawyer," I offered, hoping that might clue her in to the seriousness of my dilemma. I, unlike Aris, didn't get stressed about trivial things. If I was going to get stressed about something, it would be something consequential.

This was consequential.

"That doesn't sound good." She laid a hand on top of mine. "If you're not ready to talk about it yet, I understand, but please know I'm always here for you."

"I love that about you, Cynda. Your loyalty and compassion, your empathy and caring spirit—you're just such a special person to me. Thank you so much for bringing Aris and me together, and for inviting us to live in your polycule. I have never been happier, and there's no way I would be able to face what I'm facing without such a great support system by my side."

She brought her steepled hands to her face, pressing them against her mouth as tears glistened in her eyes. Happy tears, I hoped. "It's so lovely of you to say such wonderful things about me, Noah. I just knew as soon as I saw you and Aris together that you needed to explore that spark. I'm never wrong about these things…"

"Indeed." I chuckled.

"Then when I heard you both had less-than-supportive roommates—"

"Homophobic roommates, you mean. Let's not give them any undeserved credit." I rolled my eyes thinking about the guys we'd lived with. They didn't understand why we needed to date each other, why we couldn't just continue to date women if we liked women too.

"But you date women," my roommate Brian had said. "So…what, you're like gay now? You're not planning to bring him over here, are you?"

He said it like I got to choose who I was attracted to or

fell in love with. Or that I should only feel comfortable expressing the side of me attracted to women. That was all bullshit, of course. Cynda was instrumental in helping me understand and believe that both sides of me were equally valid and deserving of recognition.

"I hate that word—because 'phobic' means fear, and what it really is…is hate. It's homo-hatred." She gave a heavy sigh.

"Maybe. Either way…you rescued us both from what could have been a volatile situation. I will never be able to repay your kindness."

"The good news is you don't have to," she returned. "Just keep paying your part of the bills and enjoying my cooking, and we'll be all squared away." She opened her arms wide, welcoming me into her embrace.

I couldn't resist a Cynda hug. It was a momentary reprieve from worrying about Aris dating my patient…and from my legal troubles.

four

. . .

danielle

"SO DID Dr. Evans hook you up?" Raine asked as soon as I bustled in the door, dumping my heavy bag, purse and coat on the chair in the entryway. My heart was pounding from my hike up to the third floor, so I'd have to catch my breath before I could answer.

Whew, okay.

"Um, why didn't you tell me that Noah was so hot...and that Aris is poly?" I cut right to the chase. This conversation seemed loads more important than a silly medical condition. With my lungs burning, I had to prioritize.

Raine's melodic laugh filled the air. "Speaking of Aris... he texted me to see if he could get your number."

I froze in place, shock reverberating through my system. "Are you serious?"

"Would I lie about such things?" My roommate batted her eyelashes at me. "So, did you get answers for your throat or not?"

"Yes, I did. And I sure hope you wouldn't lie to me!" I

recalled the image of Aris's captivating smile when the elevator opened to reveal him in those blue scrubs. "He's absolutely gorgeous. I don't know why he'd be interested in me, though. Hell, his boyfriend is prettier than I am! And he hasn't texted or called me, anyway, so maybe he already changed his mind."

Raine held a hand up. "Chill, sis. It's been like fifteen minutes, for fuck's sake. Now, come have some tea and tell me what Dr. Evans said about your pipes."

My wonderful roommate already had the tea kettle on, and as I followed her into the kitchen, it began to whistle. The timing literally could not have been better, and we both laughed for a solid twenty or thirty seconds about it. Then I poured us both some tea, added honey to mine, and we went to sit in the living room.

"Well, he gave me an antibiotic for a sinus infection, but he wants to check what else is going on, so he's ordered a CT scan of my sinuses and an endoscopy." I sighed. "I really hope it's just the sinus infection though. I can't afford for anything else to be wrong with me. Especially not if I get a good part in this show!"

"Well, you gotta get through auditions first," Raine reminded me, then she let out a whistle almost as shrill as the teapot's. "You should see some of the costume designs for the show. They are stunning!"

"I know—I already popped one of those pills, and I'll take another before bed tonight. I'm just going to keep thinking positive. You know how hard that is for me. I'm not a glass-half-full kind of person." I sighed. "And I'm sure if you had anything to do with the costume designs, they're absolutely gorgeous."

"Thank you." She grinned. "And I know how you are, Ms. Grumpy Pants. But I'll keep trying to send you my positive vibes." Raine sipped her tea and put the cup down on the saucer. "Now…tell me what Aris said when you ran into him."

I relayed the conversation. "So did you know he's bi and poly?"

"Well, not exactly, but Bonnie did say she knew he'd dated women in the past. Do you think you'll go out with him?" she asked.

"I wonder if he and Noah are a package deal?" My eyebrows waggled as I thought about being in an Aris-Noah sandwich.

"Mmm, can you imagine being in a Noah-Aris sandwich?" My roommate's voice had a dreamy quality to it.

My eyes bugged out. "Holy shit, you did *not* just say exactly what I was thinking!"

My roommate's jaw fell open. "Get the fuck outta here! That's what you're hoping for?"

"I didn't say 'hoping…'" I realized right then that this might be one of those "be careful what you wish for" situations. "Is Noah bisexual too?"

She shrugged. "Good question. I'm sure Bonnie knows…"

"What do they call it when it's three…?" I totally spaced on the term. *Not a couple, but a…*

"Hot as fuck?" Raine supplied.

"Throuple!" I blurted out, suddenly remembering.

"Oh my god, I thought you said 'trouble' at first."

I shrugged. "Well, you never know…"

And before I could say anything else, my phone chimed in the purse I'd left in the entryway. I was so attuned to the sound, I heard it loud and clear over our laughter, even though it was several yards away. I leapt up and did an Olympic-caliber steeple chase to get into the foyer and collect my phone.

My heart was pounding as I swiped the unlock code for my phone, knowing full well it was probably something mundane like an email related to school. A girl could dream, though, right?

Unknown number. My breath hitched.

> 812-555-7865: Hi, it's Aris. Hope you don't mind I got your phone number from Raine. Enjoyed running into you today.

I squealed as I walked back into the living room, where Raine was still standing there looking flabbergasted.

"What?"

"What?! You practically set a world record to get to your phone!" Raine chuckled at her own joke. "Well? Don't hold me in suspense."

"It's from Aris!" I read her the text, analyzing every single word for hidden meaning. "Should I text him back now or wait?"

She tilted her head. "How old are you?"

"Twenty-five." I stared back at her. "What? I don't want to fuck this up."

"It's a text," she said, "not a final exam. Just text him back. Sheesh!"

I set my phone on the end table next to the sofa. "Look, you know my history with men, and what little history I have is not positive." I'd had exactly two relationships: a long-term boyfriend in high school—we broke up when I went away to college. And a broken engagement that crushed my heart around the time I graduated from college. Since then? Nada. Well, nothing worth noting, anyway.

Raine's nose wrinkled. "Well...there's no pressure, right?

It would just be hanging out. Like a friends-with-benefits thing, right?"

I blinked a few times. "What do you mean?"

"Well, he's living with Noah. They're together. I know they're poly, but—"

More confused blinking ensued. "Well, what difference does that make?"

She sighed as if frustrated by my lack of comprehension. Then she sat down on the sofa and took a sip of her tea. I plopped down and did the same, savoring the sweetness of the honey on my tongue.

"I didn't think you'd want to get serious with someone who is already involved with someone else," she said. "I mean, I could be wrong, but—"

"But what?"

"Poly is a lot of work," she warned me. "I thought you would want a man all to yourself. You know, like a traditional relationship. Marriage. Kids. White picket fence."

"Sheesh, Raine, you're kinda jumping the gun here, aren't you?" I already knew I wasn't cut out for poly. I even told him as much today when I ran into him.

I just wanted to have some fun. I deserved some fun, right? I still wasn't sure what Aris saw in me, but maybe hot Greek guys with sexy man buns thought curvy brunettes were the epitome of beauty?

"Aren't you?" She stared right back at me. "If you're thinking of it being more than just a friendship? Maybe some great sex?"

I wasn't sure why we were arguing. It sounded like we were making the same conclusion, just not reaching it in the same way. "Are you asking if I can have casual sex with Aris and not get attached?"

She bit her bottom lip, her eyes bouncing between mine.

"Yes. I guess that's what I'm asking. I know you, Dani—you have a tender heart, even if your façade is aloof and in control. I don't want you to get hurt. This just doesn't seem like a forever-type thing, you know?"

Everyone needs a best friend who can be honest with you, and Raine was the bluntest, most honest person I knew. "You're right that I get my feelings hurt easily, but if I do, I keep it to myself. I certainly won't come crying to you about it."

My gaze spun around the room, trying to find a focal point that wasn't the intense love and devotion shining in her eyes because now tears were welling in mine. To have someone care so much for me—I wasn't used to it. It was triggering something deep inside me that I tried to keep shoved down where it belonged.

"Dani," Raine set her teacup down again and stood up, "I love you so much. I see through your act where others don't. You come across as this tough, confident diva…"

I stood up too. "You don't think I can handle Aris?"

"I just don't want you to get hurt." She smiled. "That's all I'm saying."

"I'm not as weak as you think." I cleared my throat and squared my shoulders.

She reached out to touch my arm. "I know you're not weak. It takes a strong person to cover up their scars the way you do. No one would ever have a clue about your family, Dani."

I swallowed hard, sending the sniffles and tears that were burgeoning down my throat. I didn't want them right now. Didn't need them. I could turn them off and on at will. Not just because I was an actress and had been trained to, but because I grew up learning to hide my emotions.

Raine was right—she was one of the few who knew the real me with all my scars.

"As you said, it's just a text. I've hardly dated since I started this program. I need a little fun in my life. I don't know what's going to happen with Aris, but would it be a crime if I just got laid once or twice? Enjoyed myself for a few minutes?

After a deep sigh, I continued, "As soon as my MFA is complete, I'll be off to New York to start a new life and audition for shows. I'll probably have to wait tables somewhere while I audition my heart out, waiting for my big break. It's going to be rough as fuck—I know that. Maybe this is my last chance for a good old-fashioned fling while I'm still young enough to enjoy it."

"Maybe…" Raine smiled. "But you're so talented, I think some casting director is going to snatch you up right away."

"But even then I'm going to be focused on my career. I'm not going to have time for fun," I argued.

"What about the marriage, family, and white picket fence?" Raine asked.

It was a legitimate question. "I'm only twenty-five. I can do that later…after I've conquered Broadway."

She grinned. "And you will, too. I just know it." She handed me my phone from the end table. "You're right—I wasn't giving you enough credit. You should text him back. Have fun. Get laid."

I accepted the phone and unlocked it again, swallowing down more of those threatening tears. "Okay, here goes nothing."

> Me: Hey, Aris! It was nice to see you today too. How's your day going?

aris

My heart fluttered when my text was answered not long after I sent it. Thinking about that beautiful curvy brunette immediately brought a smile to my face.

"What are you smiling about?" Wendy, one of the nurses in my office, asked.

"Oh, nothing." I didn't have the type of skin to flush easily, but my cheeks felt hot nonetheless.

"Text from Dr. Evans?" Her well-groomed eyebrows arched as she stared at me like she was trying to solve a puzzle.

"No, no…" I needed to figure out what to say to Danielle, but that could wait. "I'm going to finish up restocking, and then I'm out of here."

"Have a nice evening!" Wendy waved as she headed off to greet our last patient of the day.

Noah wasn't thrilled about our relationship being so public, but nearly everyone we worked with had seen us together. Before we knew it, the rumors were flying. It was hard to keep anything secret in this medical office building. There were four doctors here: ENT, orthopedics, gastroenterology, and a urologist. And I had never met a bigger group of gossipy people. Nurses were the absolute worst, too.

I checked over all the supplies and made sure there were enough bandages, braces, gloves, and other odds and ends before gathering up my things and heading out to my bike. I was lucky to live close enough to bike to work—and the hills in Bloomington were great for my legs and stamina. I'd like to think all the bike riding improved my performance in the bedroom too.

I swung my leg over my bike and stood there for a

moment, fumbling for my phone. I wanted to text Danielle back before I left work. Maybe when I arrived home, there'd be another text from her waiting for me.

> Me: Just finished up work and I'm about to bike home. Just wondered if you'd like to hang out sometime. Coffee? Drinks?

I wanted to add: *with your naked curves pressed against me?* But that seemed a little too forward. I really didn't know much at all about this woman, only that she was a theater student and her area of expertise was musical theater. And she was absolutely stunning.

Hopefully I'd be learning more—much more—about her soon.

noah

Working in the same building as your lover does make it hard to maintain any semblance of privacy. I'd always been a private person, and although I deeply admired Aris's openness, it was just not my style. I needed to meet with my lawyer without my boyfriend asking a million questions— and Aris always asked a million questions—so I booked the appointment for right when I finished my eight o'clock surgery.

It was a simple tonsillectomy, and there were no complications, so I was on my way from the hospital to my attorney's office without anyone keeping tabs on me. I checked in and took a seat in the small waiting area across from the administrative assistant.

Maggie welcomed me with a hug—she was just that kind of person, magnanimous and effervescent, despite having a sharp and creative legal mind. She was a friend of a friend, and I was grateful for the referral.

"Come on in and have a seat, Noah!" She gestured toward the leather seat and closed the door behind us. She settled into her swanky executive chair and swiveled toward a counter behind her. "Tea? Coffee? Water?"

"I'll take a water, thanks. Just got out of surgery." I swallowed down the lump in my throat. During surgery, I felt completely capable and confident, but right now I felt like a schoolboy called to the principal's office.

She grabbed a water bottle from the small dorm-sized refrigerator on the counter and handed it to me. "So, I'll cut to the chase. I got a chance to read through the suit, and I… well, first off, I don't think you did anything wrong."

Just hearing her say those words made a sigh of relief wheeze out of my mouth like air escaping a deflating balloon. But she was my lawyer—I was paying her, and she could be biased.

"I do feel some degree of responsibility," I admitted. "But I wasn't negligent."

She shook her head. "No, not at all. So…I guess my main question is: do you want to settle, or do you want to fight it? You have malpractice insurance. We could offer a small settlement. There's no admission of guilt if you do that, by the way."

I closed my eyes and sucked in a deep breath. This was every doctor's worst nightmare. Well—maybe not worst. Worst would be losing a patient or royally fucking up in some other way *and* it being your fault. This was *not* my fault. This patient didn't follow the protocol, and she ended up needing additional surgery. That wasn't my fault.

"I can't settle out of court," I answered with very little

hesitation. I had barely considered it, and in my heart of hearts, I knew it just wasn't a direction I could ever go.

She nodded. "I understand. But I want to prepare you for what a trial is going to look like, Noah, okay?"

I folded my hands in my lap and looked at her, bracing myself for the worst.

"It's going to be slow-going. It's going to be brutally long and intensely personal. It won't just be your skills as a doctor that are on trial. It will be you as a person."

I sighed. "But why? This doesn't have anything to do with who I am as a person. It's all about my skill as a surgeon and a patient who blatantly ignored my post-surgical instructions."

She shrugged. "It doesn't matter, I'm afraid. These things always turn into some sort of character assassination."

Thoughts of Aris immediately filled my mind. I really didn't want to drag him into this. What was I going to do?

"I hope you have a strong support system. Family. Friends?" Concern was etched on her face.

"I don't really…" I bit my lip to bring my emotions back under control. Discussing my lack of family right now was not in my best interest. "I have a great group of friends."

If I could actually tell them what was going on.

"What kind of timeframe are we looking at here?" I took a deep breath, squared my shoulders, and prepared to face this head-on like I did everything in life. If I could get through losing my parents when I was a child, survive the foster care system, and graduate from medical school—I could do this.

"These things can take a while. Probably a few months to get a court date. But we'll see when I file the paperwork. Fingers crossed it will be over soon, you'll be exonerated, and you can get on with your life."

I nodded, resolved to put this behind me as soon as possible.

five

. . .

danielle

FIRST DATES ARE NERVE-RACKING. I hadn't been on one in a couple of years. Since I started graduate school, I'd been so focused on every class, every project, every single show I'd performed in, I didn't make any time for me. Raine oh-so-helpfully pointed out that Graduate Student Danielle was not nearly as fun as Undergraduate Student Danielle.

She wasn't wrong.

Now I was in the final semester of my master's program, and my fate rested on the role I got in our spring musical as well as my thesis. Perhaps I could squeeze some fun into a couple hours a week. I was vying for the role of Marian the Librarian in *The Music Man*, and if I got it, I would need to act like I was falling in love. That might be hard for me to do when I hadn't even been kissed in over two years.

I needed some inspiration.

Aris seemed to fit the bill.

And when his face lit up at seeing me nestled in the back booth at the local coffee shop a couple of blocks from campus, the butterflies in my stomach made me hope he'd fill any role I decided to give him. Or any hole, for that matter.

Oh my god, what is wrong with me?!

"Danielle, hi!" he greeted me. He continued to stand by the table as if he expected me to get up.

So I slid across the booth, my bare thighs sticking to the pleather seat—*great, didn't need those skin cells apparently*—and pushed to my feet. He wrapped his arms around me and brought me in for an honest-to-goodness hug. Not one of those wimpy hugs where your torsos don't even meet, and there's enough space between your bodies to plant a garden. No, he crushed me to his firm chest, and I was so close that the scent of his cologne was going to be in my nose for the entire day.

Not that I minded because he smelled incredible—an intoxicating combination of leather and sandalwood.

"Thanks for coming all the way over to campus," I said as I slid back into the seat. It only took a microsecond for my bare skin to re-adhere to the upholstery.

"Yeah, of course. I have a half-day today anyway. My boss had some seminar to attend." He reached up and adjusted his man bun. I couldn't help but wonder what his hair looked like down.

"So you're free all afternoon...?" I blurted without the slightest bit of sense.

Aris didn't miss a beat. "I am... Why, you wanna do something together?" His smile was like the sun parting the clouds and chasing them all away. His lips were full and kissable, his teeth straight and white. How could anyone in their right mind resist him, male or female?

"I should probably get to my practice with my accompanist so I can polish up my audition piece for the spring musi-cal." I rolled my eyes. "Adulting sucks, you know?"

"I hear you. What show are you auditioning for?"

"*The Music Man*. Nothing crazy—just have my eye on the Marian the Librarian role." I couldn't think of a better way to finish up my grad school career than having a lead in my final show. And, despite my weight, I thought this was one lead role I had a shot at.

"Ah, how…traditional." Aris grinned.

"It is definitely not the most modern choice they could make. But I'll have opportunities for more contemporary shows when I get to New York. I'm sure I'll start off-Broad-way." I was already tired of small talk. I was still thinking of how it felt to be squeezed against his firm chest.

His eyes widened in surprise. "Wow, so you're moving right after graduation, then?"

"I might stick around and see if I can get some regional theater experience. Chicago maybe, since it's close to where I grew up. I don't know, but I'm not getting any younger, and —" I cleared my throat, which was still scratchy and raw from all the drainage, "my voice isn't getting any younger either."

"Is that why you saw Noah?" he questioned, then imme-diately shook his head, and his hand flew to his mouth. "I'm sorry. It's none of my business why you saw Noah. I shouldn't have asked that."

"Actually, yes. I'm going back tomorrow for an endoscopy actually—it's right after my audition. Hopefully he can figure out why I can't seem to get over this sinus infection. My throat has been a mess all semester!" I took a sip of my coffee. "Warm drinks help. They're soothing."

"Well, I'll buy you coffee anytime." He laughed as he mirrored me, taking a drink of his coffee as well.

"What about you? I don't know much about you at all. I feel like I'm only talking about myself." I supposed we had to get through the talking phase to get to whatever came next.

A thrill danced up my spine when I imagined what "whatever came next" might entail.

"Well," he leaned forward, his hazel eyes sparkling in the late afternoon sun coming in through the window, "I'm an open book. Willing to share anything and everything with you."

The innuendo was clear. He was not in the least bit subtle, but it worked for him. Any man who looked the way he did could be as forward as they wanted—at least in my book. And it seemed like we were on the same page.

"I trust you to tell me the…um…pertinent information." I emphasized the word "pert" for some reason, then my cheeks flushed in embarrassment. I was definitely not a pro when it came to flirting. Maybe Aris could teach me a thing or two.

He reached across the table and covered my hand with his. It was warm, felt like a heater, and made me feel all toasty inside. "I already told you the most interesting things —that I'm bi and poly. But I'm a nurse in an orthopedic surgeon's office in the same building as Noah's office. I've been a nurse for four years. I'm almost thirty, and I grew up in New York before my family relocated to Florida when I was a teen."

My eyes widened. "Really? Where in New York?"

"Long Island."

He didn't pronounce it in typical New Yorker fashion. "But you don't have an accent?"

"God, no. I worked hard to get rid of that. You should hear my mom and sisters though." He laughed and then did a little imitation of them. Hearing his smooth voice with a New York accent was hilarious.

I bet he was so good with his patients. His personality was so vibrant and energetic, with a hint of confidence and assertiveness. I couldn't help but feel drawn to him as he continued to share a little more about himself.

"So what else should I know about you?" I asked, completely entranced. He wasn't just beautiful on the surface—there was plenty of personality to match his good looks.

"Well…you already know I'm in a relationship with Noah. We live in a polycule with a triad. You'll have to come over sometime—Cynda is the best cook, and when it warms up, they have a lovely deck for barbecuing and enjoying drinks. I like to stay active—you already saw my bike. I also like hiking, camping, outdoorsy stuff. It's funny because Noah is kind of a city boy—even though I'm the one who grew up near the city. He isn't into that stuff. How about you?"

"I like the outdoors," I said, immediately envisioning getting lost in the woods with Aris and all the unbelievably sexy stuff that could ensue in such circumstances. "Not sure about camping…but maybe if I had a seasoned camper to show me the ropes."

I hoped he'd get my flirt, and he seemed to as a grin spread across his face. "Mmm…that sounds like a lot of fun. I'd love to see you in a more natural setting…" His eyes darted between mine. "What else should I know about you, Ms. Delacroix?"

I loved the way he said my name. "You already can guess I'm obsessed with the theater," I shared, "but I also play the piano. And I collect antique costume jewelry—it's a bit of an obsession. I haven't had time to go to antique stores and estate sales lately because I've been so busy with grad school."

"I hate it when boring stuff gets in the way of having fun, don't you? I guess you could say I'm a bit of a hedonist," Aris admitted. "Noah can be a little uptight at times…so it would be fun to have someone to adventure with. Someone who likes and appreciates serendipity. I love Noah, but he likes to have everything planned out to the nth degree. Serendipity is where it's at, ya know?"

"Serendipity like running into you in the elevator yesterday?" I cleared my throat again. It seemed like the more I spoke, the scratchier and more uncomfortable I felt. The idea of singing sounded painful right now.

"Exactly!" He finished his coffee. "You sure you don't want to blow off your rehearsal this afternoon?"

aris

God, she was just divine. She had absolutely zero idea how absolutely stunning she was, either. She wasn't one of those girls who claimed to be clueless about their appeal but were secretly admiring themselves in every mirror they passed, either. Her long, chestnut hair fell around her shoulders in a silky waterfall. Her skin was so flawless, she didn't need makeup. She had naturally long lashes and beautiful doe-brown eyes.

And don't even get me started on her mouthwatering curves. Her breasts were full and created delectable cleavage in her low-cut sweater, and her thick thighs couldn't be hidden by her short, flouncy skirt. She wore brown leather boots that came to just below her knees.

I hadn't been with a woman in a while, and every cell in my body was calling out, begging me to bury myself in her softness and sensuality. Was there any way I could convince her to spend the afternoon with me?

Was it too early to seduce her? I used to have a pretty good track record…

Noah had given me the green light. I didn't like to use the word "permission" because he wasn't in charge of me. We were in a partnership, and we preferred to stay on the same page. He told me to pursue her if it would make me happy—and he didn't tell me that in a snarky, I-dare-you-to kind of way, but out of genuine compersion.

"Okay, so I don't want to corrupt you on our very first date," I said, "but if you do want to hang out later, let me know."

She cleared her throat for the fourth or fifth time, which made her cough. She lifted a napkin to cover her mouth while she hacked a little more. I flagged the server down and asked for some water for her.

"I'm okay," she insisted. "This is why I saw Noah. I'm just having some sinus issues. I'm not contagious, I promise." She sighed. "Sorry, I'm sure it's not very sexy."

"You'll have to try a little harder than that not to be sexy," I assured her as the server brought a tall glass of ice water with a lemon perched on the side and set it next to me. I scooted it toward her. "Here, have something to drink. I'm sure whatever Noah has prescribed will start kicking in soon."

"Yeah, he gave me an antibiotic." She took a long sip of water. "So unsexy…sorry, I—"

"Don't apologize." I held up a hand. "Actually, that little rasp in your voice is *super* sexy."

She giggled softly, then looked embarrassed that she'd laughed. "I'm sort of afraid to strain my voice, to tell you the truth. Maybe I shouldn't risk it at rehearsal. I can text my coach and accompanist and let them know."

"Are you sure? I don't want to ruin your chances at a good part in the show. You said auditions are tomorrow?"

"Yes, but I think resting my voice today is probably a better idea." She cleared her throat again, then took another sip of water.

Hmm, that ruined my plan to make her scream my name repeatedly. "Resting your voice, eh? I can work with that."

Her eyes widened. "What do you mean?"

"What I'm thinking of doesn't require any talking at all…"

I texted Noah to let him know I was going to Danielle's place. He texted back a thumbs-up and a smiley face. He was probably seeing patients and didn't have a lot of time to respond. On the drive over, I thought about the fact that this would be my first time seeing another person since I'd met Noah.

I had considered myself to be poly for a long time, but I hadn't really put it into practice. This would be a test of sorts. I asked Danielle if she was seeing anyone else, and she laughed.

"I wasn't joking," I clarified.

"I know," she continued to giggle, "but it's been so long since I've been with anyone at all that there might be cobwebs in my coochie!"

We both laughed about that. "Might be time for a spring cleaning?" I joked right back.

I parked next to her at her apartment complex and

followed her up two flights of stairs to her door. We were both a little out of breath after our climb. "Are you sure about this? I don't want you to feel like I'm pressuring you into anything."

She smiled. "No, I think this is just what the doctor ordered." Then she laughed again. "Well, not Dr. Evans. But the doctor voice in my head that is always telling me to relax and take time for me."

She unlocked the door and paused in the entryway. I leaned into her, stroking a finger down her cheek. "Well, we can make it all about you then."

Her skin heated under my touch. Bracing myself with one arm against the doorframe, I used my other hand to tuck her long hair behind one of her ears and grazed my lips against her neck. A breathy sigh slipped past her lips, and I didn't waste another moment claiming them. I'd been staring at them all afternoon, wondering what she tasted like. Notes of cream and coffee and the coconut scent of her hair filtered into my senses.

"You wanna come all the way in?" she asked, eyelashes fluttering as she pulled away.

"Sure…" I followed her inside. It was a typical two-bedroom apartment with a spacious entryway that opened to a kitchen and living room with a balcony at the far end. Two hallways branched off from the main living area, and she pulled me down the one to the right. There were three doors: one for a closet, one for a bathroom, and the third one she opened to reveal her bedroom.

It was soft and feminine with plush beige carpeting and a lavender comforter on the queen-sized bed. The furniture was all dark cherry wood, very traditional-looking. A bookcase was filled with romance novels, and on top was a collection of tiaras, all different sizes, shapes and colors.

"Wow, that is an impressive collection!" I pointed toward them.

She looked over her shoulder at the bookcase and laughed. "I have a princess complex," she said with a shrug. "Still interested?"

"I'd love to see you naked with nothing on but one of these." I was getting hard just thinking about it.

"Not sure I'm ready for that quite yet..." She exhaled softly and shut the door. With the blinds drawn, it was dark, especially since clouds were gathering to blot out the sun.

Before she could say another word, lightning cracked, with thunder rumbling right on its heels. "Looks like we made it to shelter just in time," I pointed out, lifting the blinds on one side so a bit of the sky was visible.

"Mmmm...I guess so." She cleared her throat again. "Sorry...I really hope this frog in my throat goes away before tomorrow's audition."

"Me too." I closed the distance between us. She seemed nervous, on edge. And then there was more lightning. "Wanna sit?" I gestured toward the bed, which was full of fluffy pillows and a stuffed unicorn and panda bear.

"Okay." She plopped down and patted the space next to her.

I eased myself onto the mattress next to her. "We don't have to do anything, you know. We could just lie down and cuddle."

"Really?" Her eyes darted to mine quickly.

She was not ready for more than that. The vibes emanating from her were nothing but nervous energy, buzzing around her like a swarm of bees missing their queen. But I could tell she was trying to push herself to go farther.

I kicked off my shoes and swung around so I was lying

with my head on one of the pillows. "Come here. Can I hold you?"

The sigh that puffed out of her lips sounded like relief as she crawled up beside me and reclined, laying her head right in the crook of my arm. That sweet coconut scent and something like wildflowers wafted up as she curled into my body. I rolled to my side, drawing her close to me so our torsos melted together. Her curves felt so nice against me, but my cock was straining against the zipper in my pants, wishing we were naked.

"I'm sorry I chickened out," she whispered as she closed her eyes. Another lightning flash lit the sky, and a rumble of thunder followed.

I breathed in another deep whiff of her scent. "You're not chickening out. You're here. I'm here. This feels amazing."

"You think so?"

"I absolutely do…"

She turned her wide doe eyes to mine. "You can kiss me if you'd like."

"Yeah? I'd like that." I leaned closer, cupping her cheek and jaw with my free hand. My lips brushed against hers, sending a zing through my body in time with the lightning show happening outside. With that last crack of lightning and thunder, rain began to pound against the roof, deafeningly loud since she was on the top floor of the building.

After she relaxed in my arms, I deepened the kiss, letting my tongue part the seam between her lips to delve inside. My tongue playfully explored as soft moans rose up her throat. She followed my lead in our dance, pressing closer to me until I was sure she could feel my erection through my pants.

"If I forget to tell you later," she said, sounding breathless from our kiss, "this was the best first date I've ever had…"

six

. . .

noah

"HOW WAS YOUR DATE?" I posed the question as I passed Aris the steamed broccoli. We were gathered around the dinner table with the polycule, and my handsome boyfriend had just walked in the door, sniffed the air and grinned as he plopped down next to me.

"Oh, it was lovely!" he gushed, scooping some broccoli onto his plate. "We had coffee at this little place near campus, and then we went back to her place."

Jason laughed. "I need to take notes, hold on." He pretended to get out a pad of paper and a pen. "How do you move it to the bedroom so fast? Teach me your ways." He put his hands up and performed a mock bow.

Cynda elbowed him. "What, second date wasn't fast enough for you?"

Aris took it in stride. "No sex. We just cuddled, made out, and listened to the rain. That was one hell of a storm that passed through here."

"Just be glad it wasn't snow," Darth entered the chat

room—I mean the conversation. "A few degrees colder, and it would have been."

"I really like her," Aris continued, ignoring Darth's weather report. His commentary was usually a little off, but we were all used to it. Sometimes Cynda reminded us to try to include him more, but the dude was just a little on the weird side. But, hey, they liked him, and Cynda and Jason were good people.

"That's great, Aris." Then Cynda shifted the conversation to Jason and Darth's plans to play Dungeons and Dragons at the comic book store that evening. "Say hello to Poe for me, will you?"

Jason's sister Poe played as well. She used to live with us until she moved in with her girlfriend and her girlfriend's boyfriend, Lachlan. Strangely enough, Darth had been Lachlan's roommate, so we all shifted around. Now there was one more empty bedroom in the house, which we used as a den.

My train of thought was interrupted when Aris leaned down close to my ear. His strong hand gripped my thigh as he whispered, "I'm horny as fuck, love. What are your plans tonight?"

I met his glimmering hazel eyes with my dark brown gaze. "Taking care of you?"

"Mmmmm…that's what I like to hear."

As we cleaned up the dishes after dinner, Aris couldn't keep his hands off me. He grabbed my ass, then he snapped a dish towel at it. I didn't typically bottom, but I had a feeling he needed that tonight.

It was all good. It would keep him from asking me too much about my day. I didn't want to tell him about my appointment with my attorney, and I definitely didn't want to tell him about the malpractice lawsuit.

"Shower?" I suggested when I loaded the last dish in the dishwasher.

"Thought you'd never ask!" Aris bit his lower lip as his gaze trailed up and down my body. "Been wanting to get you out of those scrubs ever since I walked through the door."

I was still wearing scrubs—a comfy pair in a deep jade color. He was wearing khaki pants and an olive-green Henley and looked pretty damn delicious too. I took his hand and pulled him down the hallway toward the bathroom, perhaps a bit too eagerly.

I started the water, knowing he liked it warmer than I did. Hopefully I'd be able to handle the heat. "So, tell me more about your date with Danielle—if you'd like."

"She's so sweet, Noah. She's kind, funny—she has this self-deprecating humor. I think she tries to come across really confident when it comes to acting and being a presence on the stage, but when it comes to her body and to intimacy…she's actually very shy. She just wanted me to hold her and kiss her."

I tried to match that up with what I surmised during the short time I'd spent with her. "Hmm…I wouldn't have guessed that from when I met her in the office. She seemed pretty assertive."

"She's super frustrated with her voice. She has an audition tomorrow for the spring musical, and it's really important. She was nervous about it—that might be another reason she wasn't in the mood for more than cuddling."

"She's seeing me tomorrow," I let slip. "Shit, I shouldn't have told you that."

"She already told me. I think her appointment with you is after her audition. You better take care of her throat, Doc. She has great aspirations!"

"I know she does, and I'll do my best. Now…I think this water is probably warm by now. Care to join me?" I began to lift my shirt over my head, and Aris froze, his bottom lip trapped under his teeth while he watched me strip off the shirt and bare my chest.

"Damn, Doc…" He glided his finger between my pecs, over the bumpy ridges of my abs, and all the way down to the waistband of my scrub pants. "These need to come off too."

"Feel free to do the honors…"

"Don't mind if I do." He bent down, sliding the pants over my thighs and knees until I could step out of them. Only my boxer briefs were left, and he made quick work of those too.

My cock thickened under his hungry gaze, and he stripped off his own clothes, revealing his luscious tan skin and white ass. I loved that he still had tan lines from the summer—it hinted at the fun we'd have this summer on Lake Monroe. My doctor partner had a pontoon boat and a ski boat, and she'd invited me out on the lake several times. This summer, I'd actually go now that I had someone to bring with me.

Well…if this all worked out.

I tried to block it out of my mind so I could enjoy the shower with my man, but it loomed like a specter in the back of my head, reminding me what was at stake.

Come summer, this could all be stripped away.

My relationship.

My housing.

My livelihood.

The woman suing me had a personal vendetta against me—I had dated her best friend, and it ended poorly. Despite her poor attitude, I treated her to the best of my ability—because the Hippocratic Oath and all that. There were some extenuating circumstances, including her family connections. But I was trying not to let any of that influence my decision to defend myself in court.

"Earth to Noah," Aris growled as he leaned in to nuzzle my neck. Hot water sprayed down on our heads, rushing in rivulets between us as his hands roamed the hard planes of my body. "What's wrong, baby?"

"Oh, sorry…spaced out there for a sec. Just thinking about work."

Aris frowned. "Don't think about work when you can think about me." He reached down and cupped my balls, squeezing ever so slightly. "I need you nice and hard."

"Oh, you don't want to top tonight?"

His brow quirked. "I mean, it is tempting…" He reached around and took an ass cheek in each hand, squeezing and pressing my body into his. "But, no, I need your cock inside me tonight. And maybe if you fuck me hard enough, you can forget about work for a minute or two." He rolled his eyes.

I felt terrible that he was feeling neglected. It wasn't my intention. "Sorry I've been so preoccupied lately. I'll make it up to you, baby."

"I'm gonna hold you to that…" He stroked my hardening cock from base to tip, making my eyes roll back in my head. If he kept that up, I was going to take him right here in the shower…

danielle

"What are you going to be singing for us today?" Raine had pulled her glasses to the end of her nose and was tapping her clipboard repeatedly with her pen. She was trying to simulate the directors who would be casting the show I was auditioning for tomorrow.

I cleared my throat and gave her my "most winningest smile"—the one my mother taught me when I auditioned for my very first show back when I was six years old. I played one of the orphans in *Annie,* and a star was born. Or something like that.

"I'm going to sing 'Goodnight, My Someone.'" I pressed play on my phone, and the music my accompanist recorded for me filtered out of the speakers. It didn't sound as nice as a real piano, but I would at least be able to stay in tune.

I belted out the lyrics, trying to keep my face and throat relaxed, even as the latter burned with strain. Immediately afterwards, I gulped down ice water from my Yeti bottle while Raine pretended to take some notes.

"Well?" I asked, prompting her to jerk her head up from the clipboard.

"Are you okay?" was the first thing out of her mouth.

My heart sank. "Was it really that bad?"

"No, you sounded lovely—just looked like you were in pain."

"Dammit! I was trying not to show it." I sighed. "I can't believe this is happening to me in my last semester." I threw myself down on the sofa and pouted. The tears stinging in the corners of my eyes only made my throat hurt worse. Thick phlegm gathered in the back of my throat, and I tried clearing it for the four millionth time.

"Stop doing that," Raine admonished me. "You're only going to strain your voice further if you keep clearing your throat like that."

"I can't help it! It's driving me crazy!" I didn't mean to sound like I was flying off the handle, but—I was. I couldn't help it. I was devastated, lost, and so upset.

Was my career over before it even began?

"Let me get you some wine," Raine offered. "Stay put. And then I want to hear about your date."

I waited for her to return, grateful my best friend was taking such good care of me. I would return the favor. We always took care of each other.

She handed me a glass of Moscato. "Now. Spill it."

I took a sip, but my lips involuntarily spread into a smile when I thought of Aris. "Oh…he's just so fucking hot, Raine. I mean, he's also kind and smart and funny, and sweet and gentle—but, damn, he makes my mouth go dry every time I see him. Not exactly helping my predicament, ya know?"

She looked about to burst with excitement. "So what ended up happening?"

"Well, he could tell I was a little nervous. I had planned to jump his bones. You know, Confident Dani made these plans. Take The Bull by the Horns Dani. But when he came over, Regular Old Dani was the one I was stuck with. So there was no bone-jumping at all."

She sighed. "Then what *did* you do?"

"It was storming…and he had me curl up in his arms, and we made out for a little bit. And then I took a nice snooze, right there against his bare chest."

"Wow, really?" She clutched her hand to her heart. "That's so fucking sweet!"

"I know!" I took another sip of the wine. "I can't believe he even likes me. I have no idea why."

"Stop it!" Raine insisted. "You are beautiful, talented, smart—you are the whole package, girl."

I rolled my eyes. "If you say so." I needed to get Confident Dani back. This issue with my throat was zapping all of my mojo.

"So when do you see him again?" Her eyes were sparkling as she awaited my answer.

"I don't know. We didn't make firm plans. I have an appointment with Noah tomorrow, though, for my endoscopy. It's right after my audition. It's going to be a crazy day. I figured I'd get through that first, and then I'll text him. But I also know he'll want to spend time with Noah too, so—"

"So there's no chance of you getting busy with both of them?"

I reached out and swatted her. "No! Noah's my doctor. Get your mind out of the gutter, girl."

"Sorry, but it's hard not to fantasize about being the meat in a Noah/Aris sandwich." She sighed. "Wait, I thought that was your fantasy too? If not, I guess I'll be forced to keep that dream alive." She fake-swooned over the back of the couch.

I swatted her again—she deserved it for teasing me. "Hey, if anyone's going to be the meat in that sandwich, it better be me!"

seven

. . .

danielle

RAINE WAS RUSHING AROUND GETTING her stuff together for class as I was rushing around getting my stuff together for my audition. "Break a leg!" she called after me as I hurried out the door and down the steps to my car.

Looking up at the sky, I wanted to cry. It was flat and gray, and the icy wind threatened snow. That storm yesterday had ushered in a cold front.

Days like this, I wondered, if there was indeed a Higher Power, why said Higher Power hated me so much. It had to be some sort of divine conspiracy against me, right? First the throat issue and now possible snow? For someone from the Midwest, you'd think I'd take it in stride, but driving in bad weather freaked me out.

With white knuckles clenching the steering wheel, I drove carefully to the audition. The whole way, I pleaded with the aforementioned Higher Power to do me a huge favor and let my audition go off without any hitches. I just needed a win right now. My anxiety was shooting through the roof at the moment. I just wanted this part so badly—my thesis would be so much better if I got a big part, and Marian was the female lead.

I fiddled with my phone as I waited for my turn. Then, I barely heard my name being called, my heart was pounding so loudly in my ears. I stood up on wobbly legs and made my way to the stage. Flashing a smile at the directors sitting at the table in front of me, I prepared myself to *knock 'em dead*. Not literally, of course. It was just another theatrical expression, like *break a leg*.

My accompanist smiled from the piano, and I nodded. The intro played, and I filled my lungs with air. And then…

Then, like some miracle unfolding its butterfly wings, my voice soared.

noah

"I hope you didn't have to wait too long," I apologized to my patient as I breezed into the room, her chart clutched in my hand.

"I was a little late, actually," Danielle admitted, her cheeks turning a rosy pink. "I had an audition today, and my voice cooperated. Maybe those antibiotics are taking care of my issue?"

"Well," I hoped that was the case, but I wasn't going to jump the gun when we hadn't run any tests yet, "we're going to see what we find in your sinuses and throat today with this endoscopy, and then you just need to complete the CT scan."

"Yes, I'm planning to do that after lunch. Hoping the snow doesn't get any worse though. They're calling for ice now, I think." She rolled her dark eyes in an adorable way.

Still, I shuddered. Driving in inclement weather was

more nerve-racking to me than performing surgery. I'd rather do the latter any day, even blindfolded with one arm tied behind my back, than drive on ice, especially black ice. It was February. Surely winter was nearly over. Indiana winters were not for the faint of heart. Wasn't it almost sixty degrees just a few days ago?

My nurse, Lucy, arrived, and we set up for the endoscopy. Out of the corner of my eye, I watched Danielle as we prepared. She was a voluptuous woman with long brown hair worn straight with a part in the middle. She had fair skin, lovely wide brown eyes and high cheekbones. She had a natural look and didn't need much in the way of makeup. I could easily see why Aris was attracted to her. She was a beautiful lady.

Erasing my thoughts about her and Aris, I performed the procedure and scoped out her sinuses and throat. After-wards, I scribbled a few notes as Lucy cleaned up the equipment.

"Well? What's the verdict?" She looked at me with her big brown eyes, blinking slowly in anticipation.

"I wish I had better news for you… Your septum is devi-ated," I explained. "I believe that is why all the drainage is going down your throat, and you're experiencing post-nasal drip. The deviated septum is blocking the mucus and causing it to drip down your throat. You said you suffer from frequent sinus infections."

She nodded. "I always have. Since I was a teen."

"We'll do the CT scan, and I can take a look on the inside to get a better idea, but the best way to correct a deviated septum is with surgery," I shared.

"Oh." She frowned. "There's nothing I can take, like another drug or something? Now's not a good time for me to have surgery." She cocked her head. "Not sure it's ever going to be a good time, in fact."

I shook my head, but I felt a pang of empathy tugging at my heart. Why? I lived for surgery. It was my favorite part of the job. "No, it's the actual anatomy that's causing your issue. At least that's my initial diagnosis. I want to get the CT scan results before I say with a hundred percent certainty."

"I appreciate you being thorough." She clasped her hands together, and all I could see was pain and fear in her eyes. "So, I guess there's nothing else I can do right now?"

I didn't like to see my patients uncomfortable, naturally, but her discomfort was affecting me more than I would have expected. Probably because I knew how much Aris liked her. There was a degree of pressure on me to fix her issues. "Let me walk you to the desk, and we'll get you set up for a follow-up appointment after your CT scan."

She huffed out a sigh. "Okay, thanks." She gathered up her things, and I opened the door, allowing her to walk out in the hallway first. Lucy flashed me a surprised look, probably because I never walked patients to the counter after an exam.

Aris was into her, and that was pushing me to take good care of her. She wasn't just an ordinary patient because of her connection to the man I loved. I supposed that made sense, then.

"Hey, Karla, can you schedule Danielle for a week out?" I asked at the counter.

The overhead light created a halo around Karla's shiny black locks, but she frowned as she studied the schedule. "You're completely booked next week."

I gritted my teeth but forced a smile so my next words

wouldn't sound harsh. "Find fifteen minutes for her, please. I'm sure you can—pull it from my lunch if you need to."

Karla looked up with a warm smile, eyes on me first and then Danielle. She scribbled something on a card. "Next Tuesday at noon, okay?"

Danielle nodded. "Thanks, I really appreciate it."

"Here," I gestured toward the exit to the waiting room, "let me walk you out. I need a breath of fresh air." I wanted to say a word or two about Aris while I had her attention, and I couldn't do that in the office when I was still acting in a professional capacity.

Her brows quirked in surprise as a smile spread across her face. But she was quiet as I pushed open the door and allowed her to exit ahead of me. Then I followed her through the waiting room and opened the door to the main hallway. We rode the elevator down to the lobby.

"Sorry, I don't mean to make you uncomfortable," I said once we were alone in the elevator.

"You're not," she assured me.

I smiled, choosing my words carefully. "I just…I wanted to tell you that I'm glad you're seeing Aris."

This time her brows drew together. "What?"

She clearly wasn't expecting me to talk about him. "Sorry, I am probably making a mess of this. I just… I'm really busy right now, and it's nice that he has something to keep him busy—"

"Are you for real right now?" Daggers formed in her dark eyes, and she looked ready to launch them at me. "Are you saying you're glad I'm able to distract your boyfriend while you have other stuff to do?"

There was venom in her words, but the elevator jerked to a stop, and the door slid open. She stormed out, and I followed her briskly, wanting to smack myself for being such a dolt.

"Wait, Danielle, that's not what I meant!" I insisted as she paced toward the front doors. The glass slid open, creating an opening to the vestibule, and as soon as she stepped in, the glass door to the outside opened as well.

A huge gust of wind smacked me in the face as I continued to pursue her, tossing out apologies. "Wait, can we talk about this for a second?"

Then I saw Aris, on his bike—*what the hell is he thinking riding his bike in this weather?*—approaching us. He wore a knitted ski hat with his fleece hood over it, tied tightly under his chin. Thick gloves covered his hands as they wrapped around the handlebars.

It all happened so fast, it was like a blur.

Danielle stepped off the sidewalk, right into Aris's path.

He couldn't stop the bike as the wet, icy snow was already falling.

Next thing I knew, he went flying into the air. He and the bike came to rest right on Danielle's leg.

I rushed to them, the snow pelting me like tiny grenades.

"Oh my god, are you guys okay?" I pulled Aris to standing, grabbed his bike, and then went to offer my hand to Danielle.

She only glared up at me with a look that could kill.

danielle

What the hell was he saying? That he was glad I could distract his boyfriend while he was busy being a surgeon? Were all doctors this fucking full of themselves? What the actual fuck?

He was shouting his apologies and explanations, but all I

wanted to do was escape. My luck with doctors had always been absolute shit, and this one just told me I needed surgery. Not what I wanted to hear when I was this close to finishing my master's degree and heading to New York to make my dreams come true.

I knew I shouldn't have trusted him.

The cold air blew in like something out of the movie *Frozen*, but I didn't care. It felt good on my burning cheeks. I needed to get the hell to my car and get home before the storm got worse. I was not about to "Let It Go" at the moment.

Shit, I still needed to go get the CT scan at the hospital.

FUCK!

I marched down the sidewalk when Aris, all bundled up in a fleece jacket, hat, and gloves, came barreling across the parking lot toward the front of the building on his bike. *Is he going to stop?*

Before I had a clue what was happening, I was stepping down onto the pavement just as Aris's bike careened into me. He went flying, and so did the bike.

But I didn't have a chance to see where he would land because I lost my balance and crashed to the ground, the icy pavement scratching up my legs and hands.

Then the wind was knocked out of me, and a crushing blow sent pain rocketing up and down my leg.

So that's where Aris and the bike landed, I thought without even looking.

Right on top of my leg.

eight

. . .

aris

PAIN SHOT through my elbow as I blinked through the stars sparkling in front of my eyes. I'd had the daylights knocked out of me, and, for a second, I wasn't even sure where I was or what happened. And then I realized I was on the hard, wet, slick pavement, half on top of my bike, and the other half was on top of someone else.

Oh my god! Danielle!

I tried to scramble to my feet, but my head was spinning too fast. Speaking of scramble, my brain kind of felt like scrambled eggs. I looked up to find Noah staring down at us both, shock on his face before he immediately went into doctor mode.

"Don't move yet. I'm calling an ambulance, and then let me assess you both." His voice was calm and authoritative, and I took a deep breath before glancing over at Danielle, who was also just now blinking her eyes open.

"Are you okay?" I tried not to move too much so I wasn't disobeying the good doctor.

She shook her head. "No, everything fucking hurts."

"I'm so sorry!" I rushed out. "I couldn't stop. I saw you, braked, and hit an icy patch."

She started to get up, but Noah—still on the phone—crouched down next to her, "Whoa, easy there. Let me check you out first."

I brought my knees up and wrapped my arms around them. My ass was cold as fuck, but otherwise I didn't seem any worse for the wear. My bike looked worse than me—it definitely had a bent frame. How the fuck could I let this happen? My heart raced thinking I might have hurt her.

We weren't too far from the hospital, so I wasn't surprised to hear sirens in the distance as Noah pulled Danielle to her feet. *I see he is helping her before me,* I chuckled to myself. I was totally fine with that and would have insisted, of course.

Guilt was stabbing into me for causing this scene in the first place. *Fucking ice!*

Danielle screamed as soon as she attempted to put weight on her leg. "Oh my god! Ouch! I think it's broken."

"I think you may be right," Noah agreed as the ambulance turned the corner and started to head into the parking lot. "We'll be getting you both checked out, x-rays, the whole nine yards."

In seconds, we were swarmed by paramedics, who lifted Danielle onto a gurney and rushed her away to examine her. "I'm okay," I insisted when they came to assess me. "Really, I can walk and everything."

"No pain?" the tall white paramedic with cropped brown hair and glasses asked.

"He's still going to go get checked out," Noah advised. "But I'll take him to the ER." He reached out a hand. "I'm Dr. Evans. Thank you for getting here so quickly."

"Not a problem. I'm Bart," the paramedic answered with a grin, shaking Noah's hand. "Okay, we'll get your friend to the ER ASAP."

"Should I ride with her?" I asked my boyfriend.

He shook his head. "Haven't you done enough for her?" It wasn't snarky—more of a joke—but it still made me feel like shit.

"I'll see you in a few," I called out to Danielle as they loaded her up in the ambulance.

Could I feel like any more of a dumbass right now? I was pretty sure it wasn't possible.

I was probably a weirdo, but I found the monotonous beeps and sounds of the hospital plus its sterile smell to be soothing. My mom was a doctor, so I'd grown up in this environment. I knew hospitals freaked a lot of people out, but they just seemed comforting to me, filled with people who could take care of me.

So, it was hard for me to really fathom why Danielle was so distressed. She gripped my hand so hard when I went to see her that I thought she might rip my fingers off.

"Don't go...please?" Her eyes darted around her curtained-off room. "Raine is coming, but I—"

"I won't go anywhere," I assured her. "They will probably see you before me since your condition is more serious. I feel fine, really. But I'm so, so sorry about what happened. I just—"

"Aris," she said, dark eyes blinking up at me, "it was an accident. Everyone has accidents. Please don't think I'm mad at you. I mean, I'm in pain, but I'm not angry with you."

There was the tiniest smirk curling her lips that offered me a bit of relief.

"I will make it up to you anyway," I promised. "I just—I hate seeing people in pain. If there's something really wrong with your leg, I'll get my boss to squeeze you in. She's booked up for months, but I know she'll make time for you, especially when she finds out I'm the dumbass who got you injured. She's the absolute best orthopedic surgeon in southern Indiana."

Danielle's eyes sprang wide open. "Surgery? You think I might need surgery?"

"Oh, I don't know. They haven't taken you for your X-ray yet. I'm just saying, you know, if—"

She shook her head. "I can't need surgery. I can't be seriously injured. I'm going to be cast in a show, and I have to be able to dance."

Just as I was about to reassure her again, the nurse came back. "We're ready for your x-ray, Danielle. Can you get yourself into this wheelchair so we can take you down?"

I offered my hand to help her out of bed. She huffed out a long sigh as she said "okay" to the nurse, but she wouldn't take my hand. She put her feet on the floor, wincing in pain, and used the bed handle to steady herself as she straightened to her full height. Then she pivoted, keeping her weight on one leg as she limped back into the wheelchair.

"You can wait here," the nurse told me as I began to follow. "Aren't you a patient as well?" She gestured to my plastic ID bracelet.

"Yes, but I—"

"Just wait there please." She pointed to the ugly blue chair. "We'll be back in a few minutes."

"Fine." I sighed as Danielle was wheeled away. She

looked over her shoulder just as they exited the room, a look of sheer terror on her face.

I pulled out my phone and glanced at a text from Noah. After getting me settled here, he'd returned to the office to wrap things up for the day, but he was coming back to pick me up.

Noah: *How are things going?*

My fingers flew over the keyboard.

Me: *She's getting x-rays. I haven't been seen yet.*

Noah: *I'll be back within an hour. One more patient to see, and I'm done.*

Me: *Take your time.*

I heaved out another sigh, feeling so defeated and restless, wishing there was something I could do. Seeing people in pain and not being able to do anything about it was a nightmare for a nurse. Then I heard the curtain draw back. My gaze snapped up to see Raine, Danielle's roommate, stepping into the small enclosure.

Her glossy black hair was pinned up in a plastic clip. "Where is she?"

"She just went back," I noted. "I'm supposed to be in the next bay, but I was waiting with her for the nurse to come take her for an x-ray. I can go back to my bay now that you're here, I guess. It's pretty cramped in here."

"Wait—what happened exactly?" Raine plopped down in the chair beside me. "She was blubbering so hard when she called, I couldn't understand half of what she said."

"Me on a bike plus ice equals epic disaster," I clarified. I pulled out the ponytail holder around my man bun and shook out my wild mane, then I ran my fingers through it in a feeble attempt to tame it. "I feel absolutely awful about it."

"What part of her is hurt?"

"Her leg—"

"Well, how is she supposed to star in the spring musical if she's in a cast?" Raine wanted to know.

"We don't even know if it's broken yet. Calm down."

"You know we live on the third floor, right? There's no elevator in our building."

The curtain parted again, and the nurse wheeled Danielle in. Her face was buried in her hands, and she didn't even look up when the nurse said, "The doctor will be in to see you in a few minutes."

Raine shot me a nervous look, then put her arm around her roomie's shoulders. "Hey, sweetie, I'm here. Can I help you back onto the bed?"

When Danielle lifted her head, she revealed a face streaked with tears. "I can do it." She hobbled onto the bed and let out a shuddering sob, the kind you get after crying hard once the tears began to wane.

"Did they say anything about your x-ray yet?"

She shook her head. "No, but the tech didn't look hopeful."

"What are you going to do about the stairs?" Raine asked.

"What am I going to do about anything?" Danielle wailed.

"Do you want me to go?" I stood up and went to her side, crouching next to her and putting my hands on her knees. My heart was somewhere on the floor—I could stomp on it, and it probably couldn't feel any worse than it already did. Did I really cause Danielle to break her leg? I would never forgive myself if she missed out on her chance at starring in the spring musical. It would be the last show of her collegiate career. I knew how important it was to her.

"You can stay with me," I offered before pulling the curtain open. "If you can't get up the stairs to your apartment, I mean. You can stay with me, and I'll take care of you. And I'll get you an appointment with Dr. Riley, my boss."

"What about Noah?" Raine asked while Danielle's head went back into her palms.

"I'm sure he'll agree," I blurted out.

"Agree to what?" I heard behind me as I backed out of the room.

Noah was standing there, his arms crossed over his chest.

noah

One advantage of being a surgeon was having free rein of the hospital. My ID badge got me into the ER with no issues, and a quick stop at the nurses' station revealed Noah was in Bay 7 and Danielle in 8. I peeked into 7 and didn't see my man, but I heard voices coming from 8, so I stood outside the curtain for a moment, realizing Danielle had just been wheeled back in from Radiology.

Through the crack where the curtain wasn't closed completely, I saw Danielle with her face buried in her hands, and her roommate Raine trying to comfort her. Then I saw Aris, in profile, standing beside her wheelchair looking completely devastated and desperate to help her, his unruly hair free of its usual confinement and waving wildly around his head.

Then he crouched down so he was eye level with her. He really liked her—that much was clear from his body language and soft, comforting tones.

Who was I to stand in the way of their budding relationship? I had been a little unsure of opening our relationship up to other partners, but Danielle was a metamour I could approve of. She seemed good for Aris.

I had my legal issues to consider. I didn't want either of

them to get wrapped up in that mess. Maybe I was better off moving out of Cynda and Jason's home, finding my own place. I'd been saving to buy a house, so sharing rent was helping me make that dream a reality. But maybe now wasn't the time. If I lost my job…my dream of home owner-ship would be out the window too.

They looked gorgeous together. A lovely couple.

Then I heard Aris say something like, "You can stay with me."

Me? Not us?

Raine asked what I would think about that, and my boyfriend confidently replied that I would agree.

"Agree to what?" I asked as Aris backed through the part in the curtain, nearly running into me.

I stepped back, waiting to hear his explanation.

"Her leg might be broken." His face was painted with concern. "I don't know what else to do but to offer to take care of her. I feel like complete shit, Noah." He stepped toward me, collapsing against my chest, and I had no choice but to wrap my arms around him to stabilize both of us before we went crashing into a patient being wheeled down the corridor between bays.

"Let's talk about this outside, okay?" I patted him on the shoulder, and he nodded, following me down the hall until I buzzed us out an external door.

The cold February wind grated against my skin, nipping like an annoying little territorial dog. "Damn, it's colder than I thought."

"At least the ice has turned to snow," Aris said as a flake landed in his thick eyelashes. He smiled and wiped it away. "I'm so sorry to put you in the middle of this, babe. This really sucks."

"I understand you wanting to take care of her," I rubbed

my hands together to keep them warm, "but we don't really have space in our room—"

"I know, but there's the fourth bedroom at Cynda and Jason's," he said. "We've all been using it as an office right now, but...Cynda would understand, right? It's only temporary. Danielle lives on the third floor, and she's probably going to be on crutches..."

I sighed. "You're right. We should help her out. Are you staying here with her till she's released?"

"Don't you think I should?"

I nodded again. "Okay, you stay here, and I'll head home and have a talk with Cynda, Jason too, if he's around. Guess our happy little family might be getting a little bigger—at least temporarily..."

"Thanks for understanding." Aris leaned in and pressed a kiss to my cheek. His lips were warm in the chilly air, heating me up from the inside out.

I didn't know what this new development meant for our relationship, but I felt like it might be a sign from the universe telling me to cool things.

Or quit while I'm ahead.

nine

. . .

noah

CYNDA WAS the stay-at-home mom of our polycule. She was the main reason kitchen table polyamory worked so well in our house—because that kitchen table was always full of delicious food. If Cynda wasn't such a good cook, I wasn't sure if I could stand to hang out with Darth every night. He was an acquired taste, to stick with the food metaphor.

She had a crockpot going with a roast of some sort, and the savory aroma of meat, onions, potatoes and carrots wafted into my nose as soon as I opened the door. I found her sitting in the living room with her feet propped up on the ottoman, engrossed in something on her e-reader. Interrupting her while she read something that appeared to be quite titillating seemed like a dick move, but I needed to iron out the arrangements before Aris showed up with his girlfriend.

I guess that's the right title for her?

Cynda's dark eyes popped up from her e-reader as I

made my way into the room and collapsed on the sofa. A huge gust of air blew out of my lips as I sank into the comfortable worn cushions and kicked off my shoes.

"You look like you had an exhausting day." She set her e-reader on the table next to the chair.

"No, don't stop reading on my account." I offered her an apologetic smile. "You looked as though you were enjoying that."

"Well, you look like you could use a friend," she rather astutely assessed.

I shrugged. "Well, who couldn't use a friend?"

"What's going on?" She sat up straight and leveled her gaze on me, letting off a distinct "and don't fuck around and try to hide it this time" vibe.

Cynda was loving, caring, and empathetic. But she also valued her time, and she didn't tolerate having it wasted.

"Aris had a bit of an accident today," I shared.

Her brows flew up into her hairline. "What? Is he okay?"

"He's at the hospital being checked out right now, but I think he's fine. The problem is that his girlfriend might not be okay."

"Girlfriend?" Leave it to her to focus on that part.

"Aris is seeing someone," I clarified. "And she was involved in the accident too."

"Well, fuck. What happened?"

"Aris ran into her, wrecked his bike, and he and the bike ended up on top of her leg."

"Shit. That sounds horrible!" She shook her head and reached for her ever-present coffee mug. This one said *Polyamory—join the party* and had a Dungeons and Dragons-esque logo that also looked a bit like an infinity symbol. Well, it was certainly an appropriate mug for what I was about to ask her.

I pushed the topic forward in the most logical manner: "She's getting x-rays at the hospital now. But we have a problem…"

Her brow quirked. "What kind of problem?"

"She lives in a third-floor apartment."

Cynda immediately stood up and set her mug back on the hand-painted coaster she'd picked up last fall in one of the little shops in Nashville, Indiana. "Say no more." She held up a hand and then started to head out of the living room.

I stood up too, following her down the hall. "Wait, what are you doing?"

"Clearing out the office," she said. "There's only a futon in there, but she's welcome to it. Or we can move Darth's bed in there for a while, and he can sleep with us. We have a king-sized bed in the master."

"Oh, I couldn't ask you or Darth to do that!" I folded my arms over my chest. "Really, I just—"

She stopped moving and turned to face me, a faint smile teasing the corners of her lips. "You were going to ask if she could stay here, right?"

"Well, there are only two steps to get up on the porch," I rationalized. "And we could keep an eye on her if she's here. Aris feels responsible for her since he caused the accident."

"Will she be here in time for dinner? Molly, Lachlan and Poe are joining us, so I made plenty of extra. That's a big-ass roast in there." She flashed a proud smile. "We'll work out the sleeping arrangements later, if you'd like, after I'd had a chance to talk to Darth and Jason."

"Are you sure? I—"

She grinned. "Noah, how many times do I have to tell you? You don't have to take care of everyone and every-thing. I can shoulder some of that burden." She cleared her throat. "Now, does that help alleviate some of your stress?" She looked me up and down as if she knew the situation with Danielle wasn't the only matter I was dealing with.

I mustered up a smile. "Yes, that does alleviate some of it."

She stepped over to me and rose up on her tiptoes to cup my cheek. "How long have we known each other, Doc?"

"I don't know, a couple of years?" We met at the gym, where we both took a yoga class.

"I know you well enough to know when something is bothering you, Noah. Now I mentioned it the other day, but my proverbial door is always open. My shoulders are always available to you. Ever hear that song, 'we get by with a little help from our friends?'"

I nodded slowly.

"Right, well, it's true. We have no chance of survival on our own, Noah. I know you think you can do everything yourself—and you have accomplished a great deal in your young life, to be sure. But we can lean on each other. I know you'd do the same for me if I needed you."

"Well, if you ever have an ear-nose-throat emergency, I'm your guy," I joked.

"I know your family is…gone," she said, her voice dropping to a whisper on the last word. "But we're your family now. And family takes care of each other. Understand?"

I smiled. "Thank you."

"Now, help me get this place cleaned up. When will you know about this mystery woman's leg?"

As if on cue, my phone buzzed. I pulled it out of my jeans pocket and took a gander at the incoming text, a frown twisting my lips downward as I absorbed Aris's message. "Well, fuck…looks like it's broken…"

danielle

It hurts. Fuck, it hurts.

When the doctor came in and told me it was fractured, I wanted to cry. Okay, so I actually did cry. Raine and Aris were on either side of me, each squeezing one of my hands in theirs.

"How is this happening?" I whimpered.

"The good news is it's a simple fracture," Aris pointed out, oh so helpfully. "So you don't need surgery. Just a cast and rest, and you'll be good as new in a few weeks."

"But the play…"

I would have to talk to my advisor. I wasn't sure I could even graduate without performing a role in the spring musical. My whole MFA thesis was based on that performance. I was to write it on how I prepared for the role, how I performed the role, and a self-reflection on how I would improve my craft for future roles.

But how could I do that without having an actual role?

"You'll have to talk to your advisor," Raine tried to soothe me, only I wasn't soothed at all because my brain had already traveled down that path, and there weren't any clear solutions.

As much as my leg hurt, my heart hurt even worse.

Aris looked down at his phone after the doctor left my discharge paperwork on the bed next to me. "Noah says he spoke to Cynda, and you're staying at our place until you can get up the stairs again."

Raine patted my hand. "Give me a list of what you need, and I'll bring it by later. I'm so sorry this happened, sweetie. It sucks beyond belief. But we'll be here for you; we'll help you get through it."

Aris grinned. "I'm not going anywhere!" he promised.

Was he being so helpful and nice because he felt obligated to after plowing into me earlier, or did he really like me? It was hard to be mad at him, especially with his beautiful wavy hair flowing over his shoulders, the slight dimples in his scruff, and those glittering hazel eyes.

Damn it, he was just too cute for his own good.

For *my own good* was more like it.

I sucked in a breath and nodded, resigning myself to my fate. I mean, it was a little bit of a bonus to get so much time with him, but I didn't want to impose on his relationship with Noah. I wasn't sure how this was going to go, but I supposed we'd be finding out soon...

I was glad my pain meds had kicked in by the time we made it to Aris's house. My leg was no longer throbbing, which was a plus, but the pills had the bonus effect of taking the edge off my nerves. And it was a good thing because there were half a dozen cars parked in the driveway and on the street by the large ranch home.

"I know it looks like we're having a party," Aris remarked as he came around to help me out of my car. Raine had driven him over to get it from his work parking lot since I never actually made it back myself, and now I couldn't drive anyway.

"Our polycule is just five people," he explained, "—me, Noah, Jason, Cynda and Darth, but we have company for dinner tonight. It's Jason's sister, Poe; her girlfriend, Molly; and Molly's boyfriend, Lachlan. Lachlan is also Darth's former roommate, and Poe and Molly used to live here, in the room Noah and I now live in. Oh, we have a cat too now! Sushi is her name."

I waved my hand in the air. "Thanks to the meds, I only absorbed maybe a quarter of that." I giggled—feeling almost drunk. Sober Dani would be freaking out at the prospect of interacting with that many people, but Medicated Dani was kinda like, "Bring it on."

He grinned. "No worries. I'll go slow when I make the introductions, and if you forget anyone, well, you have a damn good excuse."

"Fuck yeah I do." I hobbled to where he held out my crutches for me.

"There's only two steps, and I can carry you up them if you want," he offered. He walked slowly beside me as I tried to maneuver on crutches, a skill I apparently didn't excel at.

I looked him up and down. "I know you go to the gym and all, but you have no business lifting me. You'll throw your back out. And then we'll both be on the injured list."

"I'm even stronger than I look," he insisted, flexing. He was still wearing his scrubs, and his biceps strained against the cuffs of the blue shirt.

I rolled my eyes. "I can probably do two stairs with some help. But definitely not the two flights of stairs I'd have to do at my apartment. They're steep too." I shuddered at the thought.

"Well, no, of course not. That's why you're here." He grinned, flashing those damn dimples once more. "It's the least I could do after what happened."

"Again, it was an accident." A fortifying breath inflated my lungs before I grasped the handrail and hopped on my good leg onto the first step, my cast feeling like a dead weight on my other leg. Then I did the second step, utterly relieved there were only two.

"I'll get the door." Aris swung it open and waited for me to hobble into the house. It smelled like slow-roasted beef and hot yeast rolls, and I was pretty sure I'd just crossed the Pearly Gates. Laughter bubbled up from the room to my left, and a sea of faces stared back at me. The only one I recognized was Noah's.

Wow, so this is a little overwhelming, even on drugs.

On the sofa were a Black woman and two white men. She wore her hair in tiny corkscrews on top of her head and dangling earrings with multi-colored glass beads. She had an ample build and looked to be in her forties. One of the men looked tall and lanky, even sitting down, with longish mousy-brown hair, glasses and pale skin that appeared to have never seen the sun. The other had sandy-colored hair, a full beard with a reddish tint, and a shorter, broader build.

"That's Cynda, Darth and Jason," Aris introduced. "Guys, this is Danielle." They all waved at me. "On the loveseat is Jason's sister, Poe, and her girlfriend, Molly. The big guy there in the recliner is Lachlan." Jason's sister had long honey-colored hair and a pixie face, while Molly was petite but curvy with pink hair and black combat boots. Lachlan lived up to his name with his burly build, thick auburn hair and a matching beard. A striped cat with a white chest and paws was perched on his lap. I'd already forgotten the cat's name.

"And you know Noah already," Aris said just as a knock sounded at the door.

I was nearest to it, so I turned toward it in time to see my roommate through the small glass window. "Oh, it's Raine. May I let her in?"

"Of course," Aris encouraged me.

"Now we have to do intros again," Darth groaned.

"I'll take care of that," Cynda said, standing. She

welcomed Raine into her home with a smile and went around the room once more. Finally, she threaded her fingers together and addressed everyone, "Follow me into the dining room please. Dinner is served."

As we gathered around the table, I looked around at each face. This was Aris's family, essentially. These people were all part of his support system. I had Raine, of course. But I was the only child of two older parents who had me in their early forties. They put me on stage at age five or six. I couldn't remember a time that I wasn't in some show. They basically let the community theater people raise me on nights and weekends, but I spent my weekdays tiptoeing through a silent house where nothing could be touched and voices were never raised—unless I was belting out a showtune.

I couldn't imagine living in a house with this many other people my age.

It seemed wonderful and scary and foreign and wild all at once.

This was going to be quite the adventure.

ten

. . .

aris

I'D WATCHED Danielle all through dinner since she sat across the table from me, positioning herself between Raine and Molly. She apparently knew of Molly from her work in the theater program, but they'd never actually met in person. Noah was quiet next to me, not saying a word as he finished his roast, potatoes and vegetables and excused himself from the table before I even finished my first glass of wine. Sushi was perched on top of the carpet-covered tower Jason built for her, judgmentally watching us out of slitted eyes.

I'd have to ask Noah later if something was wrong, but first I wanted to make sure Danielle got settled. I helped Raine carry in her things after dinner and set everything in the room Cynda and Noah had cleaned out earlier today. It was sparse—just a futon, a desk and chair, and a small chest, but she seemed grateful.

"Can I get you anything else?" I asked after settling her on the futon. I'd put a thick foam mattress topper on the thin futon mattress and made sure she had clean sheets and plenty of blankets.

"You've been so kind and helpful." She looked down at her hands for a moment, playing with the amethyst ring she wore on her right ring finger. "I really don't deserve all this special treatment."

I sat on the edge of the futon and took one of her hands into mine. "I know we're just getting to know each other, but I feel like I should warn you that I get attached to people quickly. Ask Noah—once I befriended him at the gym, and he showed interest in me, he basically was never getting rid of me."

She giggled. "I've always been the opposite." Her confession came out in almost a whisper, casting a serious mood over the room.

"Well, we can't help our attachment styles." I thought back to some psych class I took as an undergrad. "I just want to make sure you're comfortable. If I'm too touchy-feely, just tell me. I can back off."

"No..." She gave me a sheepish smirk. "I like how touchy-feely you are..."

"You do?" If I wasn't mistaken, a soft blush was creeping across her face.

"Well, yeah... I'm not a very assertive person, you may have noticed. I have...um...issues..." She made a vague gesture to her body.

Issues? I didn't know from her gesture if she meant her body—which was lush, curvy and rather delectable—or just her general existence, but I was impressed she was opening up to me like this. It didn't seem like that was the norm for her. I had a way about me, Noah always said. People felt comfortable confiding in me.

"You get up on stage in front of thousands of people and sing your heart out," I said. "That takes serious balls as far as I'm concerned."

The little giggle was back. "Hey, I don't have balls!"

I laughed along with her. "So you say… Maybe I'll get to find out firsthand at some point?"

A smoldering gaze beamed out of her dark eyes, twisting up my insides and sending blood rushing to my cock. "Whenever you're ready, Aris."

The way she said my name almost made me shudder. *Damn, she has no idea how sexy she is, does she?*

"Seriously though…damned impressed by what you do on stage. When will you hear back about your audition?" I tried to keep the conversation focused on her.

"Probably tomorrow." Her smile vanished now that she was focusing on her injury again. "But I don't see how I can perform like this." She gestured toward her cast.

I squeezed her hand in solidarity. "How long did they tell you to stay off it at the ER today?"

"Six to eight weeks in this cast—but then I'll go to a boot for a while," she said with a sigh. "Do you think your boss would see me so I could get a second opinion?"

"Sure, of course. Or at least I can put in a good word for you with Doc Riley." I winked.

"I'm sure you're very persuasive." Her lips twisted to one side in a smirk as her gaze roamed over my body. She was flirting with me—and not even being coy about it.

She was more assertive than she thought.

I moved closer to her. "Danielle…" I tucked a piece of her long brown hair behind her ear, and she shivered under my touch.

"Yes?"

"Do you mind if I kiss you? I know it won't heal your leg

or anything, but, damn, you're just so beautiful, and I haven't been able to think of anything else since you got here." I watched her smirk become a smile when I continued, "But feel free to tell me I'm being an insensitive asshole if you're not in the mood. I know you had a rough day, and it was one hundred percent my fault. You don't owe me—"

"Just shut up and kiss me, Aris." She leaned forward until her last few words fell on my cheek, poising herself to receive my lips.

I didn't need any further encouragement. Wrapping my arms around her, I pulled her against me on the bed, my lips finding hers and ravenously taking my fill of her luscious mouth, our tongues tangling and dueling for control.

For someone who wasn't assertive, she sure was a confident kisser.

Desire surged through my body, and my cock, which was already hard, became painfully engorged. All I could think about was how long it'd been since I'd slid into a hot, wet pussy. I usually bottomed when it came to sex with Noah, and the idea of topping a beautiful woman was nearly enough to make me come right in my pants.

Fuck, what am I, eighteen?

I needed to get my act together. I needed to seduce her, get her to want me as much as I wanted her—if that was even possible.

She was wearing a long skirt, which was hiked up her thigh so her cast was visible. I tugged on it gently. "Would you be more comfortable with this off?"

Her hooded gaze met mine as she caught her breath from our kiss. "Perhaps…"

"You're sure you're okay with this? I know you're on medication, and I don't want to take advantage—"

She lifted her hips. "Take my skirt off, Aris."

I very carefully eased the elastic-waist skirt down her hips and thighs, being careful not to touch her casted leg. She lifted her pelvis a little more to free the fabric from under her ass. Once I got it to her feet, I was able to slide it to the floor. She sat up a little then, crossing her arms over her exposed torso.

I rose up onto my knees and stripped my own shirt off, smiling when her lips parted into an O at the sight of my bare chest. I was going to up the ante and see what happened. I climbed off the bed and took off my pants, leaving me standing there in a pair of hunter green boxer shorts with a gigantic bulge in the front, which pulsed when her gaze landed on it.

My words came out in a rasp, "I want to see you."

"I guess that's fair…" She opened her arms and lay there, presenting herself to me. She still wore a loose peach-colored sweater that complemented the warm undertones of her skin, but it rode up high enough to reveal the palest pink silk panties, almost the same shade as her skin. There was the tiniest lace detail at the front with an itty-bitty bow that did crazy things to my insides.

She was so soft, so feminine, like a lovely pink rose in full bloom. My fingers trailed down one thigh, and I wasn't surprised at all to find her skin was petal-soft. "Damn it, Dani…"

Her eyelashes fluttered as she looked up at me from beneath them. "What?"

"You're so gorgeous, I don't even know where to start. How about the sweater? Are you attached to it? Would you mind giving it up?" I bargained with her.

A sly smile curled her lips. "I could be convinced to part with it." She lifted it over her head and tossed it aside, her hair falling back around her shoulders as she did so. She bit her lip and stared at me—the ball was obviously back in my court.

Leaning forward, I captured her lips again, hungrily expressing my need as my pelvis pressed into hers. The contact made me throb against her. I wasn't going to last long if I didn't find some semblance of control.

What would Noah do? echoed in my head. My boyfriend never suffered from coming too fast—he was so precise and methodical in everything he did, including lovemaking. Trying to get him to lose control was like my lifelong ambition.

Then I had a rogue, fleeting thought: *wonder if Dani and I could do it together? Make him lose control…*

He'd been pretty clear he wasn't interested and was even a little leery of me staring a new relationship. Though he'd seemed to grow comfortable with the idea after my first date. I still wasn't sure why he'd changed his mind so fast…

"Aris?" Danielle broke our kiss. "Everything okay?"

"Oh, yes, sure…I was just about ready to bargain you out of that bra and panties." Her bra was one of the underwire ones with peachy-pink lace that matched the panties. Her ample breasts spilled out the top, just begging to be touched and caressed. I needed all obstacles to me doing so out of the way.

She reached behind herself and unhooked it, a devilish smirk playing on her lips the entire time. It was almost like she was leaning into her natural role as temptress with the way lust radiated from her eyes, which raked over me as if she couldn't wait to see what I would do next.

I hooked a finger in the waistband of her panties. "These too…please?"

She nodded, lifting her hips to allow me to slide them down her legs, once again being careful not to touch her cast.

Before I knew it, she was completely naked and spread out for me like a gift.

Her expression said it all: *what are you gonna do now?*

I knew exactly.

First, I leaned down to her breasts, cupping their full mounds, one in each hand. She arched her back and let out a little moan when my tongue encircled one of her beautiful, responsive pink nipples. I spent a little time coaxing it to maximum hardness as she gasped and sighed, then I gave it a tiny nibble. When she tilted her pelvis up, seeking contact, I nibbled a little harder, causing her to groan, "Aris, oh my god…please…"

"Please what?" I didn't look at her, just moved my mouth to her other breast to repeat the same process, teasing and titillating her nipple until she was writhing in a frenzy.

"Please…I need…" She raked her fingers through my hair and coaxed me further south.

Pride rushing through me at my efforts thus far, I settled between her thighs and slowly lowered myself until my mouth hovered over her mound. Her hair down there was brown and a little crinkly, but mostly straight. It looked so soft—I couldn't help but run my fingers through it, causing her to squirm. I was right—it felt like silk against my callused hands.

Her tummy was round and spilled slightly over the top of her mound, and when she spread her thighs a little wider, her rosy-pink lips glistened with moisture, awaiting my touch. I wanted to dive right in, but I knew I needed to take my time. Her hips bucked, seeking more contact, so I gave her a few light finger strokes, tracing the seam between her pussy lips.

"Aris…" she nearly hissed.

I couldn't wait to make her come undone. I was leaking

precum all over the sheets, and I would be lucky to last two minutes once I got inside her, so it was imperative that she come now all over my tongue.

One soft lick, and then I followed it up with a firmer one as her fingers continued to dig into my scalp, pushing my head closer to her pussy so she could grind against my mouth. *Holy hell, that's hot.*

"I can't normally come this way," she said, the words slurring together on a moan. "But…fuck…I'm so close…"

That was all the positive reinforcement I needed to continue. My tongue traced circles around her clit in a steady rhythm as her climax built. There were no more words, only unintelligible sounds of need and impending ecstasy as she took what she needed from me. When I sucked her clit into my mouth, she gasped, "Yes, oh, god, yes, Aris! Oh, fuck… that's it… God, I'm gonna come."

A gush hit my tongue as she bathed me in her juices, writhing, bucking, twisting against my hands that held her firmly by the thighs as I rode out the storm. Then the waves gradually subsided, and her body came to a rest, a stillness as a soft, satisfied sigh spilled from her throat.

I looked up to find her hair fanned around her, framing her face on the white pillow, her skin flushed with a rosy tint. Her arms lay limply at her sides, and she had all the stiffness of a noodle as her chest heaved with her recovering breath.

"Fuck, Aris…I never would have thought—"

"What, that I could eat pussy like that?" I licked my lips and sat back on my heels.

"I didn't know what to expect, but you blew all my expectations away."

"I haven't even fucked you yet."

"*Yet* being the operative word…"

"Does that mean you're ready now?" Still on my knees, I straightened my torso, arching my shoulders. I took my hard cock into my hands and stroked it from base to tip. A glistening bead of precum dripped down the veiny shaft.

"Give me a second to catch my breath," she begged, "and then yes…"

eleven

. . .

danielle

MY BODY WAS STILL QUIVERING from the orgasm Aris delivered with his tongue. But seeing him towering over me, stroking his thick, hard cock in his big, masculine hands was enough to send desire surging through me once more.

I took a deep breath. "Condom?"

"Should be one in that nightstand." He pointed to the small cabinet beside the futon, thankfully within reach.

I opened it and fished around until I found one, handing it to him as a mixture of nerves and anticipation flowed through me. My heart hadn't quite recovered from the intense climax, and now it was revving up for the next round of fun. I wanted to make Aris feel as good as he just made me feel.

I hadn't been with a man for a number of years, and though I used toys and took care of myself on occasion —*probably not often enough*—there was a momentary dread of whether or not it would hurt, or whether or not I would feel good to him.

I swallowed down my reservations and insecurities. I wanted this. He was right—I'd had a monumentally shitty day, and I was probably on the verge of not being able to finish my master's degree. I should at least get a couple of good orgasms out of the deal, right? The universe was telling me that yes I should.

Thank you, universe, for agreeing with me!

All of these thoughts tumbled around in my head as Aris rolled the condom down his cock before notching it at my entrance. My core tightened, preparing itself for him.

"You're sure you want this?" He pressed the head against my clit and rubbed it gently, sending a shiver of excitement through me.

"Fuck yes..." came out in a breathy moan as his eyes filled with concentration.

I watched his expression change as he breached my entrance, the way his lips parted and his eyes rolled back in his head. *Those are good signs, right?* I might have been so preoccupied with his reaction that it distracted me from my own reaction.

Inch by inch, he filled me, my walls clenching around him as tingles danced up and down my spine. I wrapped my arms around him, urging him to fully seat himself. When he hit bottom, a desperate groan rumbled up from his throat.

"Fuck, Dani...you feel so fucking good... Give me a sec to get my bearings."

I made him lose his bearings?

That has to be a check in the pros column, right?

I didn't know what he was used to. He told me it had been a while since he'd been with a woman, but how long? I didn't know.

Shut up, Dani, I told my inner voice. *Shut the fuck up and let this sexy man fuck you, for fuck's sake!*

When he finally stroked in and out, any thoughts left in my head dissolved into need that radiated from deep inside my core to the very edges of my sanity. I needed to come again. He was hitting the exact damn spot that sent thrills racing through me.

"Dani, my god…I'm not gonna last long. You have me so worked up. But I wanna make you come first," he confessed. "Tell me what you need."

"Nice and deep like that…and slow," I rasped.

"Slow, I can do…" He gulped in some air and balanced himself on his wrists as he made long, deep strokes in and out. With each one, I arched my pelvis up, taking him to the absolute depths of me, where the pleasure was so intense, it took my breath away.

"Oh, god…" He continued to grind into me, slowly, steadily, his eyes closing as he tried to delay his release. He lowered himself on top of me as I continued to rise up to meet each thrust. After brushing his lips against mine, he told me how good I felt squeezing his cock.

"Your pussy is like a gold mine," he groaned against me before nipping my lip. "It's so fucking tight and wet. You're gonna make me come, baby girl, and I'm not ready yet. I need to feel you shatter around me, milk the cum out of me."

I was close already, and his words tipped me over the edge. Heat and pleasure cascaded over me, and my field of vision went black as I rode the waves radiating from my core. I was vaguely aware of Aris's primal shout as his body jerked and he whipped his cock from me. He tore off the condom and gave his cock two quick pumps, then the tip exploded with thick white ribbons of cum. He spewed his seed all over my stomach as we both struggled to catch our breath.

I lay there for a moment, mesmerized by the pearly pattern on my skin as I studied his expression shift from exquisite pleasure to pure relief and relaxation.

"Oh, god, guess I need to clean you up." He chuckled as he eased himself out of the bed, leaning down to whisper in my ear, "Be right back, my goddess."

My whole body buzzed with peace and pleasure—not even the prescription painkillers they gave me could come anywhere near making me feel this good. But as I reveled in the aftermath, I heard talking in the hallway. It was a deep rumble of male voices.

Aris returned a moment later, still naked but holding a wet washcloth. "Let me take care of that mess I made."

The washcloth felt warm as he smoothed it over my skin, clearing away his essence. I liked seeing it—proof of what I did to him. My pussy pulsed a few times in agreement as the vestiges of my climax dissipated.

"Can I get you anything?" He curled up next to me.

"Everything okay with you and Noah?"

"Yeah, of course. He just wanted to know if I am coming to bed, or if I planned to sleep in here."

I waited for a moment to see if he was going to give me the answer, but he just nuzzled up next to me instead. It was a little strange knowing his partner was just down the hall while we fucked. I didn't know if that was something I could get used to or not.

Once all the happy orgasmic chemicals had run their course, my leg started to throb again. I tapped Aris on the shoulder. "Do you mind getting me some water so I can take my meds? Then I'll probably fall asleep."

"Sure, of course." Without complaint, he climbed off the

futon again and returned moments later with a cold bottle of water. He handed it to me, but he didn't climb back into bed.

"I need to go say goodnight to Noah," he said. "Do you want me to come back in here after that?"

I swallowed the pills, giving me time to think about my options. I felt bad asking him to stay the night and taking him away from Noah. But I also felt kind of sad and over-whelmed and anxious about my future.

I didn't even get a chance to answer. A smile crept across his face as he tilted his head. "I'll be back in about fifteen minutes, okay?"

I smiled and nodded. Damn, Aris was one of a kind.

noah

I had my hand poised to knock on Danielle's door—previously our den—but when I heard the sounds coming from inside, I knew my timing was off. I didn't want to interrupt them in the middle of sex, but from the sounds Aris was making, I could tell he was close.

Imagine my surprise when my cock sprang to life in my gray sweatpants.

I knew I shouldn't be standing here. That I should go back to my room and try again later. I just wanted to see if I should wait up for him or not.

Fuck, they sound hot together.

I leaned my head against the wall outside the room and sucked in a deep breath. Images of what my lover might look like stroking his thick cock in and out of Danielle's voluptuous body filled my mind. *Well, shit.* I didn't expect that to turn me on.

But it did.

God…what was wrong with me? I had barely felt sexual

at all since getting the news I was being sued for malpractice. The weight of the lawsuit was pressing down on me at all times, squeezing the air out of my lungs and making me ache with worry.

Aris's primal shouts signaled he was climaxing, and now my ache had been transferred right to my cock. *I need to go back to our room.*

I started to head back down the hall when the doorknob twisted, sending a jolt of adrenaline through my system. I whipped around, seeing Aris standing in all his naked glory, his cock still dripping cum as he stepped out into the hall. His face burst into a smile as soon as he saw me.

"Hey, enjoy the show?" he asked, giving me a stupid post-climactic grin.

"What? I was just about to knock, but I noticed you guys were…involved…so I was going to try again later."

"What do you need, Noah?" His eyes darted down to the bulge in my sweats—impossible to hide. Aris loved these things on me. I could guarantee myself a blowjob if he saw me walking around shirtless with these sweatpants slung low on my hips.

"I just wondered if you were sleeping in our room tonight or not, and if I should wait up for you. That's all."

"What would you prefer?" His thick eyebrows quirked before his gaze darted back down to my package, which pulsed under his stare.

Damn it. Try to be a little more subtle, for fuck's sake, I coached my dick. To no avail, I might add.

I shrugged. "It's really up to Danielle. I know she's had a trying day—though it sounds like you just improved it exponentially."

He chuckled. "I hope so. She seemed to enjoy herself."

His grin disappeared momentarily when he licked his lips. "Damn, she tastes amazing…"

"Oh, was it just oral? It sounded like you—"

His eyebrows arched.

"Oh, I mean—"

"It's okay if you were listening," he assured me. "I think it's hot—and it turned you on. Clearly."

I sucked in a breath. I couldn't really dispute the evidence of that.

"Maybe you can join us next time?" Hope dripped off the last word.

"Oh, I don't know, Aris. I don't want to intrude on your relationship with her. You know how busy I've been. I probably couldn't even find the time…"

"Well, you coulda been in there right now," he said.

"She's my patient, too, so I really shouldn't get involved with her. That wouldn't be very ethical."

"Refer her to Jess," he suggested.

Jessica was my colleague, a very competent doctor and excellent surgeon. If I had to give up my patients due to this lawsuit, they would be in good hands with Jess. At least there was that.

I still hadn't told Aris. Guilt rocketed through me, and the only bright side to that was my cock finally decided to deflate. "So…bed tonight or not?"

"I'll check and see what she has in mind, but I'll definitely come in and say goodnight to you one way or another," he promised. "Give me like fifteen minutes."

I forced a smile. "Take all the time you need."

I headed back to our bedroom, feeling defeated. My patients might not be the only thing I had to give up. The lawyer made it quite clear that my accuser would attack me as a person, not just as a doctor. If she found out I was bisexual, she could use that against me. I didn't want to bring Aris into this drama or jeopardize his career or any of his relationships.

He had Danielle now, and it would be easy for him to pass as straight if he wanted to. He might be fantasizing about having both of us, but three's a crowd, right? Maybe the best thing to do at this point was to remove myself from the equation.

aris

I snuggled up to my boyfriend after turning off the lights. I liked these moments, these little conversations before bed in the dark, when, in the absence of facial expressions and body language, you had to rely on the sound of each other's voices, each raise or lowering of pitch, each shift in inflection, to read meaning into the words. It made me feel closer to Noah, learning what patterns his voice made to express various emotions.

"You're sure you're okay if I sleep with Danielle tonight?" I checked for the third or fourth time.

"Yes, my god, Aris, how many times are you going to ask?" The slight chuckle after let me know he was only exasperated in a joking way.

"Well, I just want to be sure," I admitted. "You've been kind of preoccupied lately…and I need to make sure you're okay."

Noah's warm hand stroked down my cheek. "I'm fine. Everything's gonna be fine. I'm glad you have Danielle. It's cute to watch you guys."

"Cute? You make it sound like we're children!" I scoffed.

"Well, you definitely didn't sound like children a few minutes ago."

"You're okay with me fucking her?"

"Yes, Aris. I already told you a million times, and you saw firsthand what listening did."

"It made you hard, didn't it?" I bit my lip as my own cock twitched at the thought.

"Yes. Yes, it did."

"Are you hard now?" I reached over to check, but he swatted my hand away in a playful way.

"You promised her you were coming back. I can guarantee you, if you touch me, you will be getting fucked, and it would be a while before you got back to her."

"Right. Damn it." I sighed. Noah didn't make promises if he didn't intend to keep them.

"What?"

"Well, now I'm hard again."

"Maybe she can solve that issue for you," Noah suggested.

"Well, can I at least get a kiss good night first?" I leaned toward him, painting tiny kisses on his chest.

He wrapped his arms around me and drew me closer to him, until the smell of his body wash permeated my senses. Such a clean, manly smell. Mmmm, yeah, this hard-on was not gonna just go away.

His full, sensuous lips claimed mine, catching me off guard since I'd let my mind wander for a moment. But I didn't miss a beat, kissing him back with passion and love.

"Thank you for letting me explore things with Dani," I said as I pulled away.

"You're welcome. I'm glad you're having fun."

"See you in the morning?"

"Yeah. Hope you get at least a little bit of sleep…"

I crawled out of one bed and into another. The futon with the foam mattress on top was surprisingly comfortable. It wasn't the best for fucking because my knees sank into the memory foam, but it was more important that Danielle would be comfortable sleeping here for the next six to eight weeks.

She was breathing soundly, letting out the tiniest of snores as I snuggled up to her backside. Her cast was propped up on a pillow, meaning there wasn't one for me, but that was okay. I slung my arm around her, thinking that either myself or the medicine knocked her out for the night —or maybe some combination thereof. I would try to take that as a compliment. I knew she needed to sleep.

"Good night, beautiful," I whispered, nuzzling into her hair.

It had been a weird, wild, but wonderful day.

The next morning, I opened the door to our bedroom, hoping to hop into bed with Noah for a quick snuggle before we had to get ready for work, but he was gone.

No note, no text, nothing. He left without saying goodbye. That didn't sound like someone who was just fine with me seeing other people, right?

twelve

. . .

danielle

I WOKE UP WITH A START. *Where am I? Why is my leg throbbing?*

When it all came rushing back to me, my head began to throb too. Aris appeared through the door before I could rub all the sleep from my eyes.

"Are you okay? Do you need anything?"

My whole body was stiff. Like I'd gotten hit by a car.

Well, I *did* get hit by a bike—not quite as bad as a car, but still hard on the body. Just the slightest move made me ache. "Do you think you could help me up?"

My cast felt like a lead weight as Aris went about helping me out of bed. With me being such a big girl, it was probably going to be a workout on par with whatever he did at the gym. I assumed he went often because he had massive muscles and seemed very fit. I supposed someone who looks like a Greek god hitting me with a bike was better than someone who was rail-thin and puny.

Silver linings, Dani.

"Bathroom?" Aris questioned once I was upright and a foot or two away from the futon.

"Yes, please."

He helped me down the hall to the bathroom that he and Noah used. I peeked into their bedroom, and the sheets and comforter were rumpled on the bed, but no one was in it. And the bathroom was vacant. "Where's Noah?"

Aris shrugged. "I guess he already went to work. I tried to catch him before he left, but—" He shook his head as his frown flipped into a smile. "I'll just talk to him at work."

"I can't believe how bad I hurt today." I winced as I limped into the bathroom.

"Do you think you'll be able to clean yourself up okay?" Aris asked.

"I don't know. I am hurting so bad." I sucked in a breath. How was I going to act in a play like this? A musical, no less. Musicals required dancing. I could barely walk down the hall.

Fuck my life.

Damn, that silver linings thing sure didn't last long.

"What can I do for you?" The expression Aris's face was earnest. "Please, I want to help."

"I'm going to pee first, okay? Then maybe meds and coffee before I attempt anything else."

He grinned. "On it."

An hour later, I was sitting in the living room with my foot propped up on the ottoman. Aris had made me breakfast, served me coffee, made sure I took my meds, and helped me shower and dress. This man was amazing.

Then he went to work. So I was home alone.

Or so I thought.

At about ten-thirty, I was a half-hour into *The Price is Right* when the back door burst open. Every nerve in my body was on high alert until I heard Cynda's voice talking to the cat. "Yes, yes, I'll get you some more food, you whiny little piggy!"

Oh, good. I hadn't just become the victim of a home invasion. That would be a seriously bad twist of fate for someone who already had a broken leg.

"Good morning!" Cynda's cheery voice echoed through the mostly empty house as she found her way into the living room. "How are you feeling?"

"Sore," I admitted. "Aris hooked me up before he left though."

"Good, good. Can I get you anything?" The cat ran into the room and rubbed up against her legs, probably hoping for a treat.

"Not at the moment. Can I help you with anything?" I offered—out of habit more than ability to actually follow through.

She laughed. "Goodness gracious, no, girl! I don't expect to see you off that couch unless you need the ladies' room today, do you hear me? I just picked up some groceries, and I'm going to be in here putting them away before I do my yoga and meditation. I usually do that in the living room since there's more space. Will that be an issue?"

"Oh, no, of course not," I assured her. "It's your house. I can turn off the television and read a book or something."

She flashed a bright smile. "Thank you. Let me get these groceries taken care of. And let me know if I can bring you anything."

"Actually, now that you mention it, some more coffee would be spectacular," I said.

She smiled and went back into the kitchen just as my phone rang. With the 812 area code, I knew it was local. My heart pounded as I pressed answer.

"Is Danielle available please?" came a clear and pleasant-sounding female voice.

"This is she." I was afraid of not being able to hear her voice over the sound of my heart thumping in my ears. I swallowed hard.

"Hi, Danielle, this is Eve Wilson, the director of *The Music Man*. You auditioned yesterday morning?"

"Yes, of course." I barely squeezed the words past the lump in my throat.

"We were blown away by your audition. So I'm calling to offer you the part of Marian the Librarian!" she rushed out, like she couldn't contain her excitement.

My heart leaped into the stratosphere.

And then it came crashing back down to earth. Mighta even been on fire.

"Danielle, is everything okay? You still there?" Eve sounded concerned. And was probably already second-guessing her offer.

I closed my eyes. This wasn't fucking happening. *What do I tell her?*

"Hi, sorry, I'm just…wow. Thank you!"

"Practices start tomorrow at four p.m. in the auditorium. You'll need to bring some soft-soled shoes and wear something comfortable to dance in. We'll mainly be working on the songs this first week, plus some blocking, but our choreographer might drop by to start on the big ensemble numbers." She sounded like she was reading from a script. She continued to ramble on about a few more things, but I had stopped listening somewhere along the line.

There was no way in hell I was going to be able to take this part.

At some point in time, she said, "See you tomorrow" and hung up, leaving me sitting on the sofa sobbing. Tears were streaming down my face when Cynda returned holding two mugs of coffee.

Her smile fell as soon as she saw me sitting there blubbering, holding my phone in my hand. She set the mugs down on the coffee table and plopped down next to me, wrapping an arm around my shoulder. At the same time, Sushi jumped up on the cushion on my other side as though she wanted to comfort me too.

"What's going on? What happened?" Cynda squeezed me to her body. She smelled like fresh laundry and sunshine.

"I got the part," was all I could manage between sobs. Then a loud wail came out of nowhere as it sank in that I'd have to call whoever that was back and let them know that, in fact, they wouldn't see me tomorrow.

Fuck. How am I going to do that?

I was still shaking when Cynda pulled back to examine my tear-streaked face. "I guess that would be a good thing if not for your injury?"

I nodded. I tried to catch my breath, but it was one of those hiccuppy-shuddering ones you do when you're crying. I started stroking the cat's fur, which helped a little. And she seemed to be enjoying it.

Cynda leaned over to the end table on her side of the sofa, retrieved a tissue and handed it to me. "Do you want to talk about it, or would you rather I leave you alone?"

"I don't know..." I admitted as I wiped my eyes, followed by the snot starting to form in my nostrils. I sat back against the sofa feeling even more depleted, like I'd just run a marathon. Between the physical and emotional upheaval I'd experienced in the past few days, it was probably more stressful than running a marathon.

"Oh, sweetheart, I know we just met, but a lot of people

tell me I'm a great listener. You've had a pretty rough week, haven't you?"

I looked up at her, the tears welling up fresh again. She had such a soft, caring look in her eyes. My mother was the least maternal person I knew. Not that Cynda was old enough to be my mom—she wasn't—I didn't think, anyway. But she had that mothering vibe about her, a nurturing, empathetic but tough love-type attitude.

"It's been a little crazy. I'm supposed to be finishing up my master's this May and moving to New York this summer to try for my big break on Broadway," I explained. "But now—now I don't see how I can write my thesis because it was all based on the role I was going to get in this show. I hoped to get the lead—that would be my crowning achievement as a graduate student, but my throat has been giving me so much trouble. That's why I went to see Noah."

"I see." She smiled past me at the cat, who had now curled up against my hip. "So I guess your audition went well, then?"

"My voice actually cooperated better than it has in weeks. I think whatever Noah gave me helped—but he said I need surgery to fix a deviated septum. Honestly, I haven't even been able to deal with that because of the bike wreck. I almost forgot he even told me I need surgery! My appointment with him was just minutes before Aris crashed into me." I let out a humorless chuckle. Well, it would be funny— if it wasn't so terrible.

Cynda cracked a smile and gestured toward the coffee. I nodded, and she handed me mine so I wouldn't have to reach over my leg to get it or disturb the cat. We both took a sip from our respective mugs.

"So things aren't going the way you planned," she

summarized, still holding her mug that had a pride flag in the shape of a heart on it.

"Nope," I popped the "P" on the end of the word. "Nothing is going to plan."

"What about Aris? How does he fit into your plans?" She took another sip of coffee.

"Well…he's a sweet guy. And he's so handsome and caring. But I think we all know this is just a fun fling before I move away. And besides, he has Noah. It's not like he wants to get serious."

Cynda sighed and put her mug back down. She folded her hands together in her lap, then lifted her dark eyes to me. I didn't notice before, but she had very short, thin eyelashes. It made her eyes look so open—like she had nothing to hide.

"How much do you know about polyamory?" she asked, absolutely zero judgment in her tone.

"I know what it is, and I know Noah and Aris are poly. But what does that have to do with me? I'm not poly."

"Does Aris know that? Have you talked about your feelings at all?" Again, no judgment. Just smiles and concern.

I chuckled. "No, we've pretty much only snuggled and jumped each other's bones." As soon as it came out of my mouth, my cheeks flushed with embarrassment. It felt like I'd just confessed that to my mom.

Cynda laughed along with me. "Nothing to be ashamed of, girl. Sex is a natural human activity. Our species would have died out long ago without it, and acting upon sexual desires is something we were designed to do."

"Oh, I know…but what I mean is that Aris and I haven't talked about feelings. I know he is in a relationship with Noah."

"But that's what poly means," Cynda explained. "The

word literally means 'many loves.' Aris is a man who develops strong feelings quickly—"

I remembered him saying something about that, but I had brushed it off. He couldn't have meant "those kinds of feelings."

"Oh, well…I'm sure he knows this is temporary. We're just having fun. As soon as my leg heals, I'm…" I looked at her as it started to sink in.

With the broken leg, I might not be graduating in a couple months like I thought.

I really didn't know what my future held.

"Just make sure you're honest with him," Cynda advised. "Aris has a very tender heart. That's one of the things I told Noah when I first set them up. Noah is a very straightforward person though, thankfully. I just don't want to see Aris get hurt, that's all."

I swallowed hard. "Maybe I shouldn't be here then…" Now I was the one feeling guilty.

She gave me a soft smile. "From what I understand, you don't have a good alternative while you heal."

I looked down at my cast, those tears starting to sting again. I thought I'd gotten rid of those fuckers. "No, I suppose I don't…"

"It's fine to have fun and enjoy each other's company," she said. "As long as you're both on the same page. That's all I'm saying. With you staying here, I know you'll be spending a lot of time together. Just be honest with him. That's all I ask."

I nodded as I finished the last dregs of my coffee. "I will be. I promise."

thirteen

· · ·

noah

I SPENT the morning in surgery. Being able to compartmentalize has its advantages. All the drama with the malpractice suit went into one box, and the fact I'd gotten turned on listening to Aris and Danielle went into another. Then I opened up the box with my kick-ass surgical skills and did a fucking amazing job on another tonsillectomy. Last I checked on my young patient, she was awake and asking for ice cream. We both earned our gold stars for the day.

I headed over to my office after that. I didn't have a patient until one—a rare two-hour break. Whatever would I do with myself?

I'd been in my office for all of three seconds when there was a knock on the door. Heaving a sigh and starting to feel the tension creep into my neck and shoulders, I called out, "Come in," expecting it to be Lucy with refill requests or something of that nature.

"Hey," came Aris's soft voice as he poked his head

around the door. "You sure it's okay if I come in? You don't seem busy."

He had left a voicemail and a few texts on my phone, but if he'd gone to our shared Google calendar, he would have been fully aware that I was in surgery this morning. I was going to answer the texts eventually. Voicemails, no. I never listened to them. He knew that.

"You never answered my texts or voicemail," he said, sitting down across from me on the small brown leather sofa. His scrubs today were a medium gray color, which made his olive-colored skin look a little washed out. Or maybe he hadn't gotten enough sleep the night before—for all I knew, he was up fucking Danielle for hours.

I watched him play with his man bun, tightening the scrunchie that held it as he awaited an answer.

"Sorry, I've been busy." I didn't mean it to come out so curtly.

"What is going on with you?" he asked for the hundredth time.

"Nothing is going on with me, Aris. I'm just busy. I'm a surgeon. I have patients to see. Surgeries to perform. I had to cancel my afternoon appointments yesterday, so now I have to figure out how to cram those patients in this week."

"Oh, I suppose that's my fault," he fired back at me.

I just stared at him, blinking.

"It was an accident," he said through clenched teeth.

"I know that, Aris. But it doesn't change the fact that my afternoon and, well, now my entire life is going to be disrupted for the next six to eight weeks while you take care of your new girlfriend in our house."

"Wow." He stood up. "I didn't realize you felt that way. You're the one who told me to bring her home."

"What choice did I have?" I remained seated in my

leather executive chair while he now paced in front of the door.

"I think you would really like her if you got to know her better," he finally said.

Which wasn't at all on topic. The topic was how things were rough for me right now, and he just didn't seem to care. He was involved in his own busy times.

"You know, maybe we just need to take a break," I suggested. Not in a rude or incendiary way. In an honest way. In an *I just don't have time to deal with this right now, so can you give me some space?* way.

"You want to break up with me?" His hazel eyes flashed with hurt. "You said I could date other people. We're poly, Noah. That's what we do. And we've never had the veto power thing."

"Our relationship is still new," I reminded him. "We haven't exactly figured out what works for us. We've only lived together for a few months, and you're already bringing someone new into the picture. I'm sorry I'm so busy, and maybe I don't have the time and energy you need, so maybe you can just date Danielle for a while until things get smoother for me."

He closed his eyes and sucked in a breath, his nostrils flaring with emotion as he considered my words. "I can't believe you're doing this, Noah. You said you loved me. You're giving up on us because I'm dating a woman?"

"No, for fuck's sake! Did you hear anything I said?" I stood up now to face him. I was a couple inches taller than him, and I let him know it. I didn't need this kind of mental distraction right now when I had so much on my plate—that was why I suggested he date Danielle in the first place. *And maybe he should only date Danielle.*

"I heard everything you said," Aris answered. "But I

don't have to like it." He opened the door and started to walk out, but right before he did, he turned around and stared at me. "Goodbye, Noah."

aris

It took a lot to upset me. I was generally a glass-half-full kind of person, and, more often than not, I gave people the benefit of the doubt. The way Noah had closed himself off to me was hurtful, and now he was trying to make me feel bad about taking care of Danielle after I caused her injury.

After storming out of his office, I returned to my floor and my work, where I asked my boss if I could have the rest of the afternoon off, citing a need to take care of some personal issues.

"I was surprised to see you come in today," Dr. Meredith Riley said with empathy in her eyes. "I know yesterday was rough, but I'm glad you didn't get seriously hurt."

Because the accident happened right outside our building, everyone had heard about it. I probably had a dozen people ask me how I was doing and if Danielle was okay today.

"Would you mind seeing Danielle to look at her leg?" I asked. "You know, just so she can get a second opinion, make sure there's nothing else we can do but wait for it to heal."

"Yes, of course, Aris. Anything for you." Meredith smiled, but it didn't reach her eyes. "Have her come in tomorrow morning, first thing. I'll squeeze her in. Get me a copy of her x-ray too."

"You're the best, Mere." I reached out my arms, and she stepped into them to give me a hug. She really was the best boss I'd ever had. There were never any questions asked when we needed time off. She kept her office well-staffed, so we were never hurting for help, and because of the great work environment, no one abused her generosity.

I headed home in my car. I'd have to get a new bike—that sucked, but it could have been worse. The frame was bent. Of course, today was nearly balmy at fifty degrees, and the sun seemed to be mocking me after the ice storm yesterday. That was Indiana weather for you.

As I pulled into my driveway, I saw Raine walking out of the house. "Hey, how's she doing?"

Raine closed her eyes and shook her head. "Have you talked to her today?"

"No," I admitted, "I wanted to get work wrapped up so I could come home and spend the rest of the day with her. She's still in pain? Meds aren't working?"

"She got the part," Raine said bluntly. "And she accepted it."

"What? How's she—"

"She was caught so off guard by the phone call, she didn't have the wherewithal to tell them she wouldn't be able to perform." Raine sighed. "I don't know what to do for her. She's just sitting there staring into space—catatonic."

"Thanks for the heads-up. I'll see what I can do."

Raine reached out and patted me on the shoulder. "You're a good dude, Aris."

She climbed into her car and drove off as I stepped onto the porch and opened the door. Cynda was in the kitchen doing Cynda-things. She flashed me a concerned look, and I nodded. We seemed to understand each other. She tilted her head toward the living room, so I headed in, not prepared for what awaited me.

Danielle was sprawled out on the sofa with her leg propped on the ottoman and dozens of wadded-up tissues surrounding her. Her head was tilted back, and her eyes were closed, but when she heard me enter, they fluttered open. As soon as she saw me, she started sobbing again.

"Oh no, oh, Danielle…" I rushed to her side, gathering her up in my arms, gently because I didn't want to hurt her leg. "I heard what happened. I'm so sorry. What can I do?"

The tears erupted, soaking into my shirt as she heaved and shuddered in my embrace. I wanted to take all her pain away, and the guilt I felt for putting her in this predicament racked my whole body. I wished I could take off my good leg, let her borrow it, and then I could be the one to hobble around on crutches for the next two months.

"I have to call them and give up the role," she managed to get out, but it was punctuated by sobs. "I can't do it. I can't." She shook her head, sending tears flying all over me.

I held her close, and she rested her head on my chest. We sat there for a few minutes as the tears subsided and her breathing began to even out. I thought she might have fallen asleep when her head finally popped up.

"Can you call them for me?" came her meek little voice, the words squeaking out as she looked up at me with those big, wet doe eyes.

"Oh, darling. I feel like it should come from you, but I can if you're sure you really want me to." I stroked my fingers through her hair then tucked a strand behind her ear.

She sucked in a fortifying breath. "You're right. I'll do it. Can you hand me my phone? I think I threw it across the room when I went through my angry phase."

I saw a pink sparkly phone case on the carpet near the window. "Sure, just a sec." I retrieved it and handed it to her. "Do you want me to go or stay while you call?"

"Stay," she said. "Please?"

"Of course."

She heaved a heavy sigh of determination and scrolled through something on her phone. After punching a button, she held it to her ear. "Hello, is Eve Wilson in please?" She flashed me an uneasy smile. "It's Danielle Delacroix calling. Thank you. I'll wait."

Putting her hand over the phone, she held it away from her face. "I'm so nervous. What if they tell me I—" A garbled voice emanated from her phone's speakers. "Hello?"

My heart pounded, nervous for her. I sent her all the positive vibes I could muster.

"Yes, so, I'm calling because I had a terrible accident and my leg is in a cast… I know… Six to eight weeks. Yes, I know opening night is in four weeks. I am really disappointed too, but mainly I don't know what this means for finishing my master's… Right… Well, I'll give her a call. Thanks for your understanding… Yes, I hope so too."

Her voice was perfectly even, pleasant, and poised. There was no way anyone would have guessed she'd been crying most of the day. She didn't even have that stuffy nasal quality to her voice.

She placed the phone in her lap and tilted her head back again, appearing to be fighting more tears. "Well, I did it," she said without looking at me.

"You did an amazing job. Very professional."

"Years of acting." She blew out a sigh. "She said I'll have to speak with my advisor about the status of my degree."

"I see. Oh, I got you an appointment with my boss tomorrow morning at eight-thirty. Does that work for you?"

"That's very kind of her to squeeze me in. We can make it work. It's not like I'm going to be doing anything else, but I will need a ride." She still hadn't moved from her position with her head back against the sofa cushion.

"Of course. What else can I do for you?"

She finally lifted her head off the pillow and looked at me. "To be honest? A nap and cuddle would be lovely. With a stop at the restroom first."

I flexed my muscles. "I think I can handle that."

danielle

My headspace was currently a war zone. I had so many conflicting emotions, I didn't know whether to laugh or cry. Actually, I'd used up most of my tears already today, so laughter seemed to be the next logical choice. I wasn't even sure what Aris said when he helped me into the bedroom, but the giggles started, and I just couldn't stop.

"I didn't think it was that funny," he said as he plopped down on the thick memory foam mattress beside me.

"I think it was the way you said it, not the actual words." My stomach muscles were starting to hurt, I'd laughed so hard.

Once I calmed down, I propped myself up on my elbow facing Aris. "So…"

He smiled. "So…"

"When does Noah usually get home?" I asked.

A flicker of something passed over his face, some emotion I couldn't quite identify. But it was gone in a flash, and he smiled. "Oh, probably between five and six. He has some sort of radar that tells him exactly when to show up for Cynda's amazing cooking."

"She said she's making stir fry tonight." I licked my lips. "Sounds really good."

"I've been meaning to try some Greek recipes with her," he said, his hazel eyes locked on mine. "My whole family is Greek, and my mom and Yaya are incredible cooks. Cynda is too, of course. I figure if anyone can do their recipes justice, it's Cynda."

"That sounds amazing." I patted my stomach thinking about what Cynda's cooking was going to do to my waistline. "Well, as amazing as the food sounds, I'll probably leave here ten pounds heavier."

"So what if you do?" He tilted his head.

"Well, I'm already fat." I sighed. "I meant to lose some weight before auditioning for *The Music Man*, but…it just didn't happen. I got so busy with classes, and I—"

"Stop," he put his finger to my lips, "I think your body is absolutely perfect."

"Casting directors usually don't."

He scoffed. "Well, that sounds like a *them* problem to me."

"Well, it's a *me* problem if I can't get work," I explained. "There aren't a lot of roles for fat women."

"Not that 'fat' is a bad word at all, but you have a very beautiful curvy shape. I'd call it 'zaftig,' to be honest."

"Say what now?"

His eyes widened as they bounced between mine. "You've never heard that before? Zaftig?"

I shook my head. "Obviously, or I wouldn't be saying 'say what now!'" I gave him a little fake punch.

"It's a Yiddish word that literally means 'juicy.' I'm Greek on my dad's side and my mom's mom's side, but my mom's dad has Jewish heritage. It's a positive term. Voluptuous and beautiful. Goddess-like." He bit his lower lip and let his gaze roam over my figure. "I know that's the way I see you."

"It is?"

He nodded. "Definitely."

"Noah is so fit… He's what you're used to," I pointed out.

"Noah has a great body. He's lean and toned, not quite as bulky as I am. You know what the best part of being bi and poly is?" He looked into my eyes with such depth, such sincerity, it gave me goosebumps.

"What's that?"

"I get to fall in love with and explore so many beautiful types of bodies. Male and female. Small and large. Firm and soft." A big smile grew on his face. "Damn, I'm getting hard just thinking about it."

I almost missed his words, "get to fall in love with." The promise Cynda asked me to make rang in my ears, but I didn't say a word. Instead, I let him wrap me in his big, strong arms and hold me until I fell asleep.

She told me I should be honest about my intentions.

But I didn't want to close any doors just yet.

fourteen

. . .

noah

I WAS ABOUT to head home for the evening—late after an intense workout at the gym—when my phone rang. My lawyer. I sat in my car debating whether or not to answer it. It was almost seven o'clock—too late for her to be calling unless it was very good news…or very bad.

"Hello?"

"Hey, Noah. Maggie here. Hey, I just got off the phone with a reporter."

That was it. That was all she said.

"Uh…okay?"

"Noah, somehow they've gotten ahold of this story. They wanted my comment on it. No one has reached out to you?"

My head immediately went slamming into my palm. Rage simmered in my gut, threatening to bubble up my throat. I couldn't take it out on Maggie though. It wasn't her fault this entitled brat was trying to get me to settle out of court so she could make a quick buck. *I'm sure she never imagined in a million years that I'd push back and take it to court.*

"Noah?"

"Sorry, I…" A sigh hissed out as I tried to unscramble my brain. "I'm sorry. I'm just—uh, no, no one has reached out as far as I know, but I had a pretty busy day. I'd have to ask my office staff if they received any unusual phone calls."

"I'm afraid they're going to publish the piece," she said. "I didn't tell them much, only that you are a wonderful doctor, a gifted surgeon, and you have an excellent rating on GoodHealth dot com. I mentioned your accreditation from the American Board of Otolaryngology, and your dedication to improving the lives of your patients."

"Thanks." I really didn't know what else to say.

She audibly sighed, then paused for a moment, perhaps waiting for me to say more. But I didn't, so she admitted, "I'm just worried, Noah, because, remember how I mentioned them attacking your character?"

"Yeah."

"She asked me if I was aware that you are gay and have a reputation for sleeping with nurses and other staff who work with you in your building."

"What?! That's not true!" I fired back.

Well.

It was *mostly* not true.

Okay, I did sleep with Aris, and he was a nurse in my building, but he wasn't *my* nurse, and we didn't directly work together. *What the fuck?*

"Still there, Noah?"

"Yeah." I pinched the bridge of my nose. My head was blaring with voices telling me what an idiot I was for letting Aris be so affectionate in public. I should have known it would come back to haunt me. Even in this day and age, people still weren't comfortable with two men in love.

"I'm not gay," I finally countered. "I'm bisexual."

"Oh." My attorney huffed out another sigh. "Not sure that is any better."

"Of course it's not. Not that it's anyone's fucking business." My head was now not only blaring with voices, but pounding with the onset of a headache.

"It definitely isn't," she agreed. "But this story is probably coming out next week, and I wanted to warn you. I hope they at least get your side of the story. Hey, wait a second—"

"Wait what?"

"Isn't that charity ball for leukemia research this weekend?" she asked.

"Yeah, why?"

"You could show up with a woman—you know, as a date?" she suggested. "Make your accuser look stupid. I'm sure a lot of the local media personalities will be there, maybe even this reporter."

Her sighing was apparently contagious because I was doing it now too. "That's a terrible idea."

"Well, it's better than doing nothing." My attorney sighed again—that made like five sighs now. It wasn't exactly reassuring. "It's not too late to settle, you know. That's what she's after. And after everything you told me about her and her family, I'm surprised you didn't want to just go that route. You know, to protect your job."

I swallowed down my anger. "I'm aware. But I'm not going to give her the satisfaction. If she wants to take me to court and rake me over the coals, that's just fine. I'm fireproof."

Was I, though? Destroying my livelihood was a distinct possibility, even if I did win the case. Not to mention the fact that I was a private person and didn't like my business broadcast all over the earth. *Damn it, Aris. I knew I shouldn't have let you just pop into the office whenever you want. We should have kept our distance at work.*

Fuck.

"I've gotta go," I told her. "I'll think about it and get back to you."

I still had no intentions of surrendering.

And right now, I had no intentions of going home. Not that I had any clue where to go. Where does an introverted nerd go to drown their sorrows? Definitely not a bar…

aris

The whole polycule convened in the living room after dinner. Cynda sat sandwiched between Darth and Jason on the sofa, and Danielle and I cuddled together on the loveseat, with her cast propped up on the ottoman. Sushi was curled up on her other side.

"Do you think we should get one of those big-ass sectionals?" Jason's eyes roamed the room. "We need more places to sit."

"Sectionals do make it easier to cuddle since the space is less defined," Cynda said. "I think sectionals are more poly-friendly."

"Definitely," I agreed.

Darth rarely spoke, but when he did, it was usually to say something weird, something he thought was funny that wasn't actually funny, or to point out something obvious. Tonight, it was the latter. "Your man isn't here tonight."

"No. No he isn't." I sighed. "Thanks for reminding me."

"Is everything okay?" Cynda asked, but I was sure she could tell by taking one look at me that it wasn't.

"Not exactly."

Danielle tapped my arm, drawing my attention to her.

"You didn't say anything earlier. Did something happen between you and Noah?"

I didn't like drama. I didn't like talking about anything negative. Focusing on the positive and finding silver linings were more my jam. After leaving Noah's office earlier, I decided to just pretend like the conversation never happened.

Hey, I didn't say my coping strategy is healthy, okay?

"Well, are you going to answer?" Jason prodded.

"Fine." I looked around the room at three concerned faces and Darth, who was more in tune with his phone than any of us. Who knew what he did on that thing.

He finally looked up. "We're waiting!"

"Yes, Noah and I got into a disagreement earlier."

"About me?" Danielle was quick to ask.

"Not exactly." I scrubbed my free hand down my face. "Look, it's not a big deal, okay? We'll work it out."

"Is this your first fight?" Jason queried.

"It's not a fight. It's simply a difference of opinion."

Cynda folded her hands together in her lap. "How can we help?"

"By shutting up about it?" I forced a smile. Now would be a good time to change the conversation if I could think of a good topic. *Oh!* "So, you guys would be really proud of Danielle today."

"Oh, yeah? Why's that?" Darth asked. He was paying attention, even if his eyes were glued to his phone.

Danielle scoffed. "Oh, I hardly think I did anything worthy of praise."

"I think you were a total bad-ass." I leaned down to press a kiss to the top of her head. I loved the way she was cuddled against me, my arm wrapped around her, and her long hair spread over my shoulder.

"What did you do?" Jason's curiosity was now also piqued.

"Not much."

"Bullshit," I spoke up. "She called the director of the play who cast her in the lead to tell them she wouldn't be able to accept the part due to her injury."

"Well, duh," Darth cut in. "I mean, how's she gonna do that in a cast?"

I leapt to her defense. "It was still hard for her to do, and she did it very professionally."

"He means I didn't break down crying on the phone," Danielle corrected, then turned to me. "Have you at least heard from Noah? You know, to make sure he's okay? It's getting late. It's almost nine o'clock."

So, we were back to me and Noah, then.

I conceded, "Fine, I'll text him. I doubt he will answer, though. I'm sure he's somewhere blowing off steam."

"Where does someone like Noah blow off steam?" Jason pondered.

"Oh, I don't know. The gym? Chess with some old guy in the park? Reading the latest scientific journals? I have no idea." I pulled out my phone with my free hand, then turned to Danielle. "I'm going to move my arm for a sec, okay?"

She lifted her head so I could use both of my hands to send a text. But the cat was apparently offended by our sudden change in position, and she took off like a bat out of hell.

> Me: Hey, everything okay? Thought you'd be home by now.

I pressed send and waited for a few seconds, staring at

the screen. Nothing happened, so I laid the phone on the table beside me. "See? I told you he wouldn't answer."

Before I could orchestrate another topic change, the door handle twisted, then opened. In walked Noah with flakes of snow on his short-cropped black hair.

"It's snowing," he said, as if we couldn't tell by his appearance.

"Everything okay?" Cynda stood up. "There's some dinner left—I can heat it up for you if you'd like."

"No, no, I ate already." He flashed her a smile, but it was clearly just to be polite. Dark circles ringed his eyes. He looked stressed.

"Where ya been?" I forced my voice to stay light, nonconfrontational. "I just tried texting you."

"I know," he admitted. "I was sitting in the driveway for a while. Got kicked out of where I was hanging out."

"Starbucks?" Danielle guessed.

"Playing chess with some old guy in the park?" Jason ventured.

Noah's expression did not change. "No, the library."

"Reading scientific journals?" Darth felt the need to contribute.

Noah's nose wrinkled up. "No, just reading for pleasure. But they were closing up at eight, so I had to leave."

"Reading for pleasure?" Darth continued. "Tolstoy?"

Noah rolled his eyes. "I'll be in my room if anyone needs me."

He started to walk down the hallway, but I managed to extract myself from Danielle and leap in front of his path before he got very far. Also, "my room?" *What the fuck?*

"Do you want to tell us what's going on?" I asked in a low voice. I didn't want to put him on the spot in front of everyone, but this was getting ridiculous. "Or at least me?"

I had never seen Noah upset before. He was even-keeled. Always in control. But the look on his face right now was one of defeat. One of despair. One of abject misery.

And my big strong man who I'd never seen cry before wrapped his arms around me and sobbed.

danielle

I hated thinking Aris and Noah were fighting because of me. I'd had a rough day, week…year, really, but thinking I'd caused a rift between them felt worse than my leg and losing my lead role. When I agreed to go out with Aris, I had no idea it was going to be an emotional roller coaster. I honestly thought we'd have coffee, maybe dinner, bump uglies and get on with our lives.

I had no idea I was getting involved in all this. *gestures around wildly at this whole polycule thing, but only in my head because it would be weird and rude to do it for real*

Getting what leverage I could from the arm of the loveseat, I pulled myself to standing and grabbed my crutches from where they leaned against the wall. I was going to go talk to them both. Offer to keep myself completely separate from them so they could have space to figure things out.

"Whoa, where ya going, Danielle?" Jason hopped up and rushed to my aid.

"Just going to go talk to them…"

Cynda smiled in that motherly way of hers. "Give them a chance to talk first," she said. "They need some time. Noah is going through something, and I hope he has the strength and courage to lean on Aris right now."

"Going through what?" Jason questioned, looking from me to his girlfriend and back again.

My shoulders stiffened. "Hell, I don't know. But I'm afraid it has to do with me."

Cynda waved her hand. "Noah is a very independent person. It's hard for him to admit when he needs help."

I started crutching my way to the hallway when the low murmur of their voices continued. I didn't want them to fight about me when I was standing right here and could almost overhear them. If they'd gone to their room and shut the door, I would be forced to back off. But something inside me just snapped.

I hated being disliked. Or having anyone mad at me.

Maybe it was a female thing. Maybe it was because of the way I grew up. I didn't know the reason, but that didn't matter right now when I felt like a total home-wrecker.

They heard me coming—*duh, I was moving at approximately the speed of a tortoise*—and stopped talking when I was within a few feet of the hallway.

"Can I talk to you guys for a second?" I asked when Noah's dark brown eyes and Aris's hazel ones snapped to me.

I didn't care much for the pity on their faces, but I didn't let it stop me from what I planned to do.

"Of course," Aris said. "Do you want to come into our room? We have a nice big bed."

Noah flashed him the side-eye but said nothing.

"For you to be comfortable." Aris raised his hands up defensively. "I wasn't implying anything else. Sorry."

"Sure." I smiled, hoping I could at least convince Noah not to hate me. He didn't ask to get involved in my drama, and here I was, living with them. No wonder they were fighting!

Ugh!

It was all my fault. I could find another place to stay. Maybe my apartment complex had an empty unit—

"Here, why don't you sit in this chair?" Aris moved a small padded chair toward the bed. "You can prop your leg on the bed." He didn't wait for me to answer his rhetorical question before helping me into said chair.

Said chair was not made for big curvy rear ends, but I made do. I might still have the chair attached to my ass when I stood up, but we'd cross that bridge when we came to it.

"Sorry I worried you guys." Noah took a position on the bed, leaning against a massive mound of pillows, looking stiff and uncomfortable. "How's your throat feeling, Danielle?"

"Oh, actually it's been the least of my worries now that I've got the broken leg." I rolled my eyes as I pointed to my cast.

Aris plopped down next to Noah. "And that's my fault. Fuck, I am still so very sorry about that. I wish there was more I could do. I wish I could go back in time and—"

"I'm the one who's sorry," I blurted out.

Their gazes both snapped to mine again, this time with shock on their faces.

"Why would you be sorry? You didn't ask for this to happen!" Aris reminded me.

Noah nodded. "I'm only sorry I didn't catch him before he fell right on top of you. I wish my reflexes were a little faster."

"No, no." I shook my head. "I'm sorry for coming between you. I know you got in a fight today, and I hate that I was the cause of it—"

"No," Noah insisted. He scrubbed his hand down his face and let out a deep sigh. "Aris and I aren't really fighting about you. I've encouraged him to date you. I'm glad he has you right now."

That reminded me of what Noah said after our appointment yesterday—and my cheeks began to flush with rage all over again. I'd completely forgotten our fight after everything that happened with the accident and being rushed to the hospital. Noah had acted like I was doing him a favor by entertaining Aris while he was so busy.

It seemed like Aris was offended by this statement as well.

"What do you mean by right now?" Aris turned toward Noah, a worried look on his face. "Everything you've been saying sounds so… And this morning in your office—and now— Well, it sounds like you want to break up with me, and I—"

"That's not it," Noah sighed. He stood up and paced in the small area between the bed and the wall. "I'm sorry I've worried you both so much or made you feel like you did anything wrong. The truth is… Well, I might as well just tell you."

I looked at Aris leaning toward him with hope and care in his eyes. It was obvious these two were in love, and Aris was hurting because he knew his lover was hurting.

"Do you want me to leave?" I offered. "So you can tell Aris what's going on in private?"

"No," Noah shook his head, "stay. I might as well get this whole thing off my chest before it fucking explodes. As a matter of fact…you know what? I'm just going to tell the whole polycule at once so I don't have to repeat myself."

Aris and I exchanged shocked looks, and Noah sighed again before gesturing for us to follow him. "Come on, guys, back to the living room. Danielle, here, let me help you with your crutches."

fifteen

. . .

noah

I LOOKED around the living room at the concerned faces on the members of our polycule. Cynda was practically on Jason's lap with Darth leaning on her shoulder. He even put his phone away. And Aris and Danielle were cuddled on the loveseat, looking cozy and so damn cute together. Danielle was clearly a part of us now. Once Aris attached himself to someone...*well, just look at us.*

Even Sushi, our newest family member besides Danielle, had wandered back into the living room and had made herself comfortable next to Darth. Huh. Of all the people in the room to trust. *Interesting choice, Cat.*

I felt the love and support radiating from these five people, these five hearts—six if I counted Sushi. Okay, I still wasn't sure if Darth had a heart, but he was still here. He was still ready to find out what had been eating me up inside for the last week, twisting my guts and torturing my soul.

No one hurried me. No one looked impatient. They all waited for me to tell my story at my own pace.

"Last week, I got an email from my attorney. A former patient of mine is suing me for malpractice because her septoplasty collapsed, and she needed to have emergency surgery to repair it. She alleges that I was negligent in both my placement of the splints after surgery, and also in my discharge instructions—but, of course, those clearly state to be fucking careful with the splints holding your septum in place!

"Obviously, I performed her surgery and splint placement with the utmost care I give all my patients. She was discharged with a list of prohibited activities, and I am one hundred percent certain she did something she shouldn't have to dislodge the splints. Even blowing your nose can fuck it up. She sustained a high-volume blood loss and had to be hospitalized, and another surgeon repaired the damage.

"Now she's suing me for half a million dollars for her lost time and pain and suffering."

Not surprisingly, gasps went up around the room. Aris looked positively stricken. I had never seen his skin so pale, and the look in his eyes was pure devastation. I swallowed hard. I didn't want to see that look—that was a big reason I didn't want to tell him what was going on.

That and my almost obsessive drive to handle things on my own.

I scrubbed my hand down my face, searching for my next words to shatter the silence that had now settled over the room once the gasps dissipated.

"It's not just the money," I continued. "If it was just about money, I'd settle this suit out of court. I'm sure she's just looking to make a buck and thought I'd rather settle than dragging this through a long, drawn-out hearing. She obviously doesn't know me very well as a kid who grew up in the foster system determined to make something of myself." I snickered a little here because I believed with my whole heart this girl—and I called her that because her accusations were borne from a place of greed, entitlement and revenge—had picked the wrong man to fuck with.

"Dumb-ass bitch!" Aris interjected, and Cynda let out a whoop of support with her fist raised in the air. Jason joined in with his own fist.

"Who is she? Who the fuck does she think she is?" Jason growled.

I had to smile at how riled up they were on my behalf, but I ignored the questions about her identity. It only complicated matters. "So…my lawyer warned me that, a lot of times, these things turn into a character assassination if they go to trial. She said my life and life choices would be on full display."

Aris spoke up then, "You hate having your private life on display."

"I know," I nodded, agreeing with him, "but it's the principle of the thing, you know? I did nothing wrong. Settling out of court is not an admission of guilt, but it just doesn't feel right to me. I don't want patients to think I can be bullied into this sort of bullshit."

"That's right," Cynda joined me. "Noah, you must know that we've got your back no matter what happens."

"Well, that's part of the problem," I continued. "Tonight, my lawyer called to tell me she got a phone call from some reporter doing a story on the suit. An exposé, she called it. The patient has alleged that my distraction at work, as in dating people I work with—and she specifically said nurses, is what caused my negligence."

Aris's features pinched into a scowl. "She…what?! Is she talking about you and me?"

"I think so," I answered, "because she told the reporter I'm gay."

Cynda slapped her hand over her face. "Bi-erasure strikes again."

I chuckled a humorless laugh. "I told my lawyer that I'm actually bi, and she said, sadly, that wouldn't be any better for the bigots out there. Though, my lawyer did have a recommendation. An absurd recommendation, but a recommendation nonetheless."

"What's that?" Cynda was first to ask.

"She knows I'm going to the leukemia charity ball this weekend. I was planning to go stag—just drop in, shake a few hands, make my donation and leave…"

"But?" Jason prodded.

"She said I should take a date. A woman, specifically. Just to upend that 'gay' accusation." I facepalmed myself.

"Maybe you should," Jason suggested, shrugging.

"Why would I do that? There's nothing wrong with being gay. I should take Aris and rub it in their faces."

"Oh, that sounds fun!" Aris chimed in. "I don't have a tux, but—"

"Maybe you should take Aris and Danielle," Cynda suggested. "Really blow their minds."

"Well…" That wasn't a half-bad idea.

But Danielle was on crutches, and I only had a plus-one with my ticket. Not plus-two.

"I'd go," Danielle said, "but not sure you want me crutching around. Though—if you want to draw attention to yourself…"

"Maggie—that's my lawyer—said she figured there would be reporters and other media personalities there.

They might think twice about my patient's accusations if I showed up with a woman."

"Showing up at an event with a woman doesn't prove you're not gay," Darth interjected. "Just ask any gay man from the past."

"Well, what if they were engaged?" Cynda questioned. I could tell from her expression that she was seriously mulling over the options.

I should have known, if I opened this can of worms, I'd suddenly have a whole room full of PR experts trying to help me fashion my image. Maybe that was what I needed, though.

"Is this patient going to be there Saturday night?" Danielle asked. "At the event?"

My nostrils flared as I brought up a mental image of Alexandra Bagby. Just envisioning her made my stomach churn. I hadn't shared the worst part of it all with them. Her dad held a position of power, and he would almost undoubtedly be at the event on Saturday. Alexandra likely would be there too.

I swallowed hard, then answered, "It's possible. Even probable."

Cynda's eyes narrowed. "Who is she, Noah? She's someone important, isn't she?"

I huffed out a sigh, ready to let the cat out of the bag. And I didn't mean Sushi, who looked downright cozy curled up next to Darth. "Her dad is the CEO of Midwest Health."

There was silence as everyone's jaws dropped.

Aris was the first to speak. "You mean the guy in charge of the entire network that employs us?"

I closed my eyes, wishing it somehow wasn't true.

"Yes. That's the one."

"No wonder a reporter is interested in this story," Cynda gasped. "Fuck, Noah—this is serious."

Jason straightened his posture. "What can you do? Is there some sort of union or board that can help you?"

"I'm already in contact with someone at the American Board of Otolaryngology," I explained. "Waiting to hear back. But I just don't see how they can prove I was negligent. I think their best bet is to try to discredit me personally."

"What aren't you telling us?" Aris finally asked. "You're leaving something out, aren't you?"

I knew it would come down to this. This was the reason I wished I wasn't so stubborn. Because, if I wasn't, then maybe I would just settle this damn case and get on with my life.

"So, the real reason Alexandra hates me isn't just financial, though I'm sure she also wants my money. Her father is notoriously conservative and religious. He and Alexandra's mom have six kids. Half of them have gone into the medical field and work for him. And the other half he's helped start local businesses. But he's one of those 'pull yourselves up by your bootstraps' types. Alexandra's business was hit hard by Covid. I'm sure she's hurting for money. I'm sure that's part of her motivation for suing me."

"So what's the other reason?" Aris probed.

"I used to date her best friend, Emma," I admitted, "who started off as one of my nurses. Her dad has a pretty strict fraternization policy, so she ended up transferring to a different office when we began dating."

"And?"

"And…we broke up when she caught me…"

"Caught you what?"

I groaned. I shouldn't be ashamed of this because it

wasn't shameful. I knew Emma was upset, and I tried to explain to her, but she just wouldn't hear me.

"Noah?" Aris pressed.

"She caught me looking at gay porn," I confessed.

"So fucking what?" Aris fumed. "Fuck, I thought you were going to say she caught you fucking someone else."

"No." I vehemently shook my head. "I wouldn't do that behind someone's back. You guys know me better than that. I tried to tell her I'm bisexual, but—she ran to Alexandra, and Alexandra convinced her I'm gay and was hiding it from her because I wanted to pass as straight."

"Was this before or after you did Alexandra's surgery?" Cynda questioned.

"Literally a few days after," I answered. "This happened last year. Before I met Aris. Isn't it interesting that she suddenly had to get emergency surgery less than a week after I performed her septoplasty, and only a few days after her best friend and I broke up?"

"Fuck," Jason said. "That sucks, man."

"What took her so long to file the suit?" Cynda wondered. "If it happened last year, I mean."

"I think she decided to do it when she found out about me and Aris," I conjectured. "She's seeking money and revenge."

"That's bullshit!" Aris yelled.

"I know. So, as you can see, I'm in a bad spot. And this is why I've been so distant and preoccupied in the past week or so. I haven't treated you all like I should—especially you, Aris, and I apologize for that. And I admit I did consider breaking up with you because I don't want to put you in the middle of this. You either, Danielle—you're my patient, and—"

Cynda stood up and wrapped me in a hug. Before I knew it, all the members of my polycule were hugging me. Everyone except Danielle.

When they pulled away, I noticed she had stood up and was leaning on her crutches, a determined glint in her eyes. "You need to transfer my care to your partner ASAP so I'm no longer your patient."

"Why?" My heart sank at her demand. She wanted to fire me as her doctor because of all this drama?

"Because I'm going to that ball with you on Saturday," she said, "and if I see this Alexandra Bagby woman, I'm going to pull her aside and give her a piece of my mind."

My eyes locked on hers. "I can't ask you to do that. You're trying to heal from your injury—"

"I just lost my role as Marian the Librarian." She straightened her spine. "Let me take on the role of Noah's fiancée. We're gonna exonerate you and clear up this mess once and for all."

danielle

I encouraged Aris to spend the night in Noah's bed. He looked torn for a few minutes, like he needed to choose between us. So, I made it easy for him. Noah needed comforting tonight. I needed it last night.

I still needed it. Everything happening had shaken me to my core, but I was trying to take a page from Aris's book and be a glass-half-full kind of person. It did not come naturally to me. I remembered reading something a while back about how, if you have negative thoughts, then negative things will happen to you. But if you have positive thoughts, you can manifest positive things happening to you.

Was my negative thinking to blame for my throat issues and the bike wreck? For me being forced to give up my dream role in my last semester of school?

I would never get a firm answer to that question, but I'd spent a lot of my life imagining the worst-case scenario. My fiancé, Nathan, who broke up with me after we graduated from college, told me once that I was a buzzkill.

"You're no fun to be around, Dani," he'd told me. "You don't know how to let loose and have a good time."

Being around Aris might help me with that. He was fun and serendipitous and sincere. He was good for me. I just knew it.

As I curled up in bed, I thought about what transpired between us the night before. It was the most incredible sex I'd ever had in my life. Then he spent some time with Noah, came back, and wanted more. I'd never been with a man who wanted to have sex more than one time in a night.

So, yeah, Nathan, tell me again how I'm no fun?!

It was so quiet in the house, and my pain medication was starting to make me sleepy, but I could have sworn I heard a rhythmic sound coming through the wall. Was that Aris and Noah going at it? My nipples hardened at the thought, and a tingle of desire fluttered in my core. Thinking about them together… damn… it turned me on.

What would they do if I snuck in and watched them?

Well, there would be no sneaking around on crutches and with this damn cast on my leg.

I'd have to just lie here and imagine…

aris

"Aren't you glad you finally told me what's going on?" I slid my mouth down Noah's cock and back up again, making a distinct slurping sound at the top.

"Yes…" the strangled sound rumbled up Noah's throat. "Fuck, Aris…yes. Please…oh God, don't stop…"

"Don't stop what?" I teased him, twirling my tongue around the head of his cock. I gently squeezed his balls before making another pass down his shaft with my mouth.

"Fuck, I need to be inside you," he groaned when I stopped again. "You're killing me."

"Taking your mind off things, though, right?"

"I've been thinking a lot about something else…to be honest…" He sat up on his knees and pushed me down on the bed. He stayed there for a moment, hovering over me. The look on his face told me he had another secret, and he couldn't decide whether or not to share it.

"To be honest, what? Haven't we learned that confessing our secrets makes us feel better? And earns us blow jobs?" I batted my eyelashes at him.

"Get on your knees," he commanded. "I'll tell you when I'm balls-deep inside that ass."

"Oh, damn!" I moaned. I loved it when he took control. Not wasting any time, I rolled over onto my hands and knees and presented my ass to him.

He gripped both globes, smacking my flesh hard enough to leave a mark. When I winced, I heard a sadistic chuckle trickle past his lips. He took his time, kneading the firm muscles there, and when I least expected it, he parted my ass cheeks, and a warm, wet sensation sent a shiver down my spine. His tongue rimmed my entrance, making me weak in the knees.

"You did such a good job getting me nice and hard for this greedy hole," his voice rumbled from behind me as he used a finger to prepare me to take him. Then I heard him grab the bottle of lube from the nightstand and squirt some out. "The least I can do is get you ready for me."

"Mmm…thank you…." I gasped when he inserted his lubed finger and stretched me before inserting another finger. He fucked me with both fingers, and when he moaned, I knew he was stroking himself with his other hand.

"I need you." I looked over my shoulder at him handling his hard cock. Fuck, he had a beautiful dick. Just thinking about it inside me made my balls tighten up and my own cock rock-hard.

"Already?" Now it was his turn to tease me.

"Tell me what you were thinking about a minute ago when you said 'to be honest.'"

"Be good and take my cock first, baby." He pressed the tip against my hole, stealing my breath.

I stroked my cock, willing myself to relax so he could penetrate me. Fuck, it burned and felt good all at the same time. He leaned forward and kissed my neck as he pushed inside me ever so slowly, nibbling at the spot where it met my shoulder.

"Fuck, Aris…you're so tight. Feels so fucking good. You okay, baby?"

"Yes…fuck…oh god." I tried to stabilize my breathing as the pain and pleasure mixed, sending conflicting impulses through my body.

"Almost there…oh, fuuuuuuck…"

He slid all the way in and stilled. His steady breaths were the only sounds as he acclimated to the pressure against his cock and allowed me to relax and enjoy the sensations slowly turning from discomfort to intense pleasure.

"Okay, baby," I said over my shoulder. His fingers dug

into my hips as I gave him permission to move. "Tell me now…you're inside me."

"Yes…" He stroked in and out a few times, slow, shallow strokes, still allowing me to adjust. "So, you know how I ran into you in the hallway last night?"

"After I fucked Danielle?" I clarified.

As soon as I said the words, I felt his dick pulse inside me.

"Yes."

"What about it?" I pushed back against him, willing him to move faster.

"You know it made me hard," he admitted.

"Yes, the gray sweatpants tell all." I chuckled.

He slid halfway out and rammed in hard.

"Fuck!" I screamed.

He slowed down his pace. "I can't stop thinking about you fucking her," he said. "I woke up hard this morning dreaming about it."

"You did?"

He began thrusting a little faster. "Yes. And right now, I'm imagining what it would be like to fuck you while you're licking her pussy, or while you slide deep inside her."

"You are?"

"I am… Fuck, if I keep thinking about it, I'm going to come."

"Fuck…that's really hot." I began to stroke myself a little faster, the picture he just painted filling my mind with all sorts of interesting thoughts.

"You don't mind if she goes to the ball with me?" he asked as his speed intensified again, his balls slapping against me as his thrusts went even deeper.

"No, I'm glad you are," I admitted. "I hope you fuck her too."

"I want you there when I do," he said.

Before I could choke out any words, my climax rocked through me like a hurricane. As soon as it hit, Noah pumped into me so fast and hard, we both lost control. Only unintelligible groans and primal growls came out of our mouths now.

We just came to a fantasy starring Danielle.

sixteen

. . .

danielle

ARIS WAS SUCH A GENTLEMAN, parking as close as he could get to the building and then helping me inside. "I'll ask Doc to get you a temporary handicap permit," he offered as we rode the elevator up to my appointment with Dr. Riley.

"Thanks, I appreciate everything you've done to help me." I basked in his smile as he received my gratitude, and then he helped me off the elevator when the doors slid open.

"I'm going to take you in the back. Less walking for you," he said with a wink. He unlocked a door with his ID badge and ushered me down a hallway.

Nurses and other office staff were buzzing about as Aris guided me to Exam Room 3. "Have a seat in here, and I'll be right back to take your vitals."

A shiver of excitement coursed through me as I thought about Aris being my nurse. How did I go from hating doctors to maybe having a bit of a medical fetish? This was weird…and unexpected.

He returned with my chart and a blood pressure machine. "How tall are you, darling?"

"Five-five." I tensed up. I knew what question was coming next.

"Gonna leave the weight blank unless you want to tell me." He looked up over the chart with kind eyes.

I smiled, relief washing over me. "Blank is good."

"Let's get your temp, blood pressure and heart rate." He stuck the thermometer under my tongue and wrapped the blood pressure cuff around my arm. Adorably, he put his finger to his lips to remind me not to speak while the machine squeezed the ever-loving shit out of my arm.

"Temp is ninety-eight point three. So that's fine. And blood pressure is 125 over 84. That's pretty good. Are you comfortable?" He made a few notes in my chart and looked me over as I sat on the exam table.

"As comfortable as I can be on this paper-covered table," I joked.

"Well, how could I make you more comfortable?" His eyebrows shot up quizzically.

Something about his effervescent personality had put me in a playful mood. "Oh, I think you may have some ideas…"

"Oh, Dani!" His hands flew to his mouth in fake surprise. "So naughty!"

"Guess you can't do that at work though, huh?"

"Dr. Riley is pretty cool, but maybe not that cool." He closed the file with my chart and pressed it to his chest. "She'll be right in, okay?"

"Thanks again." I blew him a kiss.

Twenty minutes later, it was over. Dr. Riley looked over my x-ray, examined my leg, and basically told me that staying off it for six to eight weeks was the best course of action. She had Aris make me an appointment for six weeks in the future so she could repeat my x-ray and make sure it was healing properly.

"And, of course," she said, "if you have any new pain or your pain worsens, please call the office right away."

Aris sat with me for a moment after she left the room. "Are you okay?"

I nodded. "I don't know what I expected her to say. I guess maybe that I was healing magically and I'd be back to normal in a few days."

"I mean, some have said I have a magical cock," he chuckled, "but, yeah, unfortunately, that's not the way the human body works."

"I suppose not. Well, I'm preparing myself for further disappointment when I meet with my advisor, so I guess I'll just get all the disappointment over with in one fell swoop."

"I hope you'll get some good news." He helped me down from the table. "You have a ride to campus?"

"Yeah, Raine is coming to pick me up. Just need to text her to pull up to the door. She should already be here." I leaned on my crutches and started to pull out my phone.

Aris held up a hand. "Allow me, my goddess." He did a mock bow and pulled out his phone in one fluid motion. Magical cock or not, this guy *was* a magician when it came to making any lingering sadness disappear. It was almost impossible to be depressed when he was around. He was like the sun when it parts the clouds and scatters them all away.

He pressed a few buttons on his phone, then grinned. "Your chariot awaits, my goddess."

"You've gotta stop calling me that. I'm going to get a big head or something."

"Can't stop, won't stop!" He beamed as he escorted me

out the back door of the practice and down the hall to the elevator.

Once we hit the lobby, he guided me out to where Raine was indeed waiting in her black Ford Focus. He opened the door for me, got me settled inside, and pressed a kiss to my lips. "Let me know how it goes with your advisor."

"I will," I promised.

As we pulled away, he watched from the sidewalk, not far from where our collision happened just a couple of days ago.

So much had happened since then.

And yet the promise I made to Cynda was still fluttering through my memory like a butterfly taking off on its inaugural flight.

"So, now what?" Raine asked as we settled into the booth at The Trojan Horse.

Disappointing news called for a gyro with extra tzatziki sauce. I didn't make the rules.

"I wonder what Aris thinks of this place." I ignored her question. "He's Greek, you know."

"Um, yeah, you were seeming pretty smitten with each other in the parking lot back there. How's that going?" She wisely picked up on my not-wanting-to-talk-about-my-plans vibe.

"It's going very well." My traitorous cheeks flushed as soon as I said it.

"My god, Dani, you're blushing! Tell me everything." She laced her fingers together, cracked her knuckles and settled her hands on the table, leaning forward in preparation for all the news I dared to share.

"Well…"

I couldn't tell her about what was going to happen this weekend with Noah, but I could certainly dish about Aris.

"He is amazing!" I practically squealed. "He's so sweet and kind and thoughtful and—"

"This is the guy who hit you with his bike and broke your leg. You remember that, right?" she teased me.

"Yeah, yeah." I brushed away her joke with my hand. "I know it's possible he's just being so nice to me because he feels guilty, but I don't think so because he was super sweet and thoughtful before too, like when he held me during the thunderstorm instead of expecting to get laid. That was on our first date."

Her black eyebrows arched. "And has there been a second date?"

"Well, I'm staying at his house… I guess our second date was in the ER. And our third date was us sleeping together that night."

She looked like she was about to gobble up her favorite dessert. "Oh? Do tell. How did that go?"

"Well… I hadn't been with a man in a long time because I'd never been too impressed with sex. I've only had a handful of partners, my high school boyfriend, a one-night stand freshman year of college at a frat party, and then Nathan. He wasn't into giving oral—loved receiving it though. He struggled to last more than a few minutes, plus he could only go once a night."

"Ugh." Raine looked unimpressed.

"Let's just say Aris blew them all out of the water." I fanned myself because now, not only my cheeks were flushed, but my whole body felt on fire.

"Good!" She beamed. "You deserve good sex, Dani. You know that, right?"

"I do!" I agreed. "He also calls me his goddess, and he told me he loves my figure. He said I was 'zaftig.'"

"Wow, I'm impressed he knows that word." Raine sighed and seemed to swallow hard, looking down at her hands before her gaze rose to meet mine again. "I'm glad things are going so well, Dani. Now, can we talk about the elephant in the room?"

I stared at her, blinking.

"Your leg?" she reminded me. "Your living situation? Your master's degree and future career?"

I kept blinking.

"Do any of those ring a bell?"

I huffed out a long, weary sigh. "Yes, Mom."

"Speaking of your parents—"

"No, we're not gonna talk about them." I held up my hand. "Boundaries, Raine. We don't talk about the parental units. Much like," I whispered, "Bruno."

"Okay." She bit her lower lip while she stared at me, presumably trying to figure out how to rile me up some more. "So, are you still moving to New York at the end of the summer? Gonna start auditioning?"

I rolled my eyes. "Can't you just give me a moment to regroup? Let me enjoy myself for just a nanosecond?"

"Wow." Raine shook her head in disbelief. "Three days with Aris Belevonis, and you're a changed woman. I thought you said this was just a fling."

"It is," I fired back, even though I wasn't sure I believed myself. "I am taking a breather, Raine. I'm healing. I have a broken leg. I need surgery on my nose. I just had to give up my dream of playing Marian the Librarian in *The Music Man* due to these things. I just found out I'm not graduating with my Masters in Fine Arts in May like I always thought I would."

"You're handling the disappointment remarkably well," she observed, but she didn't seem one hundred percent convinced.

I licked my lips. "Well, getting some good cock can apparently do that to you."

"Huh." Raine took a sip of her ice water. "Maybe I need to look into getting me some of that too."

A couldn't help but smile. "Yeah, maybe you should."

aris

"There's my beautiful goddess!" I exclaimed as soon as I walked through the door and found Danielle in her usual spot, her leg propped up on the ottoman. Cynda was sitting in the chair across from her knitting.

"Why, thank you!" Cynda exclaimed, looking particularly cheeky.

"Two beautiful goddesses," I corrected myself.

She waved away my compliment. "I think that's my cue to go start dinner. Tacos tonight—does that sound acceptable?"

"Tacos are always more than acceptable," Danielle finally spoke, looking up from something she was watching on her phone.

"Excellent." Cynda smiled and headed to the kitchen, where I knew delicious smells would soon be wafting out to us and teasing our taste buds.

I sat down next to Danielle. Sushi was curled up in her lap. "You get home okay? What did your advisor say?"

She set her phone down and seemed to collect her thoughts as she stroked the cat's striped fur. "Oh, not much.

She told me to take an incomplete for the semester and basically try again in the fall."

"Ouch."

"Yeah. Not the best news, but…it's not like I can really prepare for auditions or think about moving when I'm dealing with this." She pointed to her cast. "It's just going to be a long eight weeks."

"Well, you'll still have the summer," I pointed out.

"There aren't any shows or classes in the summer." She sighed. The cat looked up at her in apparent commiseration.

"Gotcha." I put my arm around her. "You seem to be handling the news pretty well."

She shrugged. "Well, what am I gonna do? Cry about it? Get angry? It's out of my control. Not much I can do at this point, other than wait."

"Very true." I reached out to give Sushi a scritch behind the ear. "Hopefully we can distract you and make the eight weeks go by quickly at least."

One eyebrow arched. "We?"

"Noah and I," I clarified. "So, what are you wearing to this ball on Saturday? Do I get to see you model your dress options?"

A flash of confusion crossed her face. "Oh, fuck. I just remembered—"

"What?"

"I had some formal dresses in my closet here until winter break, when I moved a bunch of my stuff to my parents' house. I wanted to cut down on the stuff I had to move from here to New York, so I was lightening the load. I didn't think I'd need any of that stuff…"

"Hmmm." I considered our options. "Well, where do your parents live? I can take you there to get a dress for the ball?"

She laughed. "I thought I told you… I grew up near Chicago. It's like three or four hours away from here."

"Oh, shit. Yeah, I guess we don't have time to do that before Saturday."

"Um, no."

"Well, may I suggest an alternative?"

Her face brightened with hope. "What kind of alternative?"

"I'll take you shopping?"

She looked at me like I had two heads. "You'll…you'll take me shopping," she repeated.

I cocked my head and shrugged. "Yeah, why wouldn't I?"

"Aris, who the hell are you? Did an alien inhabit your body or something? Am I on candid camera? Who the hell are you?" she demanded.

I chuckled and leaned toward her, pressing a kiss to her cheek. "Dani, I care about you. I want to see you happy. Would having a new dress to wear to the ball make you happy?"

Something like surprise and delight flickered across her features. "Yes…actually, yes. I think it would."

"Then let's go!"

She wagged her finger at me. "After tacos."

I could hear the beef sizzling in the pan in the kitchen. "Oh, excellent call. Yes, after tacos. I completely agree."

seventeen

. . .

danielle

"THESE ARE KIND OF PRETTY. I'm surprised this store has a decent selection of plus-sized dresses, to be honest." I looked at the three dresses I had slung over my arm while I fingered the fabric of another one on a display rack at the back of the store.

The formalwear store was closing in thirty minutes, so I needed to try this on and make a fast decision. Thankfully, it wasn't very busy in here. I hadn't seen any other customers, and the salespeople all seemed to be at the front of the store.

"I think you'd look amazing in any of those. Are you ready to try them on? I can go get a saleslady if you need me to." He gestured toward a chair as I added the fourth dress to the stack on my arm. "Why don't you sit there while I get someone to unlock a dressing room?"

He was so freaking sweet! None of the guys I'd dated had ever been this attentive to me. Maybe it was bisexual men? If that was the case, I wasn't sure I could go back to dating self-centered straight guys.

"Thank you." I beamed up at him from the chair as he collected the dresses from my arm and hung them on a nearby rack.

"Be right back, my goddess."

While I was sitting there, I got a text from my friend Regan, who was enrolled in the MFA program at IU with me. It was a photo.

I opened it up to reveal a group of grad students in street clothes, huddled up with a sign that read, "Get well soon, Dani!" Her text message said,

> Regan: We heard about the accident, and we're so sorry. Hope you will be able to come see the show. And I guess I should be thanking you because I ended up getting recast as Marian. *heart emoji* *kiss emoji*

I flushed at the thought of Regan getting my role. I shouldn't be angry or jealous, but—

Well, I was still having a hard time dealing with this. I'd pretended things were peachy-keen-jelly-bean to Raine and everyone in the polycule, but the truth was...

I was still struggling.

Rage was starting to consume me when Aris came back with the saleslady, who introduced herself as Sasha when we first came in. I swallowed down my anger and painted a smile on my face.

Acting skills came in handy all the time.

"You'd like to try those on?" Sasha pointed to the rack where Aris had hung the four selections I'd made.

"Yes, please. Would you mind unlocking the bigger room? I'm on crutches." I pointed to my cast.

"Oh, yes, of course! No problem whatsoever." She walked over to the wall where five dressing room doors stood in a line and unlocked the last stall. "Let me know if you need another size or anything else."

She nodded and walked away. Aris helped me to my feet and carried the dresses as I made my way over to the room, pushing the door open with one of my crutches.

Holy shit, it was ginormous!

The dressing room was more like a boudoir. There was a padded bench with a vanity and round mirror, a small sofa with gorgeous luxe upholstery, a shaggy pink rug, and a crystal chandelier. In the center of the room was a pedestal, and, on the far wall, a tri-fold mirror. Everything was soft and feminine.

"This must be the bridal dressing room," I gasped, looking at the opulent surroundings. "It's freaking gorgeous!"

"Do you want me to wait outside?" Aris popped his head through the door and took a look around. "Holy shit, look at this place! I had no idea it would be so huge."

"Me either. And you might as well come in. I can probably use help with the zippers, and it's not like you haven't already seen me naked."

He chuckled. "Facts!" He hung the four dresses on a wood and brass bar beside the vanity. "I'll just sit over here. Let me know what I can do to help."

Dressing and undressing in front of people was second nature after doing a lot of theater. The dressing rooms were usually crowded, and sometimes there was such a short turn-around between scenes, you needed the costume crew to strip you out of one costume and throw you into the next. So, trying these dresses on in front of Aris shouldn't have fazed me in the slightest.

However...

I stood there holding a slinky red floor-length dress in

just my bra and panties as his gaze hungrily devoured me. Catching sight of myself in the mirror, it would have been easy for me to disparage my cellulite, fat rolls, and love handles. But with that look in his eyes of pure lust, and the way one of his hands inched toward his crotch—to cover up his erection, perhaps? How could I not try to see myself as he saw me?

A zaftig goddess.

That was the way he saw me. He told me so. And he showed me in his lingering touch, his lusty gaze, and his sweet kisses. In the way our bodies moved together, him delighting in my curves, in everything I had to offer as he took his pleasure and gave me mine in return?

Eyes locked on him, I slid the slinky material up my thighs, to my hips as I worked my arms into the sleeves. The deep V showed part of my bra—I'd have to wear a different one or no bra at all if this was the dress I chose. I turned around, revealing my bare back as I swept my long hair into a messy bun on top of my head. Now our hairstyles matched.

"Could you zip me up?"

"Gladly." He sprang off the sofa and closed the distance between us in only a heartbeat or two. The zipper offered a little resistance at the widest part of my back, but he eased it up, then gently turned me around to face him.

"Fucking gorgeous," he said. "Red is a beautiful color on you."

He stepped away so I could look in the mirror. I wasn't going to brave the pedestal with this cast on my leg, but the dress covered the cast nicely. I actually felt beautiful as I stared into the tri-fold mirror. The dress's bodice was gathered and met in a faux knot at my left hip, the pleats skimming over and accentuating my curves. It clung to my hips and a little to my belly, but then flared out beautifully at my thighs into a full skirt that skimmed the floor. The fabric was silky and shiny, but thick enough that it hid any lumps or bumps.

Holy shit. I do look like a goddess.

"Do you think Noah would like it?" I asked him, but to be honest, I couldn't take my eyes off my reflection. I'd worn plenty of bespoke costumes before, but this dress…it molded to my curves like it was made for me.

"Fuck, Danielle…it's… My god." Aris almost shuddered, like his words just refused to come out. He stepped back over to me and tilted my chin up so my eyes were forced to meet his. "Noah is a man with exquisite taste, and he is gonna want to eat you alive in this dress."

A breathy chuckle escaped my lips as I processed his words. "Is that a good thing?"

"My beautiful goddess…" He didn't answer. Instead, his lips claimed mine, stealing my breath as he wrapped his arms around me, forcing me to surrender to his passion. As he pressed against me, I realized my earlier thoughts had been correct: he was hard as a rock, his thick cock nearly bursting out of his pants when he ground it against me.

I pulled back. "So should I try the other ones on or not?" I looked over at the bar that held a black ballgown with gold sequins, a floaty light pink chiffon number, and a stunning royal blue column dress.

"Let me show you what I think of you in this dress." He reached behind me to pull down the zipper.

I glanced down at the tag, suddenly distracted by the price. "Oh, fuck! Was this on sale? It's five hundred dollars?"

"Don't worry about that." He slid the zipper down and pulled the dress until it was puddled at my feet.

I snatched it up and got it on a hanger, placing it back on

the bar with the others. When I hobbled back around, he had unzipped his pants and was stroking his cock, that look of lust in his eyes from earlier so intense, I thought he might stalk over to me, throw me down on the sofa and have his way with me.

And…well…

That was very nearly what happened.

"I need you, Dani," he growled, taking me into his arms, his teeth and lips toying with my ear as he wrapped my hand around his cock. "Feel how fucking hard you made me in that dress."

I gulped. "Um…"

"Let me fuck you," he said. "Right here, right now. Fuck, I feel like I'm about to explode."

"Oh, I don't know. What if Sasha comes back?"

"You're buying a five-hundred-dollar dress. I'm sure she works on commissions. She's not going to give a fuck what we do in here." His dimples were on full display, making it nearly impossible to argue with him.

"Uh…"

Then he did something I really didn't expect. He actually picked me up!

"What the fuck, Aris?! You're gonna break your back, for fuck's sake."

"Shhh…." He carried me over to the sofa and set me down gently. Then he pulled down his pants and stepped out of them. "Now…how can I fuck you with your leg in the cast?" He surveyed the sofa and his face lit up. "Lie down and put your leg up here." He pointed to the back of the cushions.

He yanked at my panties, wanting to slide them down, but he was in such a hurry, he just fucking ripped them off me. "Okay, I owe you a new pair. Let me see those tits."

He was so determined, so crazy with desire—I'd never seen this side of him, this dominant, almost forceful side, and I had to admit it was fucking hot as hell. I reached around and unhooked my bra, tossing it across the room as my bare breasts spilled onto my ribcage.

"Fuck, that's more like it." He knelt on the floor beside the sofa and went to work on my nipples, while his hand teased my pussy lips apart. "Holy fuck, you are already so wet!"

"Well, seeing you like this is pretty arousing," I confessed.

"Do you want me?" He knelt on the sofa cushion between my spread legs, his hazel eyes boring into mine.

"Yes...please." Just two soft words, and that was all he needed.

He guided his cock to my entrance and groaned as he plunged deep inside me with one thrust. "Oh, fuck, Danielle..."

I reached around him, my hands on his back and then sliding up to his shoulders as he thrust into me, his hips finding a steady rhythm. My hands tangled in his hair, loosening his man bun and eventually sending his shoulder-length tresses cascading around his face.

Oh, fuck. He was so gorgeous. Absolutely breathtaking. Just looking at his intense concentration as he stroked inside me was going to make me come. The desire pooled deep in my core as his cock rhythmically slammed against my G-spot. No man I'd ever been with had been able to hit it so easily—was it the way he was curved or his shape? I didn't know, but it was like his cock was an arrow and my G-spot had a bullseye painted on it.

That silly thought distracted me for a second, but then he sank his teeth into my neck, bringing me back into the moment. After a few nibbles, his lips found my earlobe, and he rasped, "I can't hold back much longer... You're gonna make my cock explode if you keep squeezing it like that."

I was completely unaware I was doing that, but just hearing him say he couldn't hold back pushed me over the edge. "God, Aris...me too..."

"That's it, baby, milk my cock, take it all..."

It was at that point I realized he wasn't wearing a condom.

Was he?

No, he wasn't. I would remember him putting one on. Right?

He collapsed on top of me, his breath heavy on my neck as he worked to control it. He stayed inside me until I worried about making a mess on the sofa, and then I was forced to rouse him from his reverie.

"Aris...hey..."

His head jerked up. "Fuck, Dani..."

"Can you get me something to clean up? We're gonna ruin this—"

"Oh, fuck!" He seemed to snap back to reality, and he was off that sofa faster than a cheetah pouncing on an antelope. He rushed over to the vanity, grabbed a wad of tissues and was back at my side in a flash to clean me up.

"I'm so sorry, Dani. Oh my god...I wasn't even thinking."

"It's okay," I assured him.

"You're on the pill?" he asked, hope in his voice.

"No, but I just finished up my period a few days ago."

His brows drew together. "Fuck...I don't like the sound of that."

"Well, I'm pretty regular. I shouldn't ovulate until next week." I shrugged.

He finished wiping up the mess he made. "Let me know if you want me to pick up a morning after pill for you."

Oh, god. I had never even thought of using something like that. Never been in a position where I needed to. But the pill made me gain weight, and I was too worried to try one of the longer-term options. I hadn't had any prospects for so long that I… Well, I just hadn't been thinking about anything other than condoms, but if I was going to have sex with Aris regularly…

But then he also had Noah in the mix.

Oh, god. Had I just made a terrible mistake?

"Don't worry about STIs," he seemed to be reading my mind. "Noah and I both got tested when we started seeing each other, and neither of us has been with anyone else since then. We were both negative for everything."

"Okay. Well, I haven't had sex in a couple years…"

"Years?!" He looked shocked. "No, that's not good. That goddess body needs to be fucked well and fucked often."

I couldn't help but laugh. He was too adorable for words. He helped me off the sofa and gathered up all my clothes for me, including my bra, which had been flung halfway across the room. "Oops, I almost forgot about your panties…"

"Yes, RIP, panties," I said solemnly as he tossed them in the trashcan beside the vanity. "Well, they're definitely going to know what we got up to."

"Probably smells like sex in here too…"

"Everything okay in there?" came along with a knock at the door.

My entire body flushed with embarrassment—and I was already pretty flushed, at least my cheeks and chest, just from the sex. I felt like I was literally on fire as I called out, "Yes, just finishing up. We'll take the red one."

Aris grabbed the hanger. "Can you get dressed on your own? I'll go pay for this."

I smiled. "Yeah, that will get her out of our hair," I whispered. When he started to head toward the door, I froze. "Hey, wait! You need my credit card!"

He grinned as he pulled a gold credit card out of his pocket. "It's Noah's. He insisted."

"I can't let him pay for a five-hundred-dollar dress!"

"He's a doctor," Aris reminded me. "You're a grad student. It's for his event. Just let him pay, love."

He didn't even give me a chance to argue. He simply patted the dress slung over his arm and briskly walked out of the room, leaving me naked with my mouth wide open, sputtering.

eighteen

. . .

noah

"HERE'S YOUR CARD BACK." Aris handed me the gold card with a sly smile on his face.

"What's the damage?" I slid it back into my wallet.

"Five hundred." He plopped down on the bed beside me as I set my wallet on the nightstand next to my phone.

"Damn…" I whistled.

"Worth every penny." He made the chef's kiss gesture and grinned.

I couldn't help but smirk. "You're awfully giddy tonight."

"Well, I like spending time with Danielle," he admitted.

I leaned in closer to him and ran my finger down his bare chest. His firm pecs were begging to be kissed and licked. I hadn't been particularly horny since I found out about the lawsuit, but after sharing my woes with my polycule, my burden had lifted somewhat—at least enough to get the blood flowing to my cock again.

I wrapped one arm around his torso and brought my

mouth to his chest, pressing kisses around his nipple. I breathed in deep, inhaling his familiar scent and something else…coconut and jasmine, if I wasn't mistaken. "You smell like her…"

"I should." He ran his fingers down my back. "I railed her pretty damn good in the dressing room."

My head popped up. "You what?"

"Fucked her in the dressing room." He grinned proudly.

I reached down and cupped his cock and balls through his thin pajama pants. "And you're getting hard just thinking about it."

"Well, you're also touching me and kissing my nipples, so…"

"You really like fucking her, huh?" I gently rubbed his lengthening shaft through the fabric.

"Is it that obvious?"

"I didn't know you were missing pussy so much." I didn't feel exactly jealous. It was more like…inadequate. Did he want me to bottom more often? Did he miss being in control? Being the one to penetrate? What was it he liked about—

"It's not just the pussy," he answered all my silent questions. "I like her, Noah." He sat up. "I like her a lot."

"*Like* like?" I asked. "Or like…*love*?"

He breathed in deeply, his chest rising and falling as his head pressed back against the padded headboard. "I mean… I know we just met. It would be weird to say I'm in love with her, right?"

I considered it for a moment. "Well, you've been taking care of her after her injury. And I do think you may be experiencing a bit of a white knight situation."

"White knight situation?" He smirked. "Is that so, Dr. Evans? And can you elaborate on this condition please?"

I sat up next to him, sliding my hand back to my side of the bed and away from his softening erection. Well, I was hoping this conversation was going to lead to sex, but…it seemed like it was leading to a discussion about feelings and other things I wasn't usually keen to discuss.

I started it though. So…the blame fell squarely on my shoulders.

"White Knight Syndrome," I explained, "you know, when someone falls in love with a partner they see as vulnerable because they get off on taking care of people."

"Well, I'm a nurse. Of course I like taking care of people!" he snapped back at me.

"And you also caused her injury, so that might play into it…"

His lips pursed. "So you don't think my feelings are real?"

"I didn't say that at all, Aris. Don't put words in my mouth. I'm only asking you to be careful and a little guarded. I know how easily you get attached. And I don't know what her MO is. Do you?"

His face scrunched up. *Because he knows I'm right.*

"All I know is that I enjoy her company. She's so… layered is the best word I can think of for her. She comes across as this confident diva, and almost a little standoffish, to be honest. But it's all to cover up her insecurity and her adorable squishy insides," he explained, unable to keep the smile from growing wider on his face the longer he described her.

He was smitten for sure. Maybe not real love. Whatever the case, I just didn't want him to get hurt.

"You're okay with me taking her to the ball?" It was a repeat question, but I wanted to make sure he hadn't changed his mind.

"Of course I am! I think it's amazing she even suggested it. You two are going to make such a striking couple, I'm sure everyone's going to want to know when the wedding is. So you better make sure to come up with specifics for all that. Or it won't seem believable." He suddenly smacked his hand to his forehead. "And a ring! You need a ring."

As soon as he said the words, I felt heat surge up from deep within me. *A ring.*

"What's wrong?" Aris's voice went from light and airy to worried in a heartbeat. He could feel the unease that just washed over me.

"I…" I shook my head, trying to get the dizzy feeling I'd just experienced to dissipate. "I actually have a ring."

His eyebrows flew up. "You do? Why would you have an engagement ring?"

I didn't bring a ton of stuff when we moved in here at Cynda and Jason's. I wasn't a materialistic person, nor a sentimental one. Maybe losing my parents and growing up in foster care meant I knew better than to get attached to people, places, or things. But I did keep a small box that had gone with me everywhere from the time I was ten years old —when I lost my parents.

I stood up, went to our closet, and pulled it off the top shelf. It was just an old metal cashbox. I wasn't even one hundred percent sure where I got it, but someone gave it to me somewhere along the line. I had never shown this to Aris before.

I laid it on the bed as Aris's eyes grew wider and wider. He laid a hand on top of mine and drew my gaze.

"Are you okay? You don't have to share anything with me unless you want to…" his voice was like a soft caress.

"I want to show you," was all I said as I spread out some old photos on the comforter, along with some other memorabilia. A medal my father got in the Army. My hospital bracelet from when I was born. And a small black velvet ring box.

"You've never really talked about your parents," Aris finally broke the silence. "And I never wanted to pry—"

I took a deep breath and opened the ring box. There, nestled in white satin was a gold ring with a half-carat round diamond.

Aris gasped. "This was your mom's?"

I nodded. "Someone decided I should have it instead of her being buried with it. I always thought she should have worn it to the grave, but…they were cremated. I guess someone thought that would be a waste of a perfectly good ring."

He just looked at me, blinking.

"Sorry, I know I'm being morbid. I don't mean to be, it's just…I'm used to it. I've had twenty-five years to process this." Damn—had it really been that long? Yeah. I was thirty-five, and they died in the car accident when I was ten. I bit my lip to push down the emotions that tried to come surging up.

What the hell was wrong with me? I had been more emotional this week than at any time since I was a gangly, snot-nosed kid. I blew out a breath, willing the feelings away. I didn't have time to deal with that right now. I had enough on my plate.

"The ring is beautiful," Aris said. "Do you think it will fit her though?"

I glanced at the ring. "My mom was actually about Danielle's size, maybe a little shorter. I think it will."

He smiled. "I know it will be beautiful on her finger. And when you see that dress…well…you may just fall in love with her too."

I highly doubted that. But I was looking forward to the look on Alexandra's face when Danielle walked in on my arm. I talked to my partner, Jessica, today about taking over Danielle's care, just in case there were any issues. I didn't want Alexandra coming back to say that I was fucking my patients now.

I didn't know if any of this was going to help my case, but at this point, I would settle for making her squirm. The paper hadn't published anything on the case yet. The reporter was still waiting to get my side of the story. Tomorrow was Friday, and I had my assistant make the appointment for the interview on Monday morning.

This weekend could change a lot for me as far as the case went. Maybe she would even drop it. Discussing it with my polycule turned out to be the right decision. They convinced me I shouldn't sweep it under the rug and take it lying down. I did nothing wrong, and I should go on the offensive.

I had nothing to hide.

I returned everything to the metal box except the ring box, which I set on the dresser. "I'll make sure it fits her tomorrow. If not, we can get a fake ring, or maybe Cynda has one she can borrow."

Aris nodded. "That sounds like a good plan." He opened his arms wide as he lay back down on the bed. "Are you tired? Wanna cuddle before we fall asleep?"

Aris loved cuddling. Cuddling was not my first choice of things to do in bed, but I did like making him feel good. I turned off the lights and climbed in next to him. He turned over, facing the wall, and I lined myself up behind him as the big spoon. He backed his ass up, grinding against me and letting out a contented sigh.

"This feels so nice, baby." His voice was soft in the dark.

I wrapped my arm around his waist and pulled him even closer so I could nuzzle his neck. His long hair tickled my cheek as I pressed kisses behind his ear and then peppered them down to his shoulder.

He groaned, pressing his ass back even farther. "If you keep that up—"

"Is that a threat or a promise?" I pushed my hard cock against his firm ass cheeks.

"Always a promise for you, my love…"

nineteen

. . .

danielle

CYNDA PUT the finishing touches on my hair and stepped back. "Okay, you can take a look now." She handed me a mirror and spun the stool around so I could check out the back in the large vanity mirror in her and Jason's spacious en suite bathroom.

She had piled my hair on top of my head in big, soft curls that spilled down in a feminine cascade, showing off my neck and the dip in the back of my dress. And she'd put a little rhinestone clip on the side that sparkled when it caught the light.

"Oh my god, Cynda! How did you learn to do hair like this?" I gasped when I saw it.

She shrugged. "My mom was a beautician," she said. "She taught me a few things."

"It's absolutely stunning!" I couldn't get over how perfect it looked. It didn't even look like my plain, boring straight brown hair. Right now it looked shiny and glowing from within. Like magic.

I stood up on shaky legs. I couldn't believe what a crazy week it had been. Had it really only been a week? Talk about a whirlwind. I went from a first date to moving in with the guy, breaking my leg, losing my lead role, and questioning all my life choices all in one week?!

I guess it's time to put on my dress and get this show on the road.

Before I could hobble into Cynda's bedroom, there was a knock at the door, and Jason poked his head in. I was wearing a robe—but, again, being a theater chick, having someone see me half naked wasn't a problem.

"Hey, Raine is here to see you off. Can she come in?"

"Yes, of course, thanks, Jason!"

I noticed he had Sushi in his arms. That cat, who was so skittish a week ago, was now letting him carry her around like a baby. How crazy was that? She wasn't the only one who'd undergone huge changes this week!

Raine burst through the door and actually froze in her tracks when she spotted my hair. Her hands flew to her mouth, and she squeezed out, "Oh my god, Dani! Your hair is gorgeous. Now that's what it should have looked like when you were in *Hello, Dolly!* Did you do her makeup too, Cynda?"

Cynda shrugged. "Just added a bit to her natural beauty."

"That smoky eye is to die for!" Raine exclaimed. "If you ever want a job at the theater, let me know. I'm doing my costuming final in May, and we sure could use a hair and makeup artist like you."

"Happy to help wherever I'm needed," Cynda said graciously as she swept out of the room, leaving behind her positive energy.

Raine handed me my crutches so I could get into the

bedroom. "Is that your dress?" She pointed to the garment bag hanging from the curtain rod on the far side of the room.

"Yes, would you mind getting it out of the bag for me?" I was glad she was here to help me get ready.

"Of course. So…how are things going with you and Aris? He's okay with you going as Noah's date tonight?"

"Yes, of course." I grinned. "He helped me pick out this dress, and he even fucked me in the dressing room."

If Raine had been sipping a drink when I tossed that little tidbit out there, she would have choked on it and sprayed it all over the place. "What happened to the demure Miss Goody Two Shoes Danielle I've known since our junior year of undergrad?"

I laughed. "I think Aris has corrupted me."

"You think?" Her gaze swept down the dress as she drew it out of the bag. "My god, Danielle…a fire-engine-red dress, too? Who are you?!"

I cocked my head. "I'm not a shrinking violet, I'll tell you that."

"Of course not. You've always been leading lady material, girl." Raine fingered the dress's silky material. "This is gorgeous."

"I just didn't believe I was leading lady material, you know?" I sighed as she brought the dress over to me and helped me step into it. "I know my voice is there. And my acting skills are top-notch. But I've always had casting directors pass me up because of my size. To combat that, I've learned to project confidence. I've done everything I could to compensate, except one thing…"

"What's that?" She waited as I wiggled my hips, pulling the dress up so she could zip it.

"I don't think I really believed in myself, believed I deserved it," I admitted. "I always thought someday I'd get the weight off, and then I'd be able to get all the roles I've ever wanted because my voice is good enough. But you know what?"

"What?"

"I deserve it now," I said with resolve. "Yes, I'm a bigger girl, but bigger girls deserve to be represented in the theater. And who says that every female love interest has to be a skinny minnie? Nothing, that's what."

"You're absolutely right," Raine agreed as she worked the zipper Aris had already loosened. This time it slid right up my back, and the fabric hugged my curves.

I slowly turned, letting the skirt of the dress curve around my legs in a beautiful swirl. "Well, what do you think?"

"My god, Danielle—you're gonna knock 'em dead tonight." She clapped her hands. "Standing O for sure!"

noah

I heard the master suite bedroom door open and straightened to my full height. Aris leaned over and adjusted my black tie. "You look smokin' hot in that tux," he whispered in my ear as he pinched my ass cheek hard enough to make me wince.

Then both of our gazes were riveted on the hallway as Danielle made her way—albeit slowly—toward us.

"Tada!" Raine jumped out of the hallway first and did a dramatic Vanna White-type flourish to showcase the diamond of the evening.

"I feel really silly in this cast and one black flat," were the first words out of Danielle's mouth.

"You can't see your shoes with the dress that long,"

Darth helpfully pointed out from the sofa, just barely looking up from his phone.

"You look stunning!" Cynda rushed in, taking photos with her phone. "Now, you two go pose by the fireplace. C'mon now."

She was just like a mom on prom night, wanting to get pics of her kid and his date all dressed up. We humored her, my arm around Danielle as we posed. I leaned in toward her, my hand on the small of her back. This close, her intoxicating fragrance wafted into my nose.

I hadn't been this close to a woman since Emma—other than in a professional capacity, of course. I didn't date during college or medical school, but I'd had a couple of longer-term girlfriends since I earned my M.D., the last of whom was Emma. None of them could really "see the light at the end of the tunnel" when it came to what they viewed as me prioritizing my career over them. I was building up my practice and creating a positive reputation for myself.

Now Alexandra Bagby was trying to destroy everything I'd worked for.

Well, not if I had anything to say about it.

After Cynda was done with her barrage of photos, she took off her paparazzi hat and put her mom one back on. "Well, kids, are we all ready for tonight?"

Danielle stood up straight, her shoulders squaring as she looked me in the eye. "We're playing roles tonight. I'm Danielle Delacroix, newly engaged to Dr. Noah Evans. We've been dating for six months, and we met at a local antiques club," she verified our story.

"Oh, the ring!" Aris remembered.

"Yes, I meant to have you try it on yesterday, but it was so crazy, I forgot." I nodded toward Aris. "Do you mind grabbing it off the dresser?"

"Ring?" She batted her eyelashes and looked down at her left hand. "I was just going to use this cheap costume piece. It's not a diamond, but the ruby matches my dress, right?"

Aris returned with the black velvet box and presented it to me. Danielle's brow arched as she looked at the box and then at me. "What's that?"

"It's a wedding ring set," I said. "It belonged to my mother. If the engagement ring fits, you can wear it tonight. If not, you can wear the ruby one."

She shrugged. "Okay."

I opened the box, and revealed the diamond solitaire ring.

"Wow, that is gorgeous!" she squealed, reaching in to pry it out of its little satin nest. She appeared to hold her breath as she slid it down onto her left ring finger. "Perfect fit. Wow!" She admired the way it sparkled in the light before turning toward me. "Are you sure I should wear it? I'm so afraid something might happen to it, and—"

I held out a hand to stop her. "I'm not emotionally attached to it. If it fits, and you think it helps the story, then, by all means, wear it."

"Wow, okay. Thank you." She held her hand up again to admire it. "It just looks so good there. Like it belongs."

I didn't miss the look Cynda flashed to Jason. Darth stood up and stretched. "Where are you guys going again?"

"The charity ball for the leukemia research society," I told him before glancing at the clock on the living room wall. "And we're running a little late. Raine, were you able to get the wheelchair for us?"

"Yes, of course. It's on the porch." She had access to the university's vast costume and prop warehouse and was able to sign it out for the weekend. Aris or I could have gotten one through the hospital network, but we didn't want that somehow coming back to Alexandra or her father.

I turned toward Danielle with a smile. "Ready to go?"

"As ready as I'll ever be, darling." She winked. "Now, remember, the most important rule of acting, especially improv—meaning there's no script—is to follow your fellow actors' leads. If they introduce something new, run with it. The key to successful improv is to always say yes."

I nodded. "I'll do my best."

Aris offered to be our driver to and from the event so we wouldn't have to order a rideshare service. I theorized he also just wanted to keep an eye on Danielle and me, plus feel like he was somehow contributing. The way he was so protective of her was really sweet.

She probably wouldn't like being my date now that she was used to Aris because I wasn't anywhere near as sweet and thoughtful as he was. But we were both playing roles tonight, so maybe I could channel my inner Aris and show her a good time by behaving the way a doting fiancé would.

Aris pulled my Acura up to the curb outside the venue, which was all lit up with luminaria and strands of white lights in the trees outside the building. The windows of the conference center were aglow with light from the massive modern-looking chandeliers that hung in a neat row in the lobby area, where people were already mingling during the cocktail hour. There was a red carpet to walk to get into the event.

I was not expecting that.

And the red carpet was lined with photographers and

members of the press. I wondered if the reporter who was writing the story about the malpractice suit was in attendance. I didn't know what she looked like, but Maggie had given me her name.

"Ready?" I leaned over to press a kiss to Danielle's cheek, and she stiffened under my touch. "Everything okay?"

"Sorry, yes. I'm just…not in character yet. I wasn't expecting you to be either." She gave a nervous giggle.

"Aris, can you get the wheelchair set up? And I'll come around and help Danielle out of the car."

"I'm on it." He threw the car into park and opened the door. Seconds later, he was rolling the wheelchair to her side of the car and helping her out. He made sure her long red dress wouldn't get caught in the wheels and gave her a kiss on the cheek.

I wasn't sure if anyone saw that, but I flashed him a glare. Just what I needed, some more rumors—ones that wouldn't help my image. *Ugh.* Being a public figure under constant scrutiny was not my cup of tea. I was sure Aris would deal perfectly well with fame—he'd make a great rock star or actor or professional athlete.

I just wanted to cut people open and fix their noses and throats.

Huh, that didn't come out quite right, but you know what I mean. I didn't need any fanfare or attention. I just wanted happy patients.

I bent down to be eye level with my beautiful date. "Ready for this?"

She had a fierce but determined smile affixed to her face. All the reporters' eyes snapped to us as we rolled along the red carpet, the flashes from their cameras temporarily blinding me. But when I looked down, I noticed Danielle was waving to them all, completely in control like she owned the place.

I sucked in a deep breath. It was going to be a long night. As we rolled up to a table of volunteers so we could check in, a security guard ambled over to us. "Do you need any assistance, ma'am?" he asked Danielle.

"Oh, no, sir. Thank you. I'm sure Dr. Evans can handle it." She looked up at me with her wide doe eyes, her natural beauty enhanced by Cynda's artistry. A sultry confidence emanated from them, making me feel a little weak in the knees.

Whoa, was not expecting that either.

I checked in with the volunteers and received our table number and drink tickets. They pointed me toward a glass box at the end of the room where I could make my donation. It sparkled on a round red velvet-draped table under an elegant chandelier.

"Let me take care of this really quickly, and then I'll get us some drinks. Where would you like me to take you?" I asked, once again bending down so I could talk to Danielle face-to-face.

She maintained her smile while she spoke to me, "If you could just wheel me over to the side for a moment, I'll get the lay of the land while you make your donation. And if you see Alexandra or her dad, make sure to point them out to me."

"Will do," I assured her.

Then she unexpectantly grabbed my hand. "And, listen, if this is going to work—we need to be noticeably into each other, you know, grab people's attention. If we go on like this, so politely and stiffly, no one is going to pay any attention to us or believe we're madly in love."

I scoffed. "Well, those reporters were definitely checking us out."

"Yes, but they were photographing everyone walking the carpet. We want them to pursue us in here too, hopefully catch us in an intimate moment." Her eyebrows waggled suggestively.

"You act like you've done this before." I licked my lower lip as I guided us past the volunteer table and a few cocktail tables to where the donation table was.

"I haven't," she insisted, "but we're playing roles tonight, remember? You're the successful doctor who is showing off his new fiancée. And I'm the doting fiancée who always wants to make her man look good. We need to act like we're in love, right?"

"Gotcha. Yes, of course you're right. Let me slip this envelope into the box, and I'll be right back."

I headed toward the glass box while pulling my donation check out of my inner suit pocket. As I slipped the check into the slot and watched it slide down on top of the other donations, I took a deep, cleansing breath. I didn't know if there was such a thing as a patron saint for actors, but I needed to pray to them tonight...

twenty

. . .

danielle

I WATCHED as Noah dropped his donation off, and then as soon as he turned to come back my way, he was cornered by three men. One was an older gentleman with wispy white hair and a cane. The other two looked middle-aged. All three were white.

I figured they were colleagues of some sort, so I just sat up tall in my wheelchair, lifted my chin and projected strength and confidence out into the room. It didn't take long for people to approach me to introduce themselves.

"Do you need any help?" one older man asked when he got within earshot.

"Help with what?" I asked in a playful way. I looked up, taking in his extreme height. I was seated, but he had to be at least six-five or six-six.

"I apologize; you do look rather capable. What table are you at?" He smiled and held out his hand. "I'm Jake Barton. I work at the university in the athletics department."

"You don't say." I smirked, my eyes trailing up and down

his athletic figure. "To be honest, my fiancé signed us in but didn't tell me what table. He's over there." I gestured toward where he was standing.

"Oh, which one is he?"

"The handsome one," I answered, letting him use his imagination.

"I see." He winked. "Well, if I can get you anything, let me know. He seems to be engaged in quite the conversation."

Noah's back was to me now, so I couldn't really see his face, but the other three men were practically caging him in. I didn't like that. I was about to roll myself over there and crash their little party when a woman came up to me. She was petite with an elegant updo like mine, only her hair was a stunning shade of auburn. She wore a pale, glittery champagne-colored gown with a slit up the thigh and high heels with pearls and rhinestones on them.

"Are you friends with Jake?" she asked after he moved on to mingle with some other attendees.

"Oh…well, I guess I am now." I smiled at her, even though she seemed a little put off by my answer. "Why do you ask?"

"I just wondered," she said. "He's single. And one of the many eligible bachelors here tonight." A couple of men started to walk past us, and she straightened her shoulders and visibly sucked in her gut.

"I see," was all I could think to say to that. Was she really here to land a rich dude?

"Have you seen Chase Walker yet?" She drew her attention back to me when the two men passed by without seeming to notice either of us.

"Um, sorry, I don't know who that is." I looked behind the woman to see if Noah was still engaged in conversation with the three men. That conversation had to either be going very well or very poorly, and I still couldn't see his face, so it was impossible to know for sure.

"You don't know who Chase Walker is?" She rolled her eyes. "Are you, like, new to town or something? Do you live under a rock?"

"Are you always so condescending to perfect strangers?" I snapped back while still maintaining a pleasant smile on my face.

"I'm sorry. I just—I thought everyone would know the Walker family. They own half of Monroe County. Very old money—goes back to the early nineteen-hundreds when Chase's great-great-grandfather founded a pharmaceutical company. Chase is in line to inherit it."

"Ah, okay."

"He's supposed to be here tonight, and he's very, very single."

I flashed my ring. "Well, I'm engaged, so single men are not really on my radar."

"Oh my gosh, let me see!" She grabbed my hand, jerked it toward her, and inspected my ring. I felt like a piece of fruit in the grocery store. "It looks like an older style ring. Is it an antique?"

"It was his mother's engagement ring," I explained.

"Oh. Well, that's very nice. I hope you two will be very happy together."

I hadn't noticed while this rude lady was jerking my hand to look at my ring that Noah had finally joined us. I heard a throat clear, and my head snapped up. My new "frenemy"—seemed to be the appropriate term—whipped around to see Noah standing there with his mouth gaping wide open.

One word came out of his mouth: "Alexandra?"

noah

Out of all the people attending this charity event—which is crawling with people, by the way—Alexandra Bagby leeches onto my date?!

"Dr. Evans," she sneered, looking me up and down. "You clean up nicely."

"I see you've met my fiancée." I flashed her a smug smile, then crouched down in front of Danielle. "Are you ready for that drink I promised? Sorry for getting trapped back there…"

"It's quite all right, my love," she said, breaking her eye contact with me to pin her eyes on Alexandra. "I've heard so much about you. Nice to meet you in person."

God bless her, I don't know how she did it, but there wasn't a trace of malice in her voice. She sounded one hundred percent sincere. *And the Oscar goes to…*

Alexandra stood there, speechless, looking very much like a fish out of water. She stepped back, glanced to her left and right, and then dipped her head before running away. Well, what constitutes running in a pair of stilettos.

"Oh my god!" Danielle burst into laughter. "That was the funniest thing ever! You should have seen your face. You should have seen *her* face!"

"Shhhh…" I warned her. "People are staring at us."

"Good, that's what we want. Now, lean down here and kiss me, and then we'll go get drinks."

I wasn't used to being bossed around, but I didn't second-guess it either. I promptly leaned forward and pressed my lips to hers as if the entire room wasn't watching us like reality TV. It was meant to be a quick smack, but she lifted an arm and palmed the back of my head, pressing me to her. The act sent a chill down my spine and a zap of arousal right to my cock.

Holy shit. Didn't have that on my bingo card for the night —and I had prepared myself for a lot of potential discomfort.

"Now, how about that drink you promised me forever ago?" She only pulled away a few inches, so her words fell along with her heated breath across my lips and chin.

"Yes, ma'am." I rose to my full height, enjoying the smug smirk on her face when she made eye contact with none other than Alexandra Bagby across the room. She was talking to her father. Oh, good. They were both watching me wheel her down the hallway toward the ballroom.

When we entered, the room was humming with conversation, underscored by a string quartet playing classical music on the stage at the front of the room. There must have been a hundred tables, all decked out with crisp white linens, floral centerpieces with fragrant lilies, and flameless candles in ornate silver holders.

"Very classy," she said as I wheeled her to table twenty-one. I started to move a chair out of the way for her wheelchair, but she shook her head. "I'll sit in a regular chair. There's not much room for the wheelchair anyway."

"I can get them to move us to a table along the wall, where there's more room?"

"No, this is fine," she insisted, lifting herself out of the chair and hobbling over to the table. "You can fold it up and put it somewhere else. I won't need it unless I need to go to the bathroom or something."

"Okay. Now, what can I get you?"

"Something strong," was the only clue she gave. It was around that time that a few others began seating themselves at our table, and I wanted to give the impression that we knew each other well, so I smiled and headed off to the bar.

She'd handled Alexandra brilliantly, so I was sure she could make conversation without me. She was a force of nature, truly. To come in here, not knowing anyone, with a broken leg and in a wheelchair—her presence was still so commanding.

I had seen her sitting meekly in my exam room and thought she was shy. I'd seen her tumble to the pavement when Aris struck her with his bicycle, and she bore the pain like someone who was accustomed to it. And I'd seen her heart broken over having to give up her dream role and postpone her master's graduation, and she took it in stride.

Yet, when I'd had an issue, she was the first to step up and offer to help.

It was easy to see why Aris thought he was falling in love with her.

Maybe he truly was?

All of these thoughts descended upon me, twisting and morphing in my brain along with the conversation I'd had with the three men who detained me at the donation table. One was a colleague, a gastroenterologist who worked in my building. The other two men were members of the hospital board.

I wanted to tell Danielle what they said, but I didn't want to rile her up any further. She was already angry about Alexandra and her father. If she knew how these three men had threatened me to settle the suit with Alexandra, she would have a difficult time concealing her rage, even if she was a seasoned actress.

I was not a seasoned actor, and I was having a hard enough time.

Bloomington, Indiana, was a relatively small town. I guessed that was why everyone felt the need to get involved in other people's business. Everyone was jockeying for power, seniority, clout. I didn't care about such things. Maybe it was my background as a foster kid shuffled from home to home from ages ten to eighteen. Maybe it was the fact that I had to scratch and claw my way through so many years of college and med school. Maybe it was because everything I had achieved had come from my own two hands, two feet, and my big ole brain.

I exchanged our drink tickets for two cocktails and headed back to the table.

I did not expect to see Danielle conversing with David Shepherd and Kurt Banks, the two board members who confronted me earlier. They were apparently assigned to our table. *Fantastic.* I fixed a smile to my face and greeted them as I set Danielle's drink in front of her and then took the empty seat beside her.

"David, Kurt, nice to see you again," I stated, trying not to sound stiff and fake. Danielle was probably less than impressed with my acting skills, but she was maintaining a pleasant smile anyway. "I see you've met my fiancée."

"Yes, Danielle has been telling us all about how you met. I didn't even know you were dating anyone, Noah," Kurt said, sounding a bit incredulous.

"I'm a private person," I said with a shrug, but I kept it light.

"Noah doesn't like to toot his own horn," Danielle jumped in. "He gets so busy with work—and I'm so busy with my master's degree that we don't get out much. So I leapt at the opportunity to attend this event with him. The leukemia foundation does such amazing work."

"Danielle was telling us she's studying musical theater at

IU," David changed the subject. "I hope we get to see you perform sometime. When is your next show?"

Danielle smiled sweetly and pointed to her leg. "I had a bit of a setback and broke my leg, but I hope to be involved in one of the fall productions. They haven't announced the fall season yet."

"And what do you hope to do with your degree when you're finished?" Kurt probed. "We don't exactly have a huge theater scene around here."

I saw Danielle's character slip for just a second when she seemed surprised by the question. But she bought herself some time by taking a sip of her drink, then jumped right in, "Oh, I'm not sure right now. I believe Noah wants to stay in the area, so I'll find something local. Of course, we want to start a family."

I nearly choked on my own drink when those words came out of her mouth, and she flashed me a "you better follow my lead" glare. I remembered her speech before we left the house. "Yes, lots of kids. Like five or six, I think."

She laughed and swatted at my arm playfully. "I think probably more like eight. Isn't that what you said, Noah?"

Now Kurt nearly choked on his drink, but David took the baton and ran with it. "Why get a master's degree if you're just going to pop out eight babies?"

It took every ounce of restraint I could muster not to punch the guy right upside the head, but Danielle didn't miss a beat. "Education is never a waste, is it?"

"Of course not, but—"

"Are you a medical doctor?" she asked David.

"I am," he said. "My specialty was cardiology."

"And how many years of education do you need for that?"

"A lot," he fired back, refusing to play along with an exact number.

"Well, that's a lot of time spent learning how to save people's lives only to sit on a hospital board and not save any." Her icy stare sliced right through him.

"Wow, I like this one, Noah. Good job," Kurt said, laughing and slapping me on the back.

"Oh, look, they're getting ready to speak." Danielle pointed to the stage, saving us from the lingering sizzle of the sick burn she just gave Dr. Shepherd. She folded her hands in her lap and trained her gaze on the podium that was being moved to where the string quartet had been playing just moments before.

A tall, wiry white man and a willowy blonde, both in their fifties, approached the podium, and the audience politely applauded. While they were waiting for the applause to die down, someone wheeled a massive black grand piano onto the stage.

"Good evening, and welcome to the Seventeenth Annual Leukemia Warriors Ball! I'm Walter Schloderman, and this is my wife Cecile. We're so glad you took time from your busy schedules to join us this evening. We have so much in store for you, including a fabulous dinner, more beautiful music courtesy of our talented musicians from the IU School of Music, and even a special guest vocalist who will perform a special number for us after dinner. Now, if you'll all turn your attention to the screen—"

A giant screen began lowering from the ceiling, taking up all the space visible behind the podium.

"—we'll watch a short presentation on some of the beneficiaries of the work we do at Leukemia Warriors. After, your servers will arrive with your first course and will take your order for your main course. Enjoy, and we'll be back later with our special performance and a speech from one of our VIP Warriors!"

Everyone applauded again as the video began to play. I looked over to watch Danielle as the faces of kids and adults, their bodies ravaged by cancer and their bald heads glowing, appeared on the screen. I saw how it visibly affected her and how her fingers clenched around her napkin in her lap. She didn't take her eyes off the screen as I reached over and laid my hand on top of hers.

Still focused on the screen, she laced her fingers together with mine and squeezed. A tear glistened in the corner of her eye.

Thankfully, the video was brief, and moments later, we were enjoying our salads and bread, our- main entrees in the works. Most of the table got up after that to mingle and replenish their drinks, leaving Danielle and me alone once again.

"I can't believe you said that to David Shepherd." My amusement rumbled in a deep chuckle at the memory.

"Well, he sounded like a misogynist pig with that remark." She rolled her eyes and drained the rest of her drink. "I am not sure what else I could have said, to be honest."

"It was perfect," I assured her. "I'm not mad."

"Those were two of the men you were talking to earlier when Alexandra descended upon me like a plague."

I had to hide my laughter at that remark behind my napkin. I had no idea she was so witty. "Yes. You wouldn't like what they said to me, so I'm not going to tell you."

"To be honest? I think I have a pretty good idea based on his attitude." Instead of the quartet returning to the stage after the video, a pianist was playing soft classical music. "I was hoping the string quartet would play some more. So," she rubbed her hands together, "what should we do to grab some more attention?"

"Honestly, the reporters got our pictures, Alexandra saw us, and her dad sent his goons to threaten me. They've all seen you with me. Everyone knows we're engaged. I think our mission is accomplished."

"There's got to be more we could do…" She looked out across the room. "Oh, hey, do you see that woman up there talking to the Schodermans?"

I nodded. They were talking to a short, full-figured Black woman wearing a gold sequined gown. "Who is it?"

"She's one of my voice instructors—she's actually the chair of the department. And she's a famous jazz singer." She clapped her hands together. "Oh my gosh, I bet she's the special guest performer. We're in for a treat!"

"Hmm…well, the Schlodermans are shaking their heads and looking upset. I wonder what's going on?"

"I hope everything's okay." She looked down at her empty drink. "Hey, do you think you could wheel me to the restroom, and maybe we could get another drink on our way back?"

"Sure, I'd be happy to." I leaned in and put my arm around her shoulder, inhaling her perfume. Tonight was weird. I was on edge, and I was pissed about the things David, Kurt and Bill said, not to mention how obnoxious Alexandra was to Danielle, but I was also enjoying myself. It was a strange conflicting sensation.

"I want to kiss you again," I admitted, a whisper in her ear.

She giggled softly, the sound like the sweetest song. "Don't let me stop you."

I didn't want to go overboard, but I also wanted to taste her lips again. I made it short, then lingered with my lips next to her ear. "How do you think it's going so far?"

"So far so good…" she whispered back.

twenty-one

. . .

danielle

I WASHED my hands and then touched up my lipstick, which had been desecrated by my drink and Noah's kisses. Not that I was complaining. Despite a few very unpleasant individuals, I was enjoying myself.

"Danielle?" a soft voice called behind me.

I'd know that voice anywhere. I whipped around to find Elaine Greene standing there. "Oh my gosh, hi, Dr. Greene!"

"I thought that was you. Good heavens, I didn't expect to see you here. I heard what happened with your leg. It's all over the music school. I'm so very sorry, love." She reached out and gently touched my arm. "So I hear you'll be staying on an extra semester."

I sighed. "Yes, I can't finish my performance requirement with no performance—and my whole thesis was going to be based on the performance too." I had to laugh at this point—what other choice was there?

"I've been sidelined too," she said, her smile falling. "I was supposed to sing tonight. I've been a longtime supporter of the leukemia foundation, and I was really looking forward to performing for this crowd." She made a *tsk-tsk* sound. "Damn sinus infection. I'm liable to break into a coughing fit at any moment, so be warned."

"Oh no! That must be going around. I'm getting over a sinus infection too!"

"Well, I hope you're healing up faster than I did. I saw my wonderful ENT, Dr. Evans, a couple days ago."

A jolt raced through me. She was Noah's patient? Oh no! I couldn't very well act like I didn't know him, and I couldn't admit to seeing him as a patient because it would blow our cover. I'd have to tell her—

"Oh my gosh! Noah is my fiancée," I gushed. "We just got engaged a few weeks ago."

"Is that so? Oh, my sweet girl! I am so very happy for you both. I had no idea you were seeing the good doctor, and he is fine, isn't he?!" Her eyes gleamed when she said this, followed by a brief spurt of laughter that morphed into one of the coughing fits she warned me about.

"Oh my gosh, are you okay? Can I get you anything?" I handed her a tissue from the dispenser by the sink.

She held it over her mouth as the last coughs shook her body. "No, no, I'm just going to skedaddle on home I think. I really thought maybe I would be able to power through, but I was doing some vocal warmups backstage, and it just wasn't happening. The Schlodermans are so disappointed."

"I'm disappointed too!" I admitted. "I love hearing you sing. Would have been the highlight of my night for sure!"

A slow smile crept across her face. "Oh, I have an absolutely brilliant idea!"

As soon as she said it, I had a feeling what she was going to suggest. And I probably would have said no, but...

I was looking for a way to call more attention to myself and Noah, wasn't I?

noah

Aris: Well, how's it going?

Me: Danielle went to the ladies' room and… she has not come back.

Aris: What?! How long has it been?

Me: A while. Do you think she's in trouble?

Aris: Is she in her wheelchair?

Me: No, I have her chair. She hobbled in there. We should have brought her crutches too.

Aris: Go get a woman to check on her. FFS, Noah. You had one job!

Just when I was about to go find a lady to look for Danielle, she hobbled out with the woman she'd pointed out earlier helping her navigate the door.

"Dr. Evans!" the lady exclaimed.

Oh, shit. She's my patient. I didn't recognize her in formal-wear, apparently, and Danielle didn't give her name earlier.

"Well, hello there, Elaine. I didn't expect to see you here. How are you feeling?" I knew she was a vocalist from seeing her in my office, but I didn't know she was a professor! I thought she meant like at church or something. I wanted to facepalm myself so bad right now.

"I'm still feeling a little under the weather," she said, "but I wanted to come out and support the cause tonight. I better go find my wife. She probably thinks I fell in!" She laughed a high-pitched twinkling laugh.

"I was starting to wonder the same about my fiancée," I said, taking Danielle's hand.

"Oh, you two are just too adorable for words!" Elaine said. "Have fun tonight!"

She headed off toward the bar, and I turned to Danielle. "So that's what was taking so long."

"Yes, I got waylaid, much like you did earlier." She cocked her head and smirked.

"Only she didn't threaten your job, I assume?" I called her smirk and raised her an eye roll.

Danielle's nostrils flared. "So that's what that was about…"

I helped her back into her wheelchair. "Let's go get a drink. I'm sure the main courses have arrived by now."

Her eyes darted over to the wall opposite the entrance to the ballroom. "I've got a better idea. Wheel me over there."

"What? Why?"

"Just do it!" She looked at me expectantly. "What did I tell you about the first rule of improv, Noah?"

"Always say yes," I repeated her earlier instructions.

"That's right. Now get to it." She laughed.

When we arrived at the door, she said, "Oh, good, it's unlocked! Open it and wheel me inside."

"What?! Why would I do that?"

"Say yes, Noah," she admonished me, and, as there were a few people lingering in the hall and a long line of folks waiting to be served at the bar, I opened the door and slipped us both inside as fast as I could.

It was a closet where they stored chairs and tables, apparently, though most of them were in use in the ballroom, if I had to guess. And it was a little stuffy in here.

"Ever play Seven Minutes in Heaven?" she asked.

"Seven what?"

She sighed. "Really?"

"I don't know what that is."

"By the time I explain it to you, seven minutes will be up!" She giggled.

"Give me the executive summary." I grabbed a chair from the short stack in the corner and pulled it up alongside her wheelchair.

"You set a timer for seven minutes, then you have to go make out with another person till the timer goes off. Usually in a closet or something. Big hit at middle school parties." She looked at me like she expected her explanation to trigger my memory.

Nope. I admitted, "I didn't go to parties as a kid."

"Never?"

I shook my head. "I was a nerd. Big nerd. And I was a foster kid, so I moved around a lot. Never really made friends."

"Oh, Noah." She shook her head and took my hand into hers. "Every single thing I learn about you is more incredible than the last."

I shrugged. "If you say so."

"When you said you lost your parents when you were young, I figured that meant your grandparents raised you, or maybe an aunt."

"No, I didn't have any family who wanted to take me," I clarified. "Or who were in a position to take me"

"Really?" There was heartbreak in her eyes.

"Well, my dad was an only child, and my mom had a brother but he was younger and not in a position to do it. And my grandparents...well... There just wasn't a good situation for me. So foster care it was."

Danielle was quiet for a moment. I knew my baggage was a lot; that was why I didn't readily share that information. It made people uncomfortable to know I had to overcome so much. I didn't want anyone's pity, and to be honest, the fact that I was smart and picked things up easily was what saved me. I loved learning.

"So did you say something about making out?" I broke the silence. "In this seven-minutes game you were talking about?"

She gave the slightest giggle. "Well, yes…but I was more meaning that when we come out, it will appear that we've been doing naughty things in here, and it will further affirm that Alexandra was lying when she said you're gay."

I stroked my finger down her cheek. "I don't really care what they think, you know. Gay, straight, bi…really don't fucking care."

"I know that. But this is about discrediting Alexandra. That's going to be important if you take this to court," she reminded me.

"True." I leaned closer to her. "So, um…about that game. How many minutes do we have left?"

"Shit, I forgot to check my watch when we came in here." She laughed and scrubbed her hands down her face. "It's probably been seven by now."

"But what if I want to make out with you first? You know, for strictly accuracy reasons."

She raised an eyebrow. "That's the only reason?"

I chuckled. "Well, no…"

Her voice was so soft and silky, "Then what else?"

I cupped her face in my hands. "When I kissed you earlier…"

"What about it?"

"It just made me want to do it again." I pressed my lips

to hers, feeling the zing ignite down my spine. "And again." Another kiss—this time, she emitted a soft moan. "And another."

"Well, it is a rather nice sensation," she agreed.

"And I find that's not all I want to do," I admitted.

She pulled back and looked deep into my eyes. "What else do you want to do to me?"

I bit my lip before confessing, "I want to see what's under that dress, for one thing."

"You gave Aris the impression you weren't interested in me," she said, her brows drawing together.

"I hardly ever admit to being wrong…" I kissed her again, this time nibbling on her lower lip. "But in this case, I was *definitely* wrong."

Before I could kiss her again, my phone began buzzing in my pocket.

"Speaking of Aris…"

An appropriate number of people saw us emerge from the storage closet looking a bit rumpled with kiss-swollen lips. Beaming, Danielle suggested I text Aris back while we waited for drinks. After those were procured, we headed back to our table, where our entrees were waiting for us.

Kurt elbowed me after the server took away his empty plate. "Guess you two didn't care about dinner being cold."

Daniclle flashed him a wink that was so perfectly executed, I wanted to kiss her all over again. We both finished dinner, accompanied by a nice glass of wine. Then I leaned down to whisper in her ear, "I'm going to go outside and call Aris back. He's climbing the walls at home worried about what's going on."'

"Are you going to tell him about us?" she whispered back.

I tilted my head. "Which part?"

"I think we should surprise him…" was all she said.

When I returned about fifteen minutes later, Danielle was gone, and so was her wheelchair. My eyes darted around the table, but I tried not to show my panic. "Where'd my fiancée go?"

"A lady came over and wheeled her away," David said nonchalantly, giving a shrug to emphasize how little he cared. Poor fragile man that he was.

Knowing Danielle, she was perfectly fine and had made a new friend, so I didn't think much about it. The Schloder-mans returned to the podium on stage at that moment, so conversation in the ballroom gradually faded.

Mr. Schloderman took the microphone. "Most of you know that my wife and I, besides being the chairman and chairwoman of the Leukemia Warriors Foundation, we are huge supporters of the arts. The new music practice facility at the university is soon to be named Schloderman Hall in recognition of our donation. One of our foundation's biggest supporters through the years has been Dr. Elaine Greene, esteemed professor of music. She came tonight to support our cause, but also to give a special thank you for our work with the music school."

He handed the microphone to his wife. "Dr. Greene was

prepared to sing 'Wind Beneath My Wings' for us tonight, but she's feeling under the weather."

The audience groaned in disappointment.

"But we are very lucky because one of her students is in attendance tonight, and she has agreed to perform in Dr. Greene's stead. So may I welcome to the stage tonight, a master's student in the musical theater program, Danielle Delacroix."

Oh. My. God.

I nearly fell out of my chair when Danielle's wheelchair was pushed front and center by a young man with a beaming smile and a suit that was just a tiny bit too small for him. He helped her stand at a microphone by the piano. Then the young man sat down on the bench, and the familiar intro to "Wind Beneath My Wings" began to play.

Danielle stood like a vision in red, perfectly backlit to give her an ethereal glow. With one hand on the microphone stand, she drew in a big breath, closed her eyes and hummed a few notes before beginning the first verse of the song.

The sound that flowed out was the voice of an angel. It pierced my heart like an arrow. I'd always thought this song was so cheesy and overdone, but not this performance. Not the power of Danielle's voice and the raw emotion on her face.

I was absolutely stunned.

Speechless.

And I don't think I moved a muscle when she finished until Kurt slapped me on the back and said, "That girl right there is a keeper."

twenty-two

. . .

aris

"OH MY GOD, I didn't think you guys were ever coming out!" I said as Noah helped Danielle into the front seat and folded up her wheelchair. I popped the trunk and then raced around the car to help him load it up.

"We didn't think we were either!" Danielle exclaimed. She was positively radiant with so much energy, I felt it bouncing off her—and it even seemed to be bouncing off Noah as well.

After Noah and I both got buckled in, I put the pedal to the metal, the tires squealing as I got the fuck out of there.

"Whoa! Be careful with my car!" Noah scolded me.

I ignored him. Naturally. "What happened in there? Why are you guys so…um…energized?" That was the only word I could think of for the energy they were emitting.

"Well, let's just say there's not a soul in that building who doesn't know who Danielle is now," Noah said with a laugh.

"And that I'm Noah's fiancée," Danielle added.

"Well, does that include Alexandra and her father?" I needed to know.

"Oh, yeah. There's no doubt. We sat with two hospital board members—you know Kurt Walker and David Shepherd?"

I groaned as a mental image of the two most stereotypical conservative white men in the universe filled my mind. "Oh, those guys are the worst!"

I got the whole scoop on the fifteen-minute drive back to our house. I couldn't believe how much happened in the four hours they were together. I noticed something else too.

They were finishing each other's sentences.

They went to this event as strangers. Well, practically strangers.

They seemed like best buds now.

Was that a good thing or a bad thing? Time would tell.

I knew one thing though: I was anxious to get some time with Danielle. I had been thinking about her in that dress and reflecting on our dressing room adventure all night, and my cock had been so painfully hard, I had to take care of myself twice.

It wasn't enough.

I needed her pussy.

I hoped she wasn't too tired, but she seemed wide awake and energized. I planned to use that to my advantage once I got her inside.

To my dismay, Cynda, Jason, Darth and Sushi were also wide awake and eager to hear how the evening went. The latter was bouncing around the room chasing a feather on a stick that Jason was whipping back and forth like a madman.

I groaned as I sat down on the sofa and Danielle and Noah animatedly shared their exhilarating tale.

There was something about a storage closet and Seven Minutes in Heaven?

My ears perked up when I heard that. Then I looked over at Danielle, and she was curled up next to Noah, and they were holding hands.

Holding hands?!

Cynda had obviously noticed too because she sent me a concerned look. I smiled. I wasn't mad about it…well, not exactly.

I just felt a little blindsided.

Was I…jealous?

I hadn't been given an opportunity to sort out my thoughts, but Danielle was still wearing that dress, and I was still envisioning ripping it off her.

Okay, probably not ripping. It was a five-hundred-dollar dress.

That Noah bought…not me…

Nah, that would still be rude.

Finally, Danielle stood up. "Okay, I'm coming down from my actor high now." She yawned and stretched her arms over her head, balancing on her good leg. When she started to wobble, Noah caught her on his lap.

I stood up as well. "Yeah, I'm going to bed too. If anyone cares to join me." I looked right at them.

Cynda shot me a look that seemed to be a warning, but I didn't care. I didn't like being left out, and right now, I felt like I was being left out.

Are they going to tell me what's going on?

danielle

"Everything okay?" I asked Aris as I leaned on him for help down the hall.

"Yeah, it's fine," he said, but it was a lie, and, as he wasn't very adept at lying, it was a pretty obvious one.

Noah turned halfway, looking at us over his shoulder. "I'll give you two a moment. I'm going to get out of this tux and take a shower."

I smiled and nodded. "Take your time." Then I gestured toward the guys' bedroom. "Let's go chat for a sec, okay?"

"In my room?" His eyebrow arched adorably.

"Yeah, if that's okay?" Was he jealous? He was acting really weird.

"I guess so." He helped me down the hallway and ushered me through the doorway. "Do you want to sit in the chair?"

"Can you help me out of this dress first?" I grabbed his arm to get his attention—he seemed to be looking everywhere but at me.

"You want to talk to me while you're naked?" he clarified.

"I just want to be comfortable. I've been wearing this a long time." I reached behind myself to tug at the zipper, but lost my balance on one foot and fell right onto the bed, laughing at my antics.

I peeked over my head and saw that Aris had cracked a smile. "Um...I don't know how well I can concentrate on talking to you if you're naked, but let me help you before you injure yourself even more, okay?"

I laughed. "Please."

I felt his warm breath on my back as he straddled my hips and slowly yanked the zipper down. There was a pause as if he was considering his next move, and then his warm lips brushed against the skin right beside my spine. Desire rippled through me, and it was like the parts of my body I'd put into hibernation mode after seven minutes in the closet with Noah were suddenly reanimated.

"Aris…can we talk first, please?"

He sighed. "We can try. But I make no promises."

I lifted myself off the bed while simultaneously trying to take my arms out of the sleeves and pull the dress down. You can imagine how effective that maneuver was. Aris rescued me, pulling me upright so he could gently lower the dress from my body. Then he hung it neatly on a hanger in his closet.

It gave me a moment to acclimate to lounging on his bed in my bra and panties. I had chosen a rather lovely matching set for the evening, crafted from exquisite black lace and satin. The entire back of the panties was stretchy lace, with two round cutouts at the top of my ass. I lay on my side with my cast on top, keeping pressure off it. In this position, my ample breasts nearly spilled out of the satin and lace cups of the bra.

When Aris turned around, the words he was about to speak seemed to get trapped in his throat. "Fuck, Danielle…"

"Yes?" I batted my eyelashes at him coquettishly.

"You are a goddess, my love, pure and simple. I just want to worship your body all night. I can't even get mad about Noah—"

"Mad about Noah?" I repeated. "Why would you be?"

"Because you two obviously have something going on." He crawled onto the bed, posing like a cat in front of me with his head lowered and his ass up in the air.

"And if we do?"

"I just…wasn't expecting it," he admitted.

"Not at all? Not even a little bit?"

He looked up at me, his hazel eyes round and clear. "I

had hoped for it a while back, but I also enjoyed having you to myself."

"So you don't want to share me?" If my voice conveyed a little bit of disappointment, it wasn't an accident.

Suddenly Aris sat up, crossing his legs like a kinder-gartner for story time. He folded his hands in his lap. It was like the seduction spell I'd been working with this lingerie was suddenly broken.

I felt exposed now. And a little embarrassed. I sat up and met his gaze. "What? Did I do something wrong?"

"Is this all an act?"

"What?" I crossed my arms over my stomach and stared at him.

"An act?" He looked around the room for a second, appearing to be collecting his thoughts.

"I don't understand what you mean, Aris." My voice was soft, almost a whisper. I'd never heard this tone from him before. It was...hard...and accusatory. "Can you explain?"

His nostrils flared as he took a deep breath. "I know we just started seeing each other, so I'm still getting to know you. And I know your world has been totally upended."

I nodded, following his train of thought so far.

"So, I saw how easily you slipped into the role of Noah's fiancée, and now you're back here, and you're all lovey-dovey with him, and you're still wearing his ring, and... well...I just want to know if all of this is an act."

Okay, his train had jumped off the tracks.

I just stared at him.

He blew out a breath and closed his eyes for a moment. Then he opened them and took my hand into his. It felt so warm and comforting—I hoped that whatever had just happened, whatever demon had just possessed him for a moment was gone. I wanted this Aris, this insecure, posses-sive Aris to be over.

I wanted my happy-go-lucky, glass-half-full Aris back.

"I told you when I first met you that I develop feelings for people quickly," he said. "It's something I'm working on, but I feel like it's also just who I am, you know?"

I nodded, biting my lower lip because I didn't know what was going to come out of his mouth next, and I was scared.

"Danielle, I know it's crazy, but I've spent a lot of time with you already, and I…I just already feel something for you. A connection. I—" He shook his head as if he couldn't believe he was telling me this.

That made two of us.

"I have done everything in my power to take care of you and reassure you, to ensure you know that I'm wild about you. That I want to take care of you. That I care about your feelings and… I…well, I love everything about you," he continued. "And…" Now he took a huge gulp, his Adam's apple bobbing in his scruff-covered throat, "and I want to make sure you're not just pretending to like me because it's some sort of acting role for you. Like just to see if you can get me to fall in love with you."

"What?" I gasped. "How could you think that?"

"Because I am," he said, his voice trembling. "And I…" He shook his head as the emotion took over his voice. "I don't know what your intentions are with me or with Noah, but I…"

Oh my god, was this really happening?

Everything Cynda told me and made me promise was pulsing in my mind, begging me to tell him the truth. To be as honest with him as he was being with me. He deserved that, didn't he?

But what *was* the truth?

Was I just acting a role? Coercing him, grooming him to feel things I never planned to reciprocate?

Was I just trying to have a good time, scratching an itch, and I never promised him anything more?

Or was I starting to feel something for him—and Noah too?

He squeezed my hand in his as he turned pleading eyes to me. "I need to know the truth, Danielle. What you're feeling. And I know you may not have answers yet because, like I said, your world has been turned upside down. I get it. I'm not trying to get you to choose me, or Noah, or both of us, or none of us.

"I just want to know where your heart is. Where your mind is. Where you think this is going because… because I think we could have a happy future." He smiled now, like he was envisioning it. "A happy future together, the three of us."

"You mean like…" I remembered that word Raine and I had laughed about. It seemed like ages ago, but it was really not that long ago at all. "You mean like a…throuple?"

He nodded, still smiling.

"Would you ever consider being in a throuple with me and Noah?"

twenty-three

. . .

noah

HERE I WAS, eavesdropping again in the hallway. But this time was a little different. First, it was my room. And, second, they knew I was just taking a shower. I couldn't take a shower all night.

Aris's voice was nothing but a deep rumble, but I could understand Danielle pretty well. Being used to performing on stage and projecting her voice, it had a natural clarity and volume.

It sounded as though she had been put on the spot, and Aris was pressing her to confess her feelings for him, whatever they might be.

It took me back a few months to a similar discussion I had with him.

Aris was a fuck-first, ask-questions-later kind of lover. He got wrapped up in the emotions; he thrived on them. He felt intensely, and those emotions gave him a sort of power over people.

Where it took most people a while to think about and

identify their emotions, he knew his right away. No reservations, no hesitations, he just took them and ran with them. It seemed Danielle and I were not that type of person, but maybe we were attracted to them.

When I examined my feelings for Aris, I realized they were there, but they were being blocked by fear. Fear that I was making a mistake. That I would have regrets. That a relationship with him would hinder my career. No more working eighty hours a week when I had someone vying for my time and attention. I had allowed Aris to wedge himself through the narrow cracks in my walls to steal a piece of my heart.

Did I want a second person trying to do the same?

Did I have enough to give both of them?

I thought about the way Danielle felt in my arms tonight. I remembered the way her soaring soprano pierced my very soul. I reflected on how she was a study of contrasts and contradictions: at one moment demure and vulnerable, at another strong and fierce.

My heart and my head were at war with each other, much like they had been over Aris. We know who won that battle.

And I had a feeling I knew who would win this one.

But I needed to know something first.

aris

My heart was in my throat waiting for Danielle to answer the question I'd posed, but when she opened her mouth to speak, the door handle turned, and in walked Noah. Water glistened on his dark skin like diamonds as he stepped into the room wearing nothing but a light blue towel wrapped around his waist. His ridged abs were on full display, a smattering of coiled hair decorating his sculpted pecs.

"I hope I'm not interrupting anything," he said without an ounce of irony. He probably had no clue that I'd just put Danielle on the spot, especially since he'd walked in to find her lounging in her gorgeous lace bra and panties.

Danielle started to slide off the bed, not an easy maneuver with her cast. "I'll get out of your hair. You two probably have a lot to discuss."

Noah smiled, his eyes roaming over her voluptuous body. "I was kind of hoping you'd stay."

It didn't take any magical powers of observation to see that he'd developed an impressive bulge underneath the towel. I noticed it right away, and the moment Danielle caught on, her reaction made my own cock leap to attention.

"Is that so?" She gave a devilish smirk and reclined again on the bed, putting her curves on full display as she reached up and released the updo Cynda had so carefully created. Her hair cascaded down around her shoulders, full of curls, making her look wild and wanton.

Then, unexpectedly, she turned to me. "Aris, I do want to continue our conversation. I need some time to think about what you've said."

That was the most honest thing she could have told me. It wasn't the answer I was necessarily hoping for, but anything else would have likely been disingenuous. I respected that. Nodding, I found myself grateful Noah had come in and lightened the mood. Not usually the role he played, but I was here for it tonight.

"So, I am feeling extremely overdressed right now," I said, pulling at my gray t-shirt.

"I think we can remedy that." Noah closed the distance

between us. I expected him to just strip the t-shirt off me, but instead he cupped my face in his hands and stared into my eyes. "I want to watch you fuck Danielle." He followed it up by seizing my lips with a demanding kiss, his fingers threading through my hair until they'd pulled it from the bun.

I moaned as I answered him, my words garbled through his kiss, "If Danielle's game..."

We broke the kiss and turned to her, once again putting her on the spot. "Hmm, I was enjoying watching you two, to be honest." She stretched her limbs out and tossed her head back, letting her long loose curls brush her back as she blew out a breath. "But I'm happy to play whatever role you'd like."

Knowing my beautiful goddess, she would excel at whatever role we decided, but it sounded like Noah wanted to play director. I whipped my shirt off over my head and tossed it aside. Then I turned to him. "Tell us what to do, what you want to see."

His dark eyes flashed with a mixture of surprise and excitement, and his tongue came out to lick his lips before his teeth sank into the bottom one. He looked like a kid standing at the ice cream counter trying to decide what flavor to choose when they all looked amazing and delicious.

"First we need to take care of these." He tugged at the waistband of my jeans.

"Take them off," I challenged him.

Eyes on Danielle while Noah unzipped my jeans and slid them down my thighs, I wondered if she really wanted us both, or if she was just going along with the flow. Was I always going to be worried she was acting?

"These too." Noah slipped his thumbs in the waistband of my boxer briefs and shoved them down my legs. I stepped out of the pile of clothes puddled at my feet, completely nude, my thick cock jutting out in front of me.

"He has a beautiful cock, doesn't he, Danielle?" Noah asked.

"He sure does. It feels amazing inside me too." Her breathy voice made a pulse of desire shoot right through me.

"I think he should fuck you," Noah decided. "But first, let me get him ready for you."

Danielle pushed up on her elbows to get a better view, seemingly eager to take in the sight of Noah dropping to his knees in front of me. As he stroked me from base to tip, he looked up at me, his dark eyes hooded with lust as his tongue darted out to catch the drop of pre-cum that had pearled on my tip.

"Save some for me…" Danielle whined from the bed.

I noticed she'd slipped her hand down inside her panties and was touching herself. Seeing that made me even harder, and I was going to have to work at controlling myself so I didn't come in Noah's mouth. I had a lot of things I wanted to do with this cock tonight, so I needed to pace myself for sure.

Noah seemed to understand, and he did nothing but tease the hell out of me, licking long strokes up my shaft with his tongue, then down to circle my balls. He sucked the tip in his mouth repeatedly and then left me hanging. He massaged my ass as he plunged down on me till I hit the back of his throat, and then he popped back off.

"You need to take Danielle's bra and panties off." He looked up at me, seeming pleased with himself for bringing me to the edge and then keeping me there.

"Yes, please," she moaned from the bed, so I stepped over and tugged her lacy panties down, carefully avoiding her cast. Then I kissed her lips as I reached around her to unfasten her bra.

When I turned to look at Noah for my next task, he had dropped the towel and was standing in his naked glory, stroking his long, hard cock with a pleased smirk on his face. "Now you need to get her ready for you."

"Yes, sir," I agreed and climbed onto the bed, straddling her nude form. My cock pressed against her thigh as I threaded my fingers through her hair and lifted her mouth to mine. Hungrily devouring her lips, I rubbed my aching manhood against her as I swallowed her moans of pleasure. She was still touching herself.

Trailing kisses in my path, I worked my way down her body as Noah joined us on the bed. I didn't know if he could stick to the observer role, but it seemed he wanted to participate a little more actively, and I was good with that. I realized when he took one of her breasts into his mouth, making her arch her back and cry out, that—and this was huge—I wasn't jealous.

It wasn't jealousy that caused the reaction I had earlier. It was insecurity. Not knowing where this was going, if she was developing feelings for me as I was for her. But right now, in this moment, I just wanted to show her how good it could be. How thoroughly satiated she would be if she had both of us to take care of her, to bring her pleasure.

Cupping her other breast in my palm, I teased her nipple to a firm peak with my tongue and teeth. Soon she was writhing beneath us, still touching herself. I didn't want her to come yet, so I reached down and grabbed her hand, intertwining it with mine and bringing it over her head so she had to wait for sweet release. My cock was throbbing and aching against her, but I wouldn't get my relief until I was inside her.

"Fuck, Aris," she gritted out. "Please…fuck me so Noah can watch. Oh my god, please…"

I heard Noah's deep chuckle beside me before he popped off her nipple much like he had my cock earlier. "Not until he tastes you, my dear."

He tapped me on the shoulder and directed me between her legs. He took over lavishing both her breasts with attention as I slid between her thighs. Now her hand, which I released, joined the other, twisting the sheets in a determined clench as she bucked against my mouth.

"Fuck, please!" she begged, but I just pressed soft kisses into her mound, waiting for her to settle before I dove into my feast.

Her fingers raked through my hair, finding a grip and pulling me to where she wanted me, directly on her clit. She rubbed greedily against my face, seeking release. Oh, what a needy little slut we'd turned this diva into, and I was loving every minute of it.

Finally, after feeling like she'd suffered enough, my tongue darted out to taste her, utterly shocked by the gush of juices that filled my mouth. "Danielle, my god, you might drown me…"

It was like she didn't even hear me at this point, she was so desperate. I glanced up at Noah to see if he was witnessing this as I was. Surely this was not an act. Her face was flushed and pinched, her eyes closed as unintelligible strings of half-curses and half-garbled moans erupted from her mouth.

"She needs your cock," Noah stated the obvious as she whimpered at my lack of contact. "Let me get you a condom."

I teased her cunt with my fingers and tongue, backing off every time she seemed close to detonating, until Noah came back with a condom. With a flair and anticipation dancing in his eyes, he unrolled it, sheathing my cock and then guiding it toward her dripping pussy.

"You want Aris to fuck you?" he asked.

She whimpered as he brushed the head of my cock against her swollen clit. "Yes…my god…please…"

"As you wish." He bit his lip as he handled my cock, penetrating her folds as I pulsed under his touch. "Don't come too fast," he instructed me.

"Well, fuck, I'll try, but—"

He kissed me hard just then, stealing my breath as I sank deep into her pussy. She gripped my hips, urging me to move. "Aris…fuck me…"

Noah slapped my ass as he knelt behind me, driving my hips and my cock into her, then pulling me back and doing it again. "That's it, fuck her tight hole, baby."

If he kept doing that, I was going to fucking lose control. There was nothing I could do to stop it.

But what he did next made it a thousand times more difficult to hold myself back. He spread my ass cheeks and swiped his finger up my crack, lingering around my hole, teasing it with his fingertip. "I think I want to fuck you while you fuck her."

"Oh, god, Noah, I will not last if you do that."

"But I'm so hard, and I want to come inside you," he argued. "Besides, I thought I was in charge here."

I closed my eyes, trying not to let the sensation of her pussy pulsating around me push me over the edge. Briefly distracting me, Noah leaned over us, stretching his long arms to reach the lube on the nightstand and being careful not to disturb Danielle's cast. My worst fear was hurting her again, so just that thought helped me stave off my climax for a little while longer—it seemed to hit the reset button.

Her eyes jerked open, and she stared at me as Noah squirted the lube on his fingers. "He's going to fuck you?"

"Yes, is that okay?"

"Oh my god, yes, I was hoping I would get to see that…" She confessed, "I've never done anal, but I have to wonder what it'd be like to do DP with you two."

"Oh, fuck." And there it was, my need to come was back tenfold.

"You're getting a bit ahead of yourself, missy." Noah laughed as he rubbed the lube around my hole and inserted one finger. I winced at the intrusion, but when he started to thrust in and out of me, I realized how damn good it felt, and how much better it was going to feel when it was his cock instead.

"If you want us to prepare you for DP, it's going to take some time," he explained as he fucked my ass with one finger, then two. "See, Aris's ass is used to my cock. It doesn't take much to get him ready. It doesn't hurt that he's already so hard and turned on by you."

My cock throbbed in response to his statement.

"But with you…it's going to take a while to work up to having one cock in your ass, let alone having one there and in your pussy."

"I want that," she said, grinding her hips up into me, trying to take me deeper into her pussy. "I want that with you two."

"Fuuuuuuuuck…" I breathed out as Noah slid his length into me.

"God damn," he groaned as he settled, waiting for me to adjust.

It stung a bit, which would help keep me from coming, but as he began to pump inside me, he was lifting my hips and driving me deeper and deeper and faster and faster into

Danielle. "Are you okay?" I asked her, making sure she didn't need us to stop.

"Oh, please…please don't stop," she confirmed. "I'm gonna come so hard, fuck…oh my god…Aris!" My name burst on her lips as her entire body tensed and then exploded beneath me, her pussy spasming so fast and so hard that I thought I might lose my mind.

Noah must have been highly aroused by her O-face and all her sexy orgasmic sounds because he began to drill into me relentlessly. "Fuck, Aris…I wanted to hold off longer, but you feel too fucking good…"

Both of them together forced my hand. My balls tightened, and my cock jerked as my entire soul shot out into the condom sheathing me. I stilled, still feeling Noah's cock spasm in my ass as he came down from his own orgasm.

"Holy fucking shit," Danielle finally spoke, her words coming out in a throaty rasp. "That was the best fucking orgasm I've ever had. I knew one man could give me an incredible orgasm, but two men? Stellar performance. No notes." Her head fell back onto the pillow. She looked completely spent.

twenty-four

. . .

danielle

I WOKE up to Sushi perched on my hip and meowing. When I moved, she jumped down and meowed at me again from the floor before she scampered off to do whatever cats do in the wee hours of the morning. "You're meowing up the wrong tree if you want me to feed you," I murmured, but my voice was hoarse.

Great.

Apparently drinking, doing an impromptu performance in public, and then fucking two hot guys all hours of the night isn't good for your voice. Who knew?

I was trapped between Aris and Noah, the former in front of me, the latter behind. My casted leg was the one on the bottom. No wonder it was throbbing. I needed some pain meds.

And to figure out what to do about all this. *gestures around at my current situation*

Aris stirred a few moments later before rolling over so

we were face to face. "Morning." He swallowed hard. "I need water."

"Me too," I rasped. "And meds. Leg hurts."

"Yeah, you kinda overdid it yesterday, love." He groaned as he scooted to the edge of the bed and pulled himself up. "I'll be right back."

"No, take me with you…bathroom," I begged.

He helped me up, and we took care of all the necessary business before returning to the bedroom, where Noah was dead to the world. "Does he always sleep like this?"

"No…sometimes he sleeps really lightly and is up half the night. You musta worn him out good," Aris said with a laugh.

"Me? He fucked your ass, dude."

"Mmm…and I loved every minute of it." Aris's hair was rumpled, and his stubble had nearly become a full beard overnight, but his dimples shone brightly on either side of his smile.

Noah mumbled something incoherently and rolled to his back.

That was when I saw it: his enormous morning wood poking at the thin sheet.

"Damn, you could have a serious campout under that tent," Aris joked. "You know, invite a bunch of your friends. Make s'mores. Tell ghost stories."

Laughter erupted up my throat, which made Noah thrash and mumble angrily. "Some of us are trying to sleep," was what it sounded like.

"He's the old man of the group, so he needs his beauty rest," Aris joked.

"I heard that," Noah snapped.

Just listening to their silly banter, something in me snapped.

Everything was up in the air for me right now. Pre-Aris and Noah Dani would be a ball of nerves. I'd be doing anything and everything in my power to avoid having to face the upheaval I was going through. I would likely be doing something dangerous, playing whatever role I could to avoid being myself and actually dealing with shit.

In the past, when I'd been in turmoil like this, I'd escaped in the following ways:

Went to the casino, pretended to be High Roller Dani and gambled away a couple thousand bucks

Went to the mall, pretended to be Rich Fashionista Dani, and bought a shit ton of clothes I couldn't afford.

Bought a bunch of ingredients and a cookbook, pretended to be Betty Crocker Dani, and ate a literal ton of baked goods.

Decided I hated men, pretended to be Butch Dani, and cut off all my hair—regretted it five minutes later.

None of those were healthy behaviors. *Well, you've taken on the role of Slutty Dani now. How is that any better?* a voice inside my head asked.

I pondered that for a moment as Aris announced he was going to take a shower. He helped me lie back down on the bed.

"Cuddle with grumpy-ass here, and I'll be back in a few."

I giggled as I curled up in Noah's arms. Was I being Slutty Dani? Was sleeping with two guys really an unhealthy way to deal with everything that had happened to me?

Noah turned toward me, pulling me closer as he pressed a kiss to my forehead. "Morning, beautiful. How'd you sleep last night?"

"Like a baby," I said dreamily. It was true. I had the best

night of sleep I'd had since…well…forever, if I was being honest.

The thought of not ever sleeping in this big bed with these two unbelievably sexy and attentive men again… well…it fucking bummed me out, to be honest.

"Me too." He sighed, pulling me even closer. Now that monster morning wood was pressing right into me so insistently, I gasped. "Oops, sorry about that. Didn't mean to poke you."

I laughed. "Sure you didn't."

"What did you think of last night?" He stroked his fingers through my hair.

"Well…" I took a moment to collect my thoughts. "Parts of it made me mad."

"Alexandra and those two asshole hospital board members?" His eyebrow quirked up.

"Yes." I really hesitated to use the word "hate," but I thought something stronger might be required to describe my feelings toward those jerks. "And part of it made me sad."

"Which part was that?" he asked.

"When you were telling me about your parents and your childhood." My words were so soft, they practically floated on the air.

He didn't respond for a few moments, but his body didn't tense, and his breathing didn't change. "I didn't mean to make you sad."

"I know. I just wish you could have grown up differently."

"Then I wouldn't be the man I am today."

"True." Silence hung between us for a moment. "I didn't have the best childhood either, to be honest. But my parents did raise me."

"Oh?"

"Yeah. They were older, and I don't think they really wanted a kid. They treated me as a small adult, and they had me on stage at a very young age. Nothing I did was ever good enough for them. They weren't very good people, in hindsight. I wish I wouldn't have tried so hard to please them."

He pressed a kiss to my forehead. "Didn't you say they live near Chicago?"

"They do," I confirmed. "I know, I talk about them like they're dead because I have as little to do with them as possible." What would they think if I brought home not one, but two men, for the holidays? Frankly, I didn't give a fuck what they thought, and that realization made me smile.

"You're smiling now though." It made him smile too. "What's going on in that big beautiful mind of yours?"

"I was thinking about the happy parts from last night."

That eyebrow was arched again. "Oh yeah? Which parts were those?"

"Oh…the parts where I told Alexandra and Dr. Shepherd off were pretty epic. As well as getting to sing in front of all those people—it made my heart happy."

"Anything else?"

"Hmm, nothing I can think of," I teased him. "Just kidding… Actually, Noah, getting to know you better was the highlight of my night."

"Oh, that's interesting, because I felt the same way about you." He leaned in and brushed his lips against mine before I had a chance to speak. And then he asked, "And were there any other parts about last night we should discuss?"

I smirked and held his gaze. "Why don't you tell me?"

He licked his lips and smiled, just seeming to enjoy the closeness we were sharing. I knew Aris could walk in at any time, and I was prepared for it, but this little stolen moment. It was gold.

"Last night was one of the most incredible experiences of my life," he finally admitted. "The charity ball, what happened afterwards, all of it."

"Really?"

"Yes…and what happened between you, me and Aris…"

"It was hot, right?" I tested.

"Unbelievably."

"So…what now?"

"That seems to be the question on everyone's mind, doesn't it?"

I laughed softly. "Aris was asking me last night if I thought we could be a…you know…"

"A what?"

"A throuple…" I held my breath while the word registered in his mind.

"I didn't think something like that would be for me," he admitted. "Especially with everything else going on in my life. You know, the whole point of last night—at least initially—was to match their expectations. To be seen as acceptable. Traditional."

"And we did that," I said. "We could leave it at that. You could claim slander or libel or whatever if that reporter publishes that piece about you."

"I'm supposed to be interviewed on Monday," he shared. "I could tell the reporter all about you and that we're making wedding plans."

"You could…" I agreed. "And, to be honest, you should. Your career is important, Noah. And, in the end, we know who you are. If you need to pander to them to protect us and protect your career, that is totally fine."

"You wouldn't think less of me?"

"No. Not at all." I put my arm around him and squeezed. "And that throuple thing? I honestly think I could."

His eyes widened with surprise before a smile crept across his face. "Don't tell me now," he said. "Tell Aris."

"Tell me what?"

Our gazes shot to the doorway where Aris stood, not in a towel like Noah had the night before, but one hundred percent buck naked.

noah

"Wow, Aris, you really know how to make an entrance." I chuckled as he stalked toward the bed, his stiff cock waving like a flag.

"Did Danielle take care of your morning wood yet?" was the first thing out of his mouth.

"No," she said. "Everyone else got to shower. Isn't it my turn? I may need some help."

"Oh, I think we can help," Aris offered. "Noah?"

On three, we picked Danielle up, me taking her legs and watching out for her cast, and Aris taking her upper body, and we carried her into the bathroom. I wrapped her leg in one of the cast covers Raine had brought for her while Aris got the shower ready.

I helped her climb in and put her under the spray, then Aris joined us and we took turns soaping up her body. While Aris kissed and rubbed her from her lips to her feet, I washed her hair.

"I'm not sure I've ever been this squeaky clean." She laughed while she rinsed the conditioner out of her hair. "Now what?"

"Did you think you were really getting out of here so easily?" Aris asked. "Look what you did to us."

We were both hard as granite.

"Hmm…well, you guys have each other. Knock yourselves out. The water is getting cold." She shivered.

Well, if Aris hadn't used most of the damn hot water we could have had some fun in there, but it was a little cramped, and it was hard for her to balance on one foot. "Fine, we'll discuss this in the bedroom after we dry you off."

"Deal," she agreed.

Aris wrapped her hair in a fluffy towel while I used another to dry off her body.

"Damn, I could get used to this kind of treatment." She took a deep, relaxed breath as she stood with one towel wrapped around her head and one around her body. "I need to comb out my hair now."

"Allow me," Aris said, "I'm used to long hair and tangles."

While he did that, I went back to the bedroom to change the sheets—I was pretty sure we were just going to mess up the new ones, but it was a risk I was willing to take.

Then I lay back down with the sheet over me, letting my cock make a tent just like this morning when I first woke up. I wanted to see what Danielle and Aris's reaction would be when they walked in and found me like this.

They seemed to be taking forever, so I reached down and took my length in my hand, wrapping my long fingers around the shaft. I remembered what Danielle had said about trying a double penetration, and I hoped she was serious. Maybe we could start training her asshole today? Thinking about it made me even harder. We'd need to get some toys…

Damn, thinking about me in her ass with Aris buried

deep in her pussy turned me on. My cock was so fucking hard, it ached.

Then I thought about what Danielle said about being a "throuple."

I was surprised that it made me ache even more.

I wanted him.

I wanted her.

I wanted them both.

danielle

Aris escorted me back into the bedroom, and I was met with a tantalizing sight. Noah in bed recreating his "half asleep morning wood" pose from this morning.

"You want to touch it?" Aris asked when he spotted the elephant cock in the room. Okay, I'd never seen an elephant cock, but Noah's looked like it was definitely the largest one I'd ever seen, judging by how far into the air that sheet had risen.

"I'd like to take a peek first and see if it's even possible..."

"Possible to what?" Noah finally let us know he was not asleep at all but listening in on our conversation.

"That depends..." I hobbled over to the bed, and, bracing myself with one hand on the mattress, I used my other to yank back the sheet. "Damn, Noah!" My head whipped back toward Aris. "You let him put that thing in your ass?"

They were both roaring with laughter at that point. I wasn't even trying to be funny. That thing was intimidating as fuck.

"Well, I don't know about this..." I was being serious now, but the boys were still laughing.

"Lie down," Noah said. "I want to taste you, get you ready for me. You'll at least try, won't you?"

"Well, yes, of course. Don't be ridiculous." I laughed as I climbed onto the bed with Aris's help and settled on the pillows. Noah stripped away my towel, and my wet hair fell against my bare shoulders, making me shiver.

He kissed me then, igniting the same sparks as his kisses in the storage closet had the night before. Damn, he and Aris were both such good kissers. I was in for a lifetime of good kisses should this throuple thing work out.

Whoa…did I really just go there?

I didn't have time to think about it because Noah was already exploring my breasts and curves while Aris made himself comfortable on his knees and presented his cock to me in all its thick, throbbing glory.

"I thought you might like some breakfast?" he asked with a dopey smile on his face. "Sausage?"

I laughed but then squealed as Noah slid one long finger inside me. He seemed to know my anatomy better than I did because he pumped a few times, and I immediately lost any semblance of control. I swear he reached some spot I didn't even know existed. Shocking the hell out of me, fluid came squirting from my pussy like a fountain.

"We got a squirter," he announced as Aris gasped.

"Holy shit, that's hot." He rubbed the tip of his cock against my mouth. "Have you ever done that before?"

"Mmm…" I couldn't answer because, as soon as I opened my mouth, he stuffed his cock inside as Noah continued to make me go crazy with pleasure with his fingers and then his tongue.

After Noah made me come two or three times, I was exhausted, and my jaw hurt. Aris was so thick, it was hard to take him very far in my mouth, and he was so excited watching Noah touch me, he was nearly choking me.

Both of these guys were like steel rods, and I wanted to make them come. "I can't believe you made me squirt. Fuck! I had no idea that was even really possible."

"Oh, it is," Noah said with a grin. "You should drink lots of fluids today so you can rehydrate."

"Spoken like a true doctor," Aris joked.

"I wanna make you guys come. How do you want it?" I asked.

Noah didn't hesitate. "I want to be inside you this time. If you think you can handle it. You could try being on top so you can control the depth?"

"That sounds like a decent plan, but I'm not sure I can with this cast. I can't be on my knees."

"Good point."

Hmm… We had an engineering problem.

"Okay, it's not you on top, but what if you lie here, and I pull you to the edge of the bed. I'll stand between your legs," Noah offered.

"I mean, we can try it…"

I sounded skeptical because I was. It also took some bravery to allow myself to be spread out like that, my whole body on display. But seeing how they were both so turned on helped.

Noah moved into position, taking both of my legs in his arms and scooting me so far down that my ass was hanging off the mattress. Aris was still beside me on his knees, stroking his cock as he watched his partner notch himself at my entrance. I held my breath as the tip penetrated me, but Noah had made me so wet with the squirting, there was very little resistance.

"Whoa…." Noah sighed as each inch of his length disappeared inside me, filling me to the brim. When he reached the very limit, I whimpered.

He nodded. "I'll be careful, beautiful. Just trust me."

I sucked in a deep breath, telling myself I'd get used to it. The last orgasm had finally completely dissipated, and my body was again suspended, ready to climb once more into the stratosphere.

"Maybe this will help distract you," Aris offered, tapping the crown of his cock against my mouth again. "I need to come, baby. Will you suck me off while Noah fucks you?"

I wanted to. I hoped I could satisfy them both. I would need to, right? For this to work.

And, god, I wanted it to work.

More than anything…

The expression on Noah's face as he slid just the tip back and forth, his features contorting in a mix of agony and pleasure, was enough to tighten up my core. Then I took Aris as deep into my throat as I could and watched as his eyes rolled back in his head.

Fuck, they were both so hot, and they both wanted me so bad.

They could just fuck each other.

But they wanted me.

Aris reached down and cradled my head under his hand, giving himself more leverage to thrust into my mouth. "That's good, baby girl. You take my cock like such a good girl. Are you gonna make me come? Will you suck all the cum from my cock? Every last drop?"

"Damn, Aris, you're gonna make me come talking to her like that," Noah groaned, "and I'm trying to enjoy this tight, wet pussy."

"Bet I can hold out longer than you can," Aris teased as

he pumped his cock in as far as he could without me choking.

Well, there was nothing I loved more than a challenge.

I was getting worked up watching their rivalry, the way they were both trying to hold back. Noah was adamant, "I wanna make her come on my cock. Danielle, how's it feeling? Can I go a little deeper?"

I could barely speak around Aris's cock fucking my throat, so I nodded and garbled affirmatively.

"Good, baby, because I'm getting close. I'm gonna fill you up with my cum."

"Fuck, Noah! What was it you said about dirty talk?" Aris growled, his jaw clenched as his dick grew impossibly hard.

"That's it, baby, take my cock," Noah tried to outdo him. "You're such a good little cumslut. Are we gonna fill all your holes up? Mmmm…"

"Fuck, Danielle—"

But I didn't hear any of the rest of their banter because my entire world shifted on its axis as an unexpected torrent of ecstasy rushed through me. Stars danced before my eyes, everything turning a kaleidoscope of colors as my core sent waves of pleasure rocking outward to my extremities and back again.

And when I came to, it was all over. I was full of cum from top to bottom.

And I couldn't have been happier about it.

twenty-five

. . .

noah

I PATTED MY POCKET, wishing I'd taken the time to put my mother's ring back in its box. Danielle caught me off-guard this morning when she handed it to me, apologizing for forgetting she was wearing it.

I wanted to tell her to keep it. But I also didn't know why that was my first instinct or what I really meant by it, and I didn't want her to freak out, so I just smiled and slipped it in my pocket. Now I was driving to work, and the sun was actually shining. It was shaping up to be a beautiful, almost springlike day, but anyone who was from the Midwest knew that late February nice weather was usually a "false spring," and we'd probably get half a foot of snow dumped on us sometime between now and April.

Heading into the building, I had an extra spring in my step. Or maybe just regular spring because I wasn't a very springy person in general. But I did feel lighter than I had in a long time, and it was all thanks to Aris and Danielle.

We'd spent all day Sunday lounging in bed and in the

living room, snacking and watching movies. You wouldn't think three people as different as we were would be able to agree on movie choices, but I learned we all loved musicals.

Well, of course Danielle did. But Aris and I did too. One of our first dates was seeing the touring production of *Chicago* when it came to the IU Auditorium. Danielle chose *Mamma Mia* for us to watch since it reflected Aris's Greek heritage. We watched a few others as well.

And Cynda surprised us by trying some of Aris's Yaya's recipes—we enjoyed moussaka, spanakopita, stuffed grape leaves, and even baklava for dessert. They were all incredible, and I'd never seen Aris so happy.

I had a full day of seeing patients ahead of me—no surgeries until tomorrow. So I headed up to my office to get started on the day. After greeting the custodial staff in the lobby as I did every morning, I took the stairs up to my floor. Then I unlocked the back door to our practice with my ID badge and went to do the same with my office door, but it was already ajar.

What the fuck? Maybe they just cleaned in here.

As soon as I stepped in, the vibe was off. I shuddered as I went to turn on the light. But as soon as I did, the high-backed leather executive chair at my desk wheeled around and revealed none other than Alexandra Bagby, her petite frame perched where my ass was supposed to be sitting.

"What the fuck are you doing in my office? Who let you in?" I seethed, my eyes shooting her a sharp glare.

She wore a smug smile on her face as she laced her fingers together and set them in her lap, not in any hurry to answer my questions. "I can go anywhere I want in Midwest Health. My dad is the CEO, you know. Helps to be well-connected." She waved an ID badge in the air.

"You need to go. You should not be here," I told her. "I

don't know what kind of stunt you're trying to pull, but rest assured I will be sharing this information with my attorney, and when we go to trial, I will countersue for harassment and stalking."

"I don't think I'd do that if I were you," Alexandra sneered. "I saw you at the ball on Saturday night with your 'fiancée.' As if I believe you'd get engaged to a fat girl." She threw her head back and laughed. "Is that the only girl you could find to pose as your fiancée at the last minute?"

"Get. Out." My nostrils flared as I struggled to keep my hands off her. I wanted to grab her by her neck and literally throw her out on her ass. Nah, that would be too kind. Throw her out the window, perhaps.

"If I don't have your settlement offer by Friday at noon," she said, her voice as cold as ice, "my father will be firing you." She stood up now and paced toward me, swinging her hips.

"We all know you're queer as a three-dollar-bill. My father is absolutely disgusted by you, and so am I. I can't believe you lied to Emma all those months you dated her. She deserves so much better than you. I hope you're not lying to that fat girl you brought with you Saturday night. I hope she doesn't actually believe you'll marry her. You're an absolute piece of shit, Noah Evans."

"Danielle is a gorgeous curvy woman," I gritted out between my clenched teeth, "and she has more beauty and grace in her pinky toe than you have in your entire body. If you think I'm going to concede to your demands because I'm scared of either you or your father, you are dead fucking wrong. I am waiting to hear back from several professional organizations, and it's your father's job that'll be on the line, not mine."

"Well, we'll see about that." She crossed her arms over her chest, scowled at me, and stormed out.

aris

What a weekend!

When I fell in love with Noah, I imagined we would be the kind of partners who could have a lot of fun together but also have the freedom to explore other relationships. With us being bisexual, it seemed like a great dynamic for both of us.

I didn't have sharing a relationship with a woman on my radar at all.

But as soon as I began to date Danielle, I realized what a perfect fit she would be in our dynamic, and in our polycule.

And, as usual, I was one hundred percent correct. I was so glad Noah saw the light. Who knows how long it would have taken if they hadn't gone to the charity ball together on Saturday night. I guess, in a weird, fucked-up sort of way, I had Alexandra Bagby to thank for that.

Flashes of the three of us together flickered in my mind all day, making it hard to concentrate on work, not to mention the great lengths I had to go to hide all the hard-ons I got in my scrub pants. Those things are pretty thin!

After work, I sent a text to my two loves, telling them I was going to the gym to blow off some steam. I'd been slacking on my workouts due to healing up from the bike wreck—I had some bruising and swelling afterwards—not to mention taking care of Danielle. It was time to get back into a routine.

Danielle was going to be with us for at least a few more weeks, and then we'd have to decide what to do. I wasn't sure when her lease with Raine ended, but...maybe she could move in permanently, or we could all go look for a place together. Noah had been saving to buy a house. Perhaps this summer would be the perfect time to start looking to buy a home in the area.

Danielle was going to be around at least through next December. I wasn't sure what her plans were after that. She'd talked about going to New York to try her luck on Broadway. Well, we'd cross that bridge when we came to it.

There were several folks at the gym eager to say hello, telling me they'd missed seeing me around. I got a great round of back and chest done, and tomorrow I'd do arms and legs. My buddy Kyle said he'd be there to spot. Driving home, I was thinking about how most of the puzzle pieces were falling into place, and, more immediately, I couldn't wait to see what Cynda was cooking for dinner.

I was starving.

My stomach was more than intrigued by the savory smells coming from the kitchen as I stepped inside the house. I nodded to Jason, Darth and Danielle sitting in the living room, then headed in to find out from Cynda what time dinner would be ready. I needed a shower…maybe Danielle would want to join me so I could give her a proper hello?

"Hey, Cynda, what's cookin', good lookin'!" I flashed her my most charming smile.

"Aris, good to see you. Have you heard from Noah today?" She stirred something in a pot. Upon closer inspection, I learned it was chili. *Yum!*

"No, why?" We often ate lunch together or saw each other on breaks, but some days we were really busy and just couldn't connect. It was no big deal either way.

"Danielle said he didn't answer any of her texts today, and I just wondered if you saw him. She's kind of upset."

She pulled open the oven door and popped what looked like a pan of cornbread inside.

"Okay, I'll go talk to her. It looked like she, Jason and Darth were watching something, and I didn't want to interrupt, so I came straight in here. I need to shower before dinner. How long do I have?"

"About thirty minutes." She smiled.

"Perfect. I'd hug you, but I'm super sweaty."

She held up her hands. "I'll take that hug after your shower then." She wiped her hands on the dish towel attached to the oven door handle. "Aris...are the three of you...good?"

"I think so. I'm..."

"Navigating a new triad," she said. "It may be rocky at first, and that's perfectly normal as everyone figures out their roles, needs, boundaries, et cetera. Let me know if you want to chat about it. Obviously, I've got a lot of firsthand experience." She gave me a wink.

"I appreciate that." I gave her a little wave in lieu of a kiss and headed into the living room to talk to Danielle.

As soon as she saw me, she worked her way off the sofa and crutched into the hallway. Darth and Jason were watching something on Hulu that they looked very engrossed in. Sushi was curled up on Jason's lap.

I didn't give her a chance to speak before I said, "Hey, I've gotta shower after the gym. You want to join me?"

"Uh...we need to talk," was all she said.

Not exactly the words a guy wants to hear as soon as he gets home from work. But we'd figure it out. "C'mon, we can talk while I shower." I helped her down the hall to the bathroom Noah and I shared.

I turned on the shower and then gave her my full attention. "I want to hug you, but I'm soaked with sweat..."

She finally looked up to meet my gaze, but she was still wringing her hands. Her phone was tucked inside her bra. I could see the top part sticking out of her lowcut shirt. *Damn, she has incredible tits.*

"What's going on, Dani?"

"Have you talked to Noah today? I've sent him at least three texts, and he hasn't answered any of them. I even tried calling, and I hate talking on the phone."

"He doesn't usually answer the phone while he's working, and he only returns texts between patients if he gets a chance. He doesn't like the office to get too far behind, so sometimes he doesn't return them until after work."

"It's been an hour now since his office closed." She pulled out her phone and looked at the screen, frowning. "I haven't really communicated with him before. I just put his number in here yesterday. Maybe he's got me blocked or something? I don't know. I'm just confused as to why he would ignore me. So, I wondered if you'd heard from him."

"Well, let me try calling him now, okay?" I offered.

She sighed. "You can take a shower first. I'm sorry to freak out about something like this. I'm sure everything's fine." She looked down at the floor. Her voice was filled with heartbreak, and it was breaking mine too.

If I knew Noah, and I figured I knew him as well as anyone, he'd just gotten busy and had forgotten other people existed. He probably forgot to eat too, but that was beside the point.

I tucked her hair behind her ear. "Okay, are you sure you don't want to join me in the shower?"

"Nah, I don't want to go through the trouble of wrapping my leg and all that. I already showered this morning." She looked down at her cast and sighed.

"No worries, I'll see you in a few then." I lifted her chin toward me. "Quick kiss? I'll try not to get sweat on you."

A tiny smile cracked her lips. "Okay. Quick kiss."

My lips brushed against hers, and desire surged through me. *Down, boy!* We'd have to revisit that later. Right now, there were showers to take, and soon, chili and cornbread to eat. I was sure Noah would turn up. He always did.

danielle

While Aris was in the shower, I got a text from Raine.

> Raine: <image> Is this Noah?

I studied the photo closely. It showed a man from behind, sitting in a chair at a table or desk with an odd machine in front of him. It kinda looked like Noah in that it was clearly a tall, Black man with short hair, and from the side I could see a hint of a well-kept beard. But I couldn't be sure since the lighting wasn't great, and the photo was a little blurry.

> Me: Um…where are you?

> Raine: I'm doing some research in the IU library for a paper I'm writing. I had to go to the Gov Docs, maps and microforms area on the second floor. And I thought this guy looked like Noah, but I didn't want to be a weirdo and go say hi if it's not him, and he looks busy.

> Me: Hold on…

I blew up the image again, trying to figure out if the

clothes were what Noah was wearing when he left the house today. I couldn't tell.

Aris came out of the shower wrapped in a towel. As much as I would have loved to snatch that towel and expose his glorious body, I was more concerned about Noah.

"Hey, can you look at this photo Raine just sent me and tell me if it's Noah?"

He gave me a quizzical look. "Huh?"

I repeated myself and held out my phone. He took it, still looking bewildered.

"Is it Noah?"

He zoomed in, and his jaw dropped. "Where is he?"

"The library at IU," I said. "How can you tell it's him?"

"He was wearing those pants this morning, and those are his Mercanti Fiorentini wing-tip shoes." Aris shrugged.

Huh. I would have never thought to look at his shoes. Though, as someone who couldn't wear two shoes right now, I was beginning to realize how much I'd taken them for granted.

"What do you think he's doing at the library? And why hasn't he returned any of our texts?" I asked.

"Didn't he go to the library the last time he was upset?" Aris tapped his chin as if in thought.

"He did. But I thought that was the public library." I couldn't get over the feeling that something was wrong with him. "Maybe we should drive over to campus and check on him."

Aris looked around, then seemed to sniff the air like a wolf. "I think Cynda's almost done with dinner."

I rolled my eyes. "Isn't Noah more important than dinner? What if something is seriously wrong?"

"I would think someone who is in crisis would go somewhere besides the library, and what's he even doing, anyway? What was that machine?"

"Raine said something about government documents?" I shrugged.

"Oh, god…I hope it's not something to do with that lawsuit." He rushed into the bedroom and started pulling clothes out of his drawers, scrambling to get them onto his body. "C'mon. I'll drive."

Well, yeah. He'd have to. I couldn't drive with a broken leg.

twenty-six

. . .

noah

MY EYES WERE GROWING BLURRY, and my head was starting to pound. I was searching for a needle in the proverbial haystack, and it was probably pointless.

I wasn't sure when the information would have been published, and I had blocked out so much from that time of my life, I wasn't even one hundred percent sure of the dates. I hadn't kept in touch with anyone from my childhood either, so I had no one to ask.

This area of the library was like a ghost town. It was just as well because, when I finally found what I was looking for —if I found it—I would have some sort of reaction.

And I honestly didn't know what that reaction would be.

I'd learned to control my emotions from a very young age. Even when I was still with my parents. My dad had a terrible temper, and my mother would get so upset when he got angry. I learned that life was much easier if you kept your feelings to yourself—or better yet—just didn't have them in the first place.

That served me well when they passed. I was numb for probably at least two or three years straight. Then my hormones kicked in, and I did deal with some anger. But I put that energy into my passions: running, reading, and learning.

The microfiche I was scanning was from a small local paper in the town where I grew up about two hours from here. This library was one of the few besides my hometown that had back issues, but they weren't indexed. So I had to guess at what date to find the article about the accident that claimed my parents' lives.

I'd seen it once. I remembered my great aunt had a copy. I stayed with her temporarily until I was placed in foster care. She was one of my few relatives, and she didn't live in the area. She only came to town for the funerals. She stayed in my home with me while everything was sorted out. She had saved the paper for a while and told me I could read it if I wanted to. But one night I remember just tossing it out with the trash.

I didn't want to read it. I didn't want any part of what was happening to me. My life was changing forever, and I had zero control over it.

Now, I was feeling the same way. Alexandra Bagby, former patient and best friend of a woman I dated, had come back into my life, and she was trying to take away everything I held dear.

And I had no recourse but the courts.

The courts that had served me oh so well as a minor when my parents passed away, and there was no living relative who wanted to claim me. Then I was shuffled around from home to home, a zombie of a kid who just wanted something of his own. All of it by court order.

Something told me to look up then, as I mindlessly

moved the microfiche across the screen. And the headline reached out and grabbed me:

Local Couple Killed by Drunk Driver on State Road 37

I heard blood rushing through my ears as my extremities went weak, my body flooded with all sorts of chemicals at the sight of my parents' names in black and white. I read through the article, which was brief, and described my parents coming home late on a Friday night from a party, my dad's coworker's retirement party, when they were struck by some drunk idiot driving the wrong way on a major highway. He was going sixty miles per hour when he plowed into my parents' car head-on. They died instantly.

At the very end of the article, it said, "The couple leaves behind a ten-year-old son, Noah."

That was it.

I was left behind. The newspaper said so.

Years of grief and repressed anger, fear, sadness crashed over me like a tidal wave as I struggled to hold it together in this quiet but very public place. Tears blurred my vision as I closed my eyes and buried my face in my palms because they just refused to stop. It didn't matter how hard I fought, they just kept coming.

No idea how long I stayed there, sobbing, but eventually I was startled by a hand pressing down on my shoulder. I lifted my chin to see Aris and Danielle standing there.

aris

"Let's get him outside," I suggested as I saw Danielle's eyes cloud with tears. She nodded, and we pulled Noah up from the wooden chair he was sitting on, lifting him to his feet. I caught a glimpse of what was on the computer screen and knew right away what he'd been doing here.

I nudged Danielle to take a look, and she did. When she looked back at me, a tear was streaking down her cheek.

We took the elevator down to the first floor, me pushing Danielle in the wheelchair we'd borrowed for the weekend and not yet returned, and went out the back of the library into the late winter night.

On the west side of the building was the university's arboretum. There wasn't much growing there at this time of the year, but the gazebo might offer us a private place to talk and let Noah collect his thoughts.

The crisp air felt cleansing as we made our way around the building, me still pushing Danielle on the sidewalk and Noah walking beside me. Danielle climbed out of the chair when we reached the steps to the gazebo. After I helped her up them, we guided Noah to a stone bench. He hadn't said a word yet, not from the time I laid a hand on his shoulder in the library till now.

Danielle wrapped her arm around him and snuggled in close. "It's freezing out here, Noah. Let me warm you up."

He finally broke his silence. "What would they think of me? If they could see me now?"

"Oh, sweetheart…" My heart broke for him as I contemplated what he had gone through as a young, vulnerable child. "I know they'd be so damn proud of you now. How could they not? Look at all you've achieved, Noah."

Danielle nodded in agreement. "Noah, they would be blown away by what an amazing human you turned out to be, how smart you are, how generous, how gifted. I'm so, so sorry they aren't here to witness the incredible man they created."

He was quiet for a moment, then he stood up. I wasn't expecting to see tears streaking down his face, but there they were, shining in the soft light illuminating the gazebo.

"I just…" He shook his head, tears flying off his cheeks as he paced back and forth, his breath coming out in short white puffs as he spoke. "I never allowed myself to grieve or feel sorry for myself. I simply decided I was going to take care of myself, and I would never have to rely on anyone else ever again. I wanted to be completely independent—never need anyone."

He shook his head again as he continued pacing. "I hated not having control over where I lived or what I did or where I could go or what I learned. I didn't want strangers making those decisions. I didn't want to be beholden to anyone. I didn't want to be close to anyone…"

He looked at us briefly now, huddled together on the stone bench—which was freezing, by the way—as we attempted to keep each other warm, and Danielle softly sobbed as Noah's words pierced her soul.

"I never envisioned myself married. Or having kids. I just wanted to have my career, use my gifts to help people, and keep to myself. That is what I pictured." He pinched the bridge of his nose and drew in a deep breath as the tears seemed to subside. "I definitely didn't think I'd ever have two incredible people like you walk into my life and want to love me and take care of me.

"I didn't think I'd be part of a family like we have at Cynda's and Jason's, where we care about each other's problems and we lean on each other. And for me to realize that I actually *do* need you guys? That I wasn't going to get through this lawsuit without support? God…"

He leaned against the gazebo railing and actually burst out laughing.

Wasn't expecting that!

"I didn't want to admit I needed help. Or support. But you guys did it anyway. You knew I needed you, and you didn't hesitate to give me what I couldn't even ask for. And you did it out of pure altruism. Not because I could give you something in return. But because you actually care about me…and…."

"And love you," I finished for him, rising from the bench to wrap my arms around the man I loved with all my heart and soul.

Danielle worked herself off the bench to standing and limped over to us, her arms outstretched. "Of course we'll take care of you. All you've done since I met you is take care of me. It's time to return the favor."

danielle

After Noah shared with Aris, myself, and the rest of the polycule the stunt Alexandra had pulled this morning in his office, a plan started to take shape in my mind. I spent the night ruminating about it, and in the morning, it was time to put it into action.

I waited until Noah left for work, and then I sidled up to Aris and laid it on him.

"You want to confront Alexandra, make her call off the suit, and convince her dad not to fire Noah?" Aris asked over morning coffee. Everyone else in the polycule had left for work or whatever else they had on their agendas.

"Yeah. Do you know where we can find her?" I cracked my knuckles like a badass mob boss who was about to go hunt down a rat. I mean, badass in the sense I had come up with this plan and wanted to execute it. The not-so-badass part was that I couldn't drive or get around very well, so I needed Aris's help.

Aris looked decidedly unconvinced. "Yeah, I know where she works, but I need to get to work, and I—"

"You already said your boss is cool," I cut him off. "I met her. She's great, and I think she'll understand if you need to go defend your boyfriend's honor. As a matter of fact, that's exactly what you should tell her is your reason for calling out today. Do you want me to talk to her?"

He rolled his eyes and chuckled. "I just...I don't know if it's a good idea to get involved like this."

"You heard Noah last night. It's hard for him to ask people for help. He would never ask us to confront her or her dad. Which is exactly why we need to do it. Noah is the best doctor I've ever seen. And he should not be losing his job. As a matter of fact, Dr. Greene, one of my voice professors, told me a lot of the music school folks see him. I bet you I could get them all to help out too."

Aris shook his head. "I don't think this is a good idea, Dani."

I crossed my arms over my chest, determined to see this through. "Just take me to her workplace. And I'll do everything else."

"So, this is where she works, huh?"

"Yep," Aris popped the "P" at the end of the word.

I looked at the sprawling complex. "What is it?"

"It's a spa and 'wellness' center." He actually used air quotes around "wellness."

"And what does she do here?" I did not particularly want to go in there. I could just tell it wasn't going to be my vibe.

"They do spa services. Aesthetic procedures—Botox, laser treatments. Liposuction. Other weight-loss stuff."

"Why did I have a feeling you were going to say that?" I shivered. I knew something about her rubbed me the wrong way.

"Yeah, Noah thinks Alexandra wants the money so bad because Covid nearly wiped out her business. She lost a lot of clients, and, in this economy, with all the inflation, they aren't coming back. People can't afford this kind of crap, and it's not like there are a ton of rich people in Southern Indiana."

I scoffed. "Good point."

"I'm sure her daddy financed it for her originally, but I think he's cut her off."

"So you think I can just walk in there and ask to speak with her?" I sucked in a breath. I was going to have to dig deep to gather up every bit of confidence and moxie I had to make this happen.

"I'll come with you. I have a way of..." He laughed. "Well, you know."

I considered whether or not that would help our cause. "But she doesn't already know you, right?"

"Nah, I think she knows of me and that Noah is dating me, but not what I look like. I've known people from work and from the gym who come here for treatments. When Noah finally admitted who the disgruntled former patient suing him was, I knew the name. It's a fairly small town. People talk. She doesn't have the best reputation."

"You don't say..." I inflated my lungs again with fortifying air. "Well, let's do this."

The inside of the spa was very Zen-like with soothing music and the tranquil sounds of rushing water, thanks to a fountain in the middle of the waiting room. Bonsai trees and orchids decorated the reception area, decorated in soft shades of blue, gray and green.

We approached the counter, where a young blonde receptionist smiled at us. She wore a headset for answering the phones and was clearly speaking to someone else as she held up one finger to ask us to wait. A moment later, she said, "Welcome to the Garden. How may I help you?"

"I have an appointment with Alexandra," I namedropped.

"Oh." The receptionist frowned and looked at her computer screen. Her brows furrowed, and she squinted for a moment before looking back up at us. "I don't see you on her schedule."

Aris took the reins. "Are you sure? I told her to pencil us in for nine o'clock, but sometimes she forgets. We go back a long way. Just tell her Aris is here to see her."

She hesitated, and then Aris continued, "You don't know who I am, do you?"

She stared at him blankly, but her smile never faltered. Well, he was pretty nice to look at, and she was clearly mesmerized by his dimples and beautiful hazel eyes, not to mention that man bun perched on top of his head.

He whipped out his phone. "I can give her a quick call since you don't seem to—"

"No, no, it's fine. I believe you," she said with a sheepish smile. "Let me take you back to her office."

I shot Aris a grin, and he smiled back. Then he pushed me in the wheelchair—*I was gonna have to give this thing back to Raine eventually, huh?*—down a long hallway lined with Asian-inspired artwork. We headed toward an office with French doors inset with stained glass that featured cherry blossoms.

"She's right through there. Have a nice day." She nodded at us and walked away.

"Well, that was easy enough." I punched him playfully on the shoulder. "Now I'll do the hard part."

He opened the door and pushed me through.

Alexandra was busy examining her nails and watching something on her computer that she quickly silenced. "Um…hello?"

"Hello, Alexandra," I said as Aris rolled me closer to her desk. "I wanted to have a word with you."

A huge, fake smile spread across her face as she adjusted herself in her plush chair and turned to face me head-on. "What can I do for you, hon?"

"Well, first off, don't call me 'hon.'" I cleared my throat. "Let's start there, shall we?"

"Sorry. You don't need to be so hostile," she said in a fake sugary voice.

"Don't I though?" I let her squirm for a moment as she tried to figure out what I was going to say next. "I heard you don't believe I'm engaged to Noah Evans."

"Well, I—I just said that, um—"

"You know, I think the community would be very interested to know that a small business owner trespassed in a local doctor's office to extort money from a well-loved surgeon under the threat of losing his job because your daddy is technically his boss. I think they'd also be very interested to know that someone who runs a quote-unquote wellness—" yes, I made the air quotes too! "—spa made a point of disparaging said doctor's fiancee's weight more than once. I also find it hard to believe your father would want his name sullied around the community in connection with this scheme."

"Well, I—" Her face flushed, and her nostrils flared as she scrambled for some sort of rebuttal.

"I'm sure your father has no idea what you're up to with

this suit, and you mistakenly believed Dr. Evans would want to settle this out of court, sweep it under the rug so he didn't get on your father's bad side."

Alexandra's lips thinned. "My dad hates gay people. He would be happy to fire Noah just for being gay."

I scoffed. "Yeah, well, pretty sure he can't do that, not even in Indiana."

"My malpractice suit gives him a reason to," she fired back.

"But you're lying about him making a mistake, aren't you?" I sneered. "You know he didn't do anything wrong, did he?"

"Well, no, but I did have to have emergency surgery." She shrugged.

"Because you didn't follow the aftercare directions," Aris entered the chat. "I bet you did something stupid like blow your nose too hard or—oh, I bet I know what it was—"

"You don't know jack shit!" she fired back.

"I see women like you in the gym all the time," he continued. "The kind who are so scared of gaining an ounce, they work out like complete lunatics. You're not supposed to work out too hard or lift weights after a septoplasty, are you?"

Her features pulled into a pinched scowl. "This isn't about me! This is about Noah being a shitty doctor and human!"

"So you admit he didn't fuck up your surgery!" I pressed.

"He cheated on my best friend!" She was so worked up now, she had started to cry. Her face was scarlet red, and her eyes were bloodshot and glassy.

"Cheated how?" Aris demanded.

"He's gay!" she screamed at me, pointing her finger in my face. "He's going to cheat on you too!"

"Did he actually cheat on her?" I asked.

"Well, he was watching gay porn…"

"Okay, Alexandra, I don't have all day." I straightened up my spine and folded my hands together in my lap. "I'm going to tell you what's going to happen next: you're going to get on the phone with your lawyer and call off the suit, and call off your dad. Then, you're going to call that reporter and retract your statements about Noah. If it's too late, then you're going to write a formal apology to him and ask them to print it.

"And if you don't agree that's what's going to happen next, we're going to go to that reporter and tell them all about your scheme to extort money and how you used your father's influence to do so. It's going to put you out of business, and it's going to make your dad look bad too. And if you're truly the Daddy's Girl I think you are, you're going to want to avoid angering him."

"It's too late. Daddy already knows about the lawsuit, and he knows Noah is gay." Alexandra rose, her hands clenching into fists at her hips. "And he's already agreed to fire him by the end of the week if he doesn't offer a settlement of at least two hundred thousand dollars."

"Your father saw Noah at the charity ball with me!" I reminded her.

"He doesn't believe you're engaged to him. And neither do I." She crossed her arms over her chest.

I went to twist the engagement ring on my finger and suddenly remembered I'd given it back to Noah yesterday morning. "Fine, here's what's going to happen, then. We're all going to drive over to your father's office right now, and we're going to straighten this out once and for all, or I'm going to the press, and I will not rest until I ruin your livelihood like you've attempted to ruin my fiancé's!"

Aris's head whipped toward me as the words spewed out of my mouth. He looked utterly impressed. He reached down and grabbed my hand as Alexandra bowed her head and reluctantly conceded.

I didn't believe her father knew half of what was going on.

And we were going to prove it.

twenty-seven

. . .

aris

Me: Hey. Feel like I need to give you a heads up.

Noah: Oh no. Why do I have a bad feeling?

Me: Danielle, myself and Alexandra are on our way over to her daddy's office to discuss you and your lawsuit.

Noah: Please tell me you're joking.

Me: Nope. It's gotten a little out of control, but let's just say what Alexandra did yesterday set Dani off something fierce. And then when she learned what Alexandra does for a living…

Noah: Oh god.

Me: Exactly.

Noah: What do you want me to do?

> Me: Ball is in your court, love, but Danielle plans on telling him that you'll be suing for defamation if the newspaper publishes that you're gay and behaved inappropriately at work. Alexandra didn't say she knows about us, but I'm sure your dad has heard rumors. I'm…well, I'm a little worried about my own neck here too. And yours, of course.

> Noah: Sigh.

> Me: Alright we're driving over now.

> Noah: I'll figure something out.

I put my car in drive and backed out of the parking space. Meanwhile, I noticed Danielle's fingers were flying furiously over her phone.

"What are you doing?"

"Don't worry about it," came her reply.

"Dani, I think what you did back there is amazing, but you're freaking me out, and I have to be honest with you—I'm starting to worry a little about my job too, you know. Mr. Bagby could also fire me. I work for Midwest Health too."

She held up a hand. "Aris, I need you to trust me right now. I know what I'm doing. I have this all planned out. It's like I'm directing the show. I have a vision, and I've set the stage with all the props we need."

"Did you just turn this into a theatrical production?" I asked incredulously.

"Yeah, it's called *Saving Noah's Private Life*."

danielle

We met Alexandra in the parking lot. I was surprised, in a way, that she actually showed up. But I was prepared if she didn't. I had everything I wanted to say to Mr. Bagby all mapped out, and I wouldn't be alone. I had recruited help.

Alexandra scowled as soon as we made eye contact. "Follow me."

"I do all the talking," I told her as Aris pushed me in the wheelchair.

She started to protest, but I cut her off, "That's part of the deal. Do you want to keep your business?"

"You accused me of extortion? Well, you're blackmailing me!" she whined.

Aris patted her on the back. "Just smile and look pretty, okay? We're about to go by the security desk, and I'm sure everyone here knows who you are."

I smiled at Aris as we passed the main reception desk of the Midwest Health executive offices. We stepped into an open elevator, and Alexandra pressed a button for the top floor. Of course, Daddy's office was in the penthouse.

We all made our way down the hall to where another receptionist sat at the front of a rotunda. This building was insane. I couldn't imagine how many millions of dollars it took to build it, when the hospital was falling apart. I'd just spent time in the emergency room getting my leg looked at, and it was not updated at all. It was dank and dingy, but of course, Mr. CEO was all decked out in a luxurious penthouse. *Figures.*

This was going to be fun. I couldn't wait. Maybe when this was all over, I'd go to law school. Forget the musical theater degree. I'd go fight for the little guy using my silver tongue and my expansive repertoire of acting skills.

Alexandra breezed past the receptionist. "We're going to talk to my dad." She waved her hand dismissively.

"Uh, okay," was all the middle-aged brunette woman said, shrugging.

Alexandra knocked twice and then opened the door. "Dad! These people want to talk to you," she announced.

Mr. Bagby, whom I had seen briefly at the charity ball, turned his sharp gray eyes on us from his massive mahogany desk. He was wearing a charcoal-gray suit with a red tie, and everything about him screamed wealth and power.

"Hello. Are you two friends of my daughter's?" he asked in a somewhat pleasant voice.

"Not exactly," I said. "Do you mind if we sit down? I mean, I'm already sitting, but do you mind if my friend sits?" I gestured toward the chairs in front of his desk.

"Of course. Of course. Can I get you anything?" He was certainly a lot more polite than his daughter.

"No, just a moment of your time, please." Aris sat down after wheeling me closer to the desk. Alexandra remained standing.

"Alexandra, dear, what is this about? Who are these people?" His eyes locked on his daughter, who stood wringing her hands a few feet from him.

"Father, you know about my lawsuit against Dr. Noah Evans," she said.

"Oh, that's how I know you!" Mr. Bagby clasped his hands together. "You're the lovely young woman who sang at the charity ball on Saturday night."

"I am." I gave him a pleased smile, fighting hard to maintain my composure and accomplish this with as much grace and decorum as possible. Noah could thank me later when he didn't have to worry about this bullshit anymore.

"My name is Danielle Delacroix. I'm Noah Evans's fiancée, sir."

"Yes, I heard something about that." Mr. Bagby scratched at his chin. "Alexandra told me he was gay after he and her friend broke up." He raised his hand. "Don't agree with it. But I hear he is a fine doctor and a gifted surgeon."

"Daddy, you *know* what he did to me!" Alexandra shrieked.

"I know what you think happened," he silenced her. "And I know you had to have a second surgery."

"Sir, we're here because your daughter is trying to force my fiancé into settling her case out of court. And she is using you for leverage, saying you'll fire him for being gay." I cleared my throat and settled my gaze on his. "I'm sure you'll agree it's a ridiculous and baseless threat. For one thing, Noah is an excellent surgeon, and for another, he's not gay. He's engaged to me, a woman! Now, I'm sorry that his relationship with your daughter's best friend did not work out, but I'm sure we can all agree it has nothing to do with his surgical abilities—"

"Now, who are you?" Mr. Bagby turned to Aris, who had been sitting there silently, listening to me handle this whole situation like a total boss.

"Oh, I'm Noah's friend. And Danielle's friend. Um, probably best man at their wedding." He grinned, revealing his adorable dimples.

"What's your name, son?" Mr. Bagby asked in that patronizing way older men sometimes spoke to younger men.

"I'm Aris Belevonis, sir."

"Oh." He sat there for a moment, brows furrowed and a confused look on his face.

"Daddy, he's the nurse Noah has been seen with at his

practice, you know, in the building that's part of Midwest Health? The company you're the CEO of?" Alexandra spouted off. She crossed her arms over her chest and shot us both a smug grin before turning back to her father. "Don't you have a strict fraternization policy at Midwest Health?"

Mr. Bagby didn't acknowledge his daughter's comments. "Aris? Are you Dr. Riley's nurse?"

"Yes, sir, but—"

"And what is the nature of your relationship with Dr. Evans?"

noah

I punched the elevator button for the top floor, hoping I wasn't too late. When the car arrived, I rushed in, and suddenly I was surrounded by more people stepping on behind me. As I looked closer, I realized I knew these people. I knew all of them.

My jaw dropped open as I recognized my partner Jessica, Aris's boss Dr. Meredith Riley, Lucy and Karla from my office, plus Elaine Greene, my patient we'd seen at the charity ball on Saturday night. And with her were several other patients who worked in the music and theater departments at IU.

There were no fewer than eight people on the elevator with me whom I knew in some capacity.

"And there are more on their way," Dr. Greene said to me when my face morphed into what must have been a rather befuddled expression.

"We aren't letting you go down without a fight," Jess said, patting my back.

I swallowed down my emotions as the elevator door slid open, and we collectively marched toward the rotunda at the end of the hall. "We're here to see Carl," I told the receptionist, giving my boss's first name.

"Oh, he's uh—"

"I know what he's doing," was all I said, and the entire crowd of us continued forward, opening the door and marching in en masse, right up to Carl Bagby's desk just as Aris was about to speak.

"What is the meaning of this?" Midwest Health CEO's thunderous voice boomed around us.

Danielle sat in her wheelchair, looking over her shoulder at the people assembled behind me. She arranged this, didn't she? She brought all these people here on my behalf.

"Mr. Bagby," Danielle said before anyone could answer his question, "we are all here to speak to Noah's incredible skills as a physician and surgeon. And I'm here, as his fiancée, to tell you, despite whatever rumors have been spread about him, Dr. Evans is very much a model employee who embodies the family values you embrace here at Midwest Health."

She shot me a look that said, *See? This is working! But I'm not finished yet…*

"Furthermore, I'd also like to bring to your attention the fact that I was recently the victim of an accident that occurred in your facility's parking lot due to negligence on your part. The parking lot was not cleared of ice, which led to me breaking my leg. So, if we want to talk about negligence, let's start there. I would be willing to forgo filing a suit against your company if your daughter is willing to drop her lawsuit against Noah."

Gasps went up all around me as a proud smile crept across Aris's face. I stood behind Danielle, placing my hands on her shoulders in support.

Carl Bagby stood up and looked over the crowd of

people assembled in his massive office. His office was so big, it wasn't even crowded with this many people here. And as he surveyed each face, the next elevator delivered six or eight more people, all either patients of mine or staff in the building where I worked, including the custodians.

"You can't fire Dr. Evans," Elaine Greene spoke up from the congregation of my supporters. "He's the best ENT I've ever seen, and, as a vocalist, I've seen every single one between Indianapolis and Bloomington."

"He has not only taken excellent care of me," said another patient of mine, Tom Janssen, "but he also did an amazing job on my daughter's tonsillectomy when she was eight years old."

"He's the best boss I've ever had," said Lucy, my nurse. Karla, my scheduler, nodded in agreement.

Carl put his hands on his desk as his eyes darted from face to face before landing squarely on me. "Looks like you have a lot of folks in your corner, Noah."

"I do," I agreed. "I'm a very lucky man."

"So," Mr. Bagby said with a smile spreading on his face, "it's not true that you've been distracted at work by having an inappropriate relationship with a male nurse in another doctor's office? You're engaged to be married to this lovely lady with the voice of an angel?"

"Tell him," Danielle urged.

Aris looked back at me, trying to smile to cover up the hurt in his eyes. "Tell him," he said, nodding.

"Sir, with all due respect, my sexual orientation has nothing to do with my job nor my skills as a surgeon or physician. I'm not involved in any inappropriate relation-ships. To be clear, my relationships are absolutely none of your business," I stated.

"That's right," Dr. Greene said from behind me.

"However," I paused and swallowed hard, "both of my partners are in this room with me right now, and I don't think it's fair that it's 'acceptable' for me to be publicly engaged to one, but it's not 'acceptable' for me to profess my love for the other in public."

A little gasp sounded from somewhere, and when my head turned toward the sound, I identified Alexandra as the culprit.

"Sir, the truth is, I'm bisexual. I'm polyamorous. And I happen to be in love with a beautiful, talented woman—" I put one hand on Danielle's shoulder, "and a smart, handsome, kind man." I put my other hand on Aris's shoulder.

I turned my steely gaze back to Mr. Bagby. "And if you want to fire me because of that, well…go ahead…but I'll see you in court if you do."

Danielle smirked. "And so will I."

I didn't get a chance to say another word because the entire room erupted in thunderous applause, and Alexandra ran out screaming and crying. But the best part was when Aris and Danielle both mouthed "I love you" to me at the exact same time.

epilogue

. . .

six weeks later

aris

SPRING WAS FINALLY HERE. Yes, we did get another snow after that lovely late February warm snap we had around the time that Alexandra Bagby dropped her malpractice suit against Noah, and Noah confessed his love for both Danielle and me in front of his boss, his colleagues, his patients, and most of his office staff.

Today we were celebrating something else momentous: Danielle got her cast off.

Cynda and Jason had fired up the grill, and we'd invited Raine, Poe, Molly, and Lachlan to cook out with us. Noah had invited his attorney, Maggie, and her husband, Leo, to join us. And Danielle had invited Elaine Greene and her wife to join us as well.

It was quite the crowd, but I knew it was going to be a

fun time. I'd even ordered a cake for Danielle that I hoped she would get a kick out of—and not be too mad at my joke.

Tomorrow, she was auditioning for a job teaching drama and musical theater to summer camp students at IU. She still wasn't one hundred percent sure what she was going to do after she finished up her MFA in December. She had thought about going into teaching or perhaps applying to law school.

She was going to have that deviated septum repaired at the end of the summer, between the end of camps and the beginning of the fall semester. Noah's colleague Jessica would perform the surgery. She knew there was a chance her voice might never be one hundred percent the same as it was before. And she was coming to terms with that, just like she did her broken leg and losing the lead role in *The Music Man*.

"You look beautiful tonight!" I greeted her when she came out of the bedroom wearing a lovely sundress.

"Look, I'm wearing sandals!" she gushed. "I know, it's only sixty degrees, but I can wear two shoes again! Do you have any idea how exciting that is?"

I gave her a kiss, and we walked down the hallway together to where Noah and Raine were having a heated discussion in the living room about some obscure nineteenth-century book. Elaine and her wife, Isobel, joined us.

"Danielle, you look absolutely gorgeous!" Elaine gushed. "And I know you're going to nail your audition and interview tomorrow for the camp job. I've already put in a good word for you with the camp director." She winked.

"Oh my gosh, thank you!" Danielle brushed a strand of hair behind her ear and grinned.

"Well, isn't that a beautiful ring!" her voice professor cooed, taking Danielle's hand to get a closer look at it. "Is it an antique?"

"It was my mother's engagement ring," Noah said.

"Oh, so you two really are engaged!" Elaine clasped her hands together in joy. "You don't know how happy that makes me. I'll sing at your wedding if you'd like!"

"Now slow down there," Noah said with a laugh. "I originally gave it to her as a prop for the charity ball."

"I returned it to him after the ball," Danielle confessed. "But when I was doing his laundry and found it in his pants pocket, I put it back on for safekeeping."

"Yes, and after that all went down in Bagby's office a few weeks ago? I told her to keep it. We'll make it official someday." He shot her a wink and put his arm around her. Then he wrapped his other arm around me. "But whatever we do, it will be all three of us. No one gets left out. No one gets left behind."

Elaine grinned from ear to ear. "That is just the most beautiful thing. You three make such a cute—"

"Throuple," Raine supplied. "That's the right word!"

"The cake is here!" Cynda announced from the kitchen. "Come see it!"

I grabbed Danielle's hand. "Now look, I don't want you to get mad about the cake, okay? I mean it as a joke... You know you're going to kick ass at your audition tomorrow."

"Why would I be mad?" She scrunched up her eyebrows adorably as she took my hand and Noah took her other, and we all three walked into the kitchen together.

There, on the table, was a huge white sheet cake with lavender roses—Danielle's favorite color.

And in curlicue writing, it said,

Break a Leg, Danielle!

"Aris! Oh my god, how could you?" She punched my arm playfully, and all of us burst into laughter.

noah

Later that night, I was anxious to get all of our guests out of the house so I could be alone with my lovers. We had been working on preparing Danielle for her dream come true—and now that her cast was off, it was time to fulfill that fantasy for hopefully the first of many times.

She walked into the bedroom of her own accord from the shower, looking sexy as fuck in a lavender satin robe. Her damp hair was piled on top of her head, and her skin was glowing.

Aris had everything we needed laid out on the nightstand. And he was already stripped down to his birthday suit. He didn't generally require much coercing to get naked. His hair was down around his shoulders, his olive skin already tan from being outside, setting off the golden-brown scruff on his jaw.

That left me, still wearing what I'd worn to the party: black jeans and a fitted button-down shirt. Danielle headed toward me, a mischievous look in her eyes. "You know you're completely overdressed for the occasion, right?"

"Oh, was there a special DP costume I was supposed to wear?" I joked. "Should I have asked Raine to design something for me? Tell me, dear director—this is your show, after all."

She slapped my arm playfully. "Very funny." Then she wasted no time deftly unfastening the little buttons down the front of my shirt and pulling it open to reveal my chest and torso.

"Damn it, you're just so fucking hot." She pressed kisses to my pecs and down my stomach, gently lowering herself to her knees.

Aris was quick to grab a pillow for her to kneel on. "Don't want you to hurt yourself, my goddess."

She looked up at him with adoring eyes. "Thank you."

With that, her focus was back on unbuttoning my pants and freeing my cock, which was growing stiff at the idea of fucking her tight ass. Every time I'd used a toy on her and worked on stretching her to prepare for me, I fantasized about this night, about being the first cock to drill into her ass while Aris fucked her pussy, only a thin wall of flesh separating us.

She stroked me from base to tip, making me lengthen and harden under her touch. A tentative taste, and her eyes rolled back in her head. "Mmm, I love the idea of getting you all hard and ready to fuck me."

"Just not too much. I want to be able to last, okay?" I tilted her chin upward so she had to meet my gaze and hear my request.

"I'll do my best." Her tongue flicked out to tease me, and just before my eyes shut, I caught a glimpse of Aris sitting on the bed watching, his hand moving up and down his thick shaft.

"Damn it, Dani, you sure know how to suck cock." I threaded my fingers through her hair and guided her up and down my dick, trying not to choke her with my excessive length.

"I want some of that too." Aris stood next to me, presenting his enormous erection for her to taste.

Danielle went back and forth between us, and when she was sucking Aris's cock, he played with mine. And vice versa. We did that until we were both about to lose control.

She sat back on her heels and looked up at us. "My turn?"

"Yes, my goddess." Aris pulled her to standing and

smacked her ass while she climbed up on the bed, which she could do so much easier now without the cast on her leg.

This was our first time fucking her without it. It opened up a lot of doors, like doggy and the DP we were about to try. Aris lay down on his side of the bed and pulled her over toward him. "Straddle me. Ride my face."

She climbed aboard with no hesitation, lowering her pussy to Aris's hungry mouth. As she rode him to multiple orgasms, I perched between Aris's legs and made him come with my mouth, knowing full well he could get hard again when it was time to fuck Danielle senseless.

It was so fucking hot sucking him off while she fucked his face. And by the time he finished, my own cock was aching, swollen, and had left a trail of precum all the way down his leg. *Oops!*

I took my dick in my hand, trying to relieve a bit of the pressure. "I hope I can last…"

"Where do you want me now?" Aris asked. "I'm already getting hard again. Damn it, Dani. You're so fucking hot. How many times did you come? You taste so fucking good."

"Three?" she answered with a sheepish smile.

"Climb aboard." He gestured toward his cock, and she moved down his body, lifting up onto her knees. She took him into her hand and began to stroke. Meanwhile, I was trying to figure out if I should have done the same thing as Aris—gotten off first so I could last longer in round two.

No, I was determined to make this work. I'd waited too long, and I didn't want to take the chance of not being able to go a second round. Aris was younger and more reliable when it came to that. Hell, he could come four, five, six times a night if I had the energy to keep up with him. Having Danielle here to help keep Aris satisfied was a huge bonus.

"Fuck, Aris, you feel so good," she moaned as she guided

his cock into her pussy, sliding down on it until her thighs rested on his. She sat there motionless for a few seconds, just acclimating to the feeling of him inside her.

"Go ahead and start fucking him—but go slow," I instructed as I moved into position behind her. "I'm going to get you ready to take me."

She did as told and slowly lifted herself up and down. A squeal burst from her throat when I spread her cheeks and rimmed her tight hole. "Oh, god," she groaned, "if you keep that up, I'm going to come again."

"Go ahead," I said. "You get to have as many orgasms as you want. That's the reward you get for being a woman."

"Damn right," she gritted out. "We deserve all the orgasms."

I smiled as I licked her again, feeling her whole body quiver against my tongue. Then I took out the lube and began to gently insert my finger.

"Go slow," she sighed as she rode Aris.

"Yeah, good idea, go slow," Aris agreed. "I'm already ready to bust another nut! Fuck!"

I laughed as I positioned my cock at her back entrance and pressed forward a little. She gasped at the sensation, and I backed off a bit. "Relax, baby, this is going to feel so good. You're going to be so full of cock. Just think about how good it'll feel."

"Fuck..." she groaned as she pressed back against me and took the tip inside.

I gripped her hips, steadying myself. Holy shit, this was going to be a test of my endurance. Just the tip felt so exquisite, I could have come right then and there.

"More," she moaned. "Please...Noah...fuck me. I need your huge cock in my ass."

"That's not exactly helping the whole self-control situation," I gritted out as I pushed deeper inside. She could barely take me in her pussy…but somehow she seemed to be doing better with this.

"Yes, oh god!" she screamed, her head thrown back as we both began to move in sync, both sets of our hands on her hips, controlling her movements.

I couldn't believe how amazing this was, and how Aris and I had been missing out on this dynamic our entire relationship. I felt more connected to him now, with Danielle between us, than I ever felt when just the two of us fucked. How was that possible?

"This was meant to be," Aris rushed out as his body tensed. "Fuck, I can't last… Your pussy is so tight. Fuuuuuuck!"

That set off a chain of reactions with Danielle reaching her climax, the spasms squeezing my cock like a vise. I could barely move at all, she was coming so hard, and before I could bring myself back under control, cum shot up from my balls like a rocket being launched into space. I held on for dear life as my cum gushed out, and stars, planets and entire universes appeared in my field of vision.

Our first DP would not be our last…

danielle

"My god, that was amazing!" I lay back against Aris's chest while Noah curled up on his side and wrapped his arm around me. I loved that we were all connected, our breaths synchronizing as we came down from our orgasms.

"You know how much I love you both, right?" I asked with a breathy sigh.

"Of course we do," Aris said.

"Do you remember accusing me of acting the role of your girlfriend a couple months ago?" I lifted my head just enough to make eye contact with him.

He scoffed. "Well, I saw how you acted so expertly as Noah's fiancée, so I had to wonder…"

"I'm sorry I made you feel that way. I had been going through a weird time in my life, you know? Breaking my leg, finding out I need surgery on my sinuses, possibly having to change careers…"

"It's totally understandable, Danielle. I still feel bad that I pushed you to make a decision before you were ready," Aris apologized.

"And I'm sorry I was so closed off to everything at first," Noah confessed. "It took me a while to really embrace that this is who I am, and that I need and want two partners. Hell, it took me a while to convince myself I needed or wanted *one* partner!"

We all chuckled. Noah ran his hand along my stomach while Aris played with my hair. I loved having both of them. They were the perfect complement to me, and they took such great care of me. But now…now would be the greatest test of our relationship. Even though we had already overcome so much… there was a new challenge for us to face. Hopefully together.

I swallowed hard before finally blurting out, "Well, I wanted to tell you guys something important tonight. Something that may change the trajectory of our lives forever."

"You made a decision about your career?" Aris guessed, his eyebrows arched.

"Well…sort of…"

"Don't hold us in suspense," Noah said.

I took a deep breath and went for it. "Well, it's just that I… I kind of just got cast in a new role."

"A new role?"

"We all did, actually."

Noah jerked up. "What do you mean, Dani?"

"Well…"

Aris looked at Noah, and Noah looked at Aris as I scooted up on the bed and put a little space between me and them. I needed to be able to see their faces.

"Dani, just tell us! What role?" Noah demanded. He did not like being in the dark about anything. Or having to wait for anything.

I smiled and took Aris's hand in my left hand and Noah's hand in my right. "I've just been offered the role of Mother."

"Who's mother?" Aris asked excitedly. "Is this for the summer drama camp?"

Noah shook his head, and then his eyes began to widen. He reached over to put his other hand on my stomach. "Are you saying what I think you're saying?"

"Um, yeah, so…how do you guys feel about playing the role of Father?"

They looked at each other, both too stunned to speak.

"Yeah, I don't know how it happened either…but I didn't get my period this month, and the test was positive. No idea what's in the script as far as the genetic situation is concerned…" A nervous smile curled my lips.

"Well, I love you," Aris squeezed my hand and put his other hand on my belly, right on top of Noah's, "so I know I'm going to love his new role too. And it doesn't matter what 'the genetic situation' is."

"Well, I love both of you, so count me in," Noah agreed. "The three of us in the roles of parents? We're gonna bring down the house."

. . .

THE END

Raine, Maggie and Leo's story is next:
books2read.com/PolyAmFam3

Join Phoebe's newsletter here: bit.ly/PhoebeAlexanderNews

about the author

USA Today Bestselling Author Phoebe Alexander writes romance about characters like her: with extra curves and life experience. Her stories often include themes of ethical nomonogamy, such as polyamory. She believes love is love, and everyone deserves a happily ever after, no matter your size, shape, age, or color.

Phoebe lives near the beach on the East Coast with her husband and multiple fur babies. When she's not writing, she works as an editor and consultant for indie authors. She also volunteers to run a 6000-member indie author support group.

Phoebe enjoys hanging out with her three adult sons, as well as travel, Broadway musicals, dark chocolate, swimming, hiking, college basketball, and making Seinfeld references whenever possible, especially in her books. Her single greatest fantasy is just having some free time. Join her newsletter for bodypositive memes and plenty of dog pics!

facebook.com/phoebealexanderauthor

instagram.com/authorphoebealexander

bookbub.com/authors/phoebe-alexander

tiktok.com/@authorphoebealexander

threads.net/authorphoebealexander

also by phoebe alexander

Mountains Series

Mountains Wanted

Mountains Climbed

Mountains Loved

Christmas in the Mountains

The Navigator

The Explorer

The Adventurer

Mountains Transcended

Eastern Shore Swingers Series

Fisher of Men

The Catch

Siren Call

Sailors Knot

Turning the Tide

Spicetopia Series

Penny & Pryce

Sugar & Spice

Virtue & Vice

Fire & Ice

Naughty & Nice

Dares & Dice

Loyalty & Lies

Spice Up Our Marriage Series

Project Paradise

Rule Breaker

The Playground

Keeping Secrets

Alpha Bet Guys Series

A Hole

The Big O

Need the D

Hard F

Ride the C

Polyam Fam

The Scottish Play

Break a Leg

Standalones:

Authority Issues

Clean Grammar for Dirty Minds

9 781949 394764